MW01181515

CAUGHT STEALING

by

BEN J. MARTIN

Caught Stealing
Ben J. Martin
ISBN: 0-9661852-3-4

You may purchase copies of "CAUGHT STEALING" by mail-order. Call toll free, 1-888-600-9922. All major credit cards accepted. Or visit our website www.caughtstealing.com $7.99 per book plus $3.00 postage and handling.

Publisher's Cataloging-in-Publication
(Provided by Quality Books, Inc.)

Martin, Ben J.
    Caught stealing / by Ben J. Martin. -- 1st ed.
    p. cm.

    1. Hispanic American baseball players--Fiction. 2. Discrimination in sports--Fiction. 3. Baseball players' spouses--Fiction. 4. Baseball--United States--History--Fiction. 5. Fortune hunters--United States--Fiction. 6. Equitable distribution of marital property--United States--Fiction. I. Title.

PS3563.A7235C38 1998   813'.54
                    QBI98-10506

ADAMS PRESS
Chicago, Illinois

DEDICATION

It would be a mistake to assume that because your name does not appear here that I have forgotten you, your friendship, or, the impact you've had on my life.

To all of you, my love and gratitude forever.

Polly Pollard Christopher and her Uncle, Pete Rhodes. My son, Michael and his wife Becca. My daughter Marilyn. My grandchildren, Madison, Tanner, and Hannah. Mr. & Mrs. James J. Ellis and Mr. & Mrs. David DeLozier, Ahmed M. Khan.

Sharon Roberts, Dee Ann Skipton, Jack Hogan, Pepe Frias, Tony Armas, Julio Valdez, Pat Gillick, Tom Henzie, Glenn and Gracie Ballenger, Bill Kircher, Patrick Conner, M.D., Katy Haley, Wensy and Peggy Marsh.

Woody Justice, William Wear, Sr., Randy Ebright, Lillian Warren, Dick Rollings, Billy Joe Fitch, Andy Anderson, Gerald Gleason, Harry Reed of Nevada, and

Howard Coble of North Carolina, Mr. & Mrs. Tom Rhodes of Arizona.

Harry Smith, Jack Breedlove, Dan Morgan, Billy and Barbara Long (and their folks), Karen Meads, Jarrel Saladin, Donald Woolf, Mr. & Mrs. Bob Nelson, J. Max Price, Brendon and Carol Ryan, Joe Turner, John Savoy, Shirley Simmons, Mickey Owen, Jim Gray, Robin Rice.

Ralph and Darlene Scott, Ben and Amelia Pendleton, Donna Kay Cotner, Dottie Justice, Robert V. Groce, Greg Weld, Bob Francis, Kerry L. Holder, Dr. Hugh Stephenson, Jr., M.D., Dr. Steven Attwood, M.D., Dr. Jay Milne, M.D., Dr. Fred McQueery, M.D., Dr. Bob Benedett, M.D., Henry Westbrook, Dee Wampler, Porter Wagoner.

Deceased

My parents, Ike and Ethel Martin, Jack Skidmore, Bill McNeal of Salem, Missouri, Jack Powell, Floyd W. Jones, Denzil Mitchell, Bill Veeck, John Hosmer, Scott Traylor, Red Foley, Tom Greenwade, and Thomas Brady.

My sincere and heartfelt thanks to all of you.

Ben J. Martin
1998

CAUGHT STEALING
Synopsis

Manny Hernandez was so frail and sickly as a child that he was too weak to join his brothers working in the sugarcane fields of the Dominican Republic. Instead he spent his time practicing pitching baseball.

When Manny was signed by a U.S. Professional Baseball Club he was sent to the deep south for assignment to the minor leagues. It was then that he first experienced the abrupt culture shock of racial prejudice.

Manny struggled against this and finally sought a solution by marrying Vivienne, a Caucasian camp follower who in reality was purely a predator vixen just waiting for this kind of opportunity.

By the time Manny achieved millionaire status through free-agency, Vivienne had borne him two children who Manny adored.

Vivienne manipulated Manny through his love for his children and her sexual favors to Manny's lawyer, Sammy Snider. This led to her divorcing Manny while he was away playing baseball and concealing it from him until he returned home after the World Series to find the locks changed and he not welcome and virtually penniless.

How Manny overcomes these problems and ultimately achieves the personal, romantic, and professional goals he had originally strived for are told in the rest of the story, including his falling in love with a female sports reporter.

The author maintains that the work is fiction based on facts, he saw, knew of, or participated in while an agent for Professional Baseball Players in the 1970's and 1980's.

This book is a gripping love story, social commentary, and warning to any person who could be victimized by a predator spouse and a crooked lawyer before they are.....*Caught Stealing*.

Table of Contents

Table of Contents

PREFACE

Between the years 1979 and 1986, Ben J. Martin, the author of this novel, was a baseball player-agent. His clientele were primarily of Hispanic origin, and most of them were from the Dominican Republic. Mister Martin's first client was Pepe Frias, a major league shortstop with almost fifteen years experience on American baseball diamonds. Pepe's first-born son is named Ben J. Frias. When Ben Martin cautioned Pepe about tacking his long German name, Bernhard Joseph, on that little Dominican baby, Pepe just laughed and said, "We named him Benito Jesus, and call him Ben J."

The author's last client was Julio Valdez, a major league shortstop until he was falsely accused of the crime of statutory rape by a runaway sixteen-year-old "groupie". However, in the spring of 1984, Julio was totally exonerated of the crime. The judge threw out the case at the preliminary hearing, based upon insufficient evidence. Regrettably, the bad publicity caused Julio's parent club, the Boston Red Sox, to relegate him to the minor leagues until his ultimate release from the Red Sox organization. When this occurred, Julio was signed by the Chicago Cubs, due in large measure to the sensitive open-mindedness of Gordon Goldsberry, General

Manager of the Cubs, a man of great depth and understanding of the human experience. Consequently, Julio finished his playing career in 1987, with dignity, at the Triple A level Iowa Cubs in Des Moines.

In July of 1986, a trial was held in Boston to determine if civil damages should be assessed against Julio Valdez and/or the Red Sox as a result of the alleged statutory rape. The case against the Red Sox was dismissed by the judge at the end of all testimony. The case against Julio was referred by the judge to the jury. The jury, once again, exonerated Julio in short order. His name was cleared and his family's honor restored. Thus, Julio Valdez successfully defended himself in two Massachusetts courts, one criminal and one civil. Despite his innocence, Julio was defenseless against the politics that perpetually surround a professional baseball player, resulting in the premature end of what had been an extremely promising career.

Pepe and Julio were both from the Dominican Republic. Pepe was from San Pedro de Macoris. (This town produces more major league players than any other small town in the world.) Julio was born and raised in the capital city of Santo Domingo.

All this, simply to say that this is a story based on fact.

Mister Martin has not breached any attorney-client privilege, but has drawn from actual occurrences between many of the players he represented. This story has been embellished, added to, and often departs from the actual facts, the intention being to make it more interesting reading.

It is not the story of Pepe and Julio, but rather it is a fiction born from the experiences of every ball player.

Marvin Miller, the founding Executive Director of the Major League Baseball Player's Association from 1966 through 1982, has often been quoted as saying "... players were easily the most exploited group I've ever known," when referring to his early days in baseball. It may also be said that the most exploited among the players were the Hispanics.

It is illegal for any foreign national to work in the United States without a work permit. A contract with a baseball club qualifies a player to be issued a work permit by the United States Department of Immigration, thus enabling him to play America's favorite pastime, and he is usually handsomely remunerated. When the contract is ended, the player must leave the country within seventy-two hours.

While the Major League Players Association (called the Union) has made great strides in the financial status of its members, a new phenomenon has been created. The newly wealthy, especially the Hispanics, became fair game for unscrupulous gringo ladies who did, and still do, prey upon them.

There is, to this day, a collateral society in baseball of predator ladies who do very well for themselves monetarily, until they are .... "Caught Stealing."

Chapter 1 -- THE SUMMONS - AUGUST 1980

Manuel Hernandez was enjoying his seventh year as a highly successful major league baseball player. He was a short-relief pitcher, par excellence. On a good day Manny, as he was known to his numerous friends and associates, would pitch the final one or two innings as the closing pitcher of a ball game. In other words, he was expected to deliver at least part of one, but not over two, strong innings as a closer.

On this day in 1980 Manny was riding the team's bus from his Chicago hotel on Wacker Drive to Wrigley Field. His club, the St. Louis Cardinals, was scheduled to play the final game of a three-game series. The first two games had been divided, and on this extremely hot and humid August afternoon the Cubs would play host for the rubber game.

Manny had been signed by the Cardinals during the previous winter as a free agent. Consequently, he was now flying high on life, experiencing the confidence which comes with a financially-sound, five-year guaranteed contract.

Manny appreciated that the guarantee meant he would not be released or traded to another team without his consent, and his salary would remain the same until the contract expired. His financial and emotional security were safe with the knowledge that he would earn a salary which ran to seven figures annually.

As the sweating driver eased the team's bus into the parking lot at Wrigley Field, Manny sighed, thinking that the ride had ended too soon; he liked the bus ride for the opportunity it afforded him to observe the hustle and bustle of the Windy City. The driver pulled up close to the clubhouse door, and the players disappeared into the ever-present crowd of autograph-seeking fans. The shy Manny stepped into the throng and began the signing ritual he had practiced since coming to the major leagues over six years earlier. As he slowly made his way to the clubhouse, he reached his left hand for the programs, balls, caps or the plain pieces of paper thrust at him by his overzealous fans. Smiling and slowing his stride, he signed the varied mementos with the pen carried in his right hand.

Manny was an extremely handsome, light-skinned Afro-Dominican gentleman. His father was very dark, and his mother's ancestors came from Greece. He bore a strong resemblance to the younger movie star, Sidney Poitier. Manny also was a very popular ball player and his fans were most appreciative of his willingness to give autographs. He always managed to charm the clamoring crowd of fans by tousling a curly head here, giving genuine answers on baseball questions and a friendly shoulder hug there. Manny loved his fans, especially the young children.

Manuel Hernandez had made the headlines in Chicago's morning tabloids because on the night before, he had pitched two scoreless innings in relief, resulting in a victory for the Cardinals.

"Hey, Manny," one young boy shouted, "you goin' for the Cy Young?"

Manny smiled at the youngster and at the thought of even being considered for such a post-season honor. With characteristic modesty, he lowered his eyelids and replied, "I'm trying... we'll see."

Manny signed so many autographs, he was beginning to feel the onset of writer's cramp.

Another child handed Manny a baseball card to autograph. Manny took the card, looked at the picture of himself taken during his rookie year, and said, "Hey man, who's the kid in this picture? Gee, it's me! I sure am gettin' old."

Ruffling the boy's dishwater-blond hair, he returned the signed card and continued walking, accompanied by the crowd's cheers and laughter.

Preparing to enter the clubhouse door, Manny was confronted by a swarthy stranger, who had boldly stepped in front of him. In a voice reminiscent of a U.S. Army Drill Instructor, the stranger rudely demanded, "You Hernandez?"

Manny had previously noticed this short, fat man standing next to the clubhouse door, chewing on what was left of a large cigar; he had incorrectly assumed that this was another avid fan. Now he was sufficiently close enough to him as to be assaulted by a foul odor emanating from the man's mouth. Halitosis, generated by a combination of onions and stale tobacco, caused Manny to wince as he breathed in and replied, "Yes sir, that's me."

For the first time, he noticed the brown legal-sized envelope, which contained a sheaf of papers. The man roughly pushed the envelope against Manny's chest, knocking him sideways. He managed to steady himself with one hand and took hold of the envelope with the other. He again assumed that the man, with graying chest hair protruding through his partially unbuttoned and dirty shirt, was soliciting his autograph. As soon as Manny had the documents in his hand, the unkempt man with two days of facial stubble quickly stepped aside and said in a voice loud enough to be heard clearly by all of Manny's fans and teammates: "I'm an officer of the court; your wife is suing you for divorce. Better git somebody to read this to you if you don't understand English."

For a moment, all Manny could think was that the man looked more like a ten-dollar gambler lounging against a betting window at Arlington Park than an 'officer of the court'. Suddenly it dawned on Manny just what the man had said, and he shook his head in utter disbelief and bewilderment. "There must be some mistake," he said.

"No mistake; you better do what I told you." This last remark was shouted by the fat man, for all to hear, as he quickly departed the clubhouse area.

Still puzzled, Manny stepped into the corridor which led into the clubhouse. He had just spoken to his beautiful and loving wife, Vivienne, on the phone the night before. He had called her from his hotel room and there certainly had not been any discussion of divorce. 'So what is this?' he

7

wondered. Suddenly the obvious occurred to him. 'Of course, Hernandez is such a common Hispanic name,' he thought, 'that's it, a case of mistaken identity.'

His brief moment of relief ended abruptly when he stepped through the door and had the papers snatched from his hands. Baxter Burrows, a lanky white teammate who played outfield, was, both on and off the field, the Cardinals' self-appointed know-it-all. The skinny hawk-nosed Burrows ripped open the package of papers as Manny unsuccessfully attempted to retrieve them. Burrows announced in his loud rasping voice: "Gentlemen, the league's premier relief pitcher is about to join the ranks of the emotionally and financially-encumbered unmarried.

"Hey Manny," he grated on, "how's it feel to lose that ten million dollars?"

Almost in tears with embarrassment, Manny finally wrangled the papers, in the now torn envelope, away from Burrows' long slim fingers, then made his way to the locker room. Burrows, a bigot, could be heard laughing all over the clubhouse.

Manny intensely disliked this freckled-faced, curly red-headed outfielder, who possessed a six-foot, five-inch meatless skeletal frame, and a loud mouth. His facial features did not seem to go together either. His forehead was not too high, and his long wide beakish nose dominated his face, which did nothing to compliment his thin, yet somewhat sensual, mouth. Baxter continually squinted at anyone who would listen to him, through his too small, too close-together brown eyes. He was also extremely liberal-minded and had some very warped ultra left-wing views and radical opinions on just about every subject under the sun, not the least of which comprised race relations, religion, politics, sex and environmental issues. All this hot air, despite the fact he had only completed six months at Detroit University on a baseball scholarship, Baxter Burrows also was emotionally bankrupt and completely devoid of sex appeal, although his overtly explicit descriptions and boastful stories of his many conquests with 'bimbos' spoke to the contrary. He was definitely not the team's 'Mister Popularity'. He was an excellent outfielder, however, but this was his one and only redemption.

A very shaken Manny slowly made his way to his private locker. For a few minutes he just sat on the bench staring at the torn brown envelope containing the unimaginable paperwork. He attempted to clear his head and concentrate long enough to look over the papers for himself.

'How,' Manny asked himself, 'could Vivienne possibly do this to me?' He thought about her and his two adorable children, Joseph and Marie.

* * *

Vivienne was born in Medford in the state of Oregon. She was the product of an alcoholic father who, when he deemed it necessary to work, was employed as a heavy equipment operator in the road construction business. When he was drunk, her father frequently beat her mother, a small defenseless, mousy woman.

Vivienne, an attractive dark blonde with blue eyes, possessed all the right curves in all the right places. She had long shapely legs, was intelligent and scholastically bright, having maintained an A-standing in school. But, for all this, she was unable to comprehend why her mother tolerated such abuse, and vowed to herself that as soon as she graduated high school, she would leave home and the culturally-deprived city of Medford. She wanted a real and successful life, and possibly a career. Her plans were to marry as soon as she could find a decent man, one who did not drink, and who would, hopefully, hold a respectable position such as an attorney or a school teacher.

All of Vivienne's plans reached fruition six months after high school graduation. Two days following her departure from high school, a Greyhound Bus took her to San Francisco, where she played sexual games with many of the Forty-Niner football stars. At an after-game winner's party, to which she was invited by her latest conquest, she fell madly in love with Tod Tindle. Tod was employed by the United States Postal Service and held a management position in the Marketing Department of the main San Francisco Post Office. He stood six feet, three inches tall, and was graced with high cheek bones and a neatly groomed head of prematurely silver-white curly hair. He was unmistakably handsome, due in large part to features he inherited from his Cherokee Indian mother. His large trim angular frame was a gift from his European father, who now owned and operated a grocery store in Springfield, North Carolina. Tod was a playboy with misogynistic tendencies.

Tod and Vivienne married on February 19, 1970, but, unbeknownst to Vivienne, her husband of two months was once again enjoying the companionship and sexual favors of various rich women of the Nob Hill society set. He also began drinking excessively, and Vivienne soon found herself physically abused. The physical abuse continued and was accompanied by mental and sexual spousal battery. Due to her youth and lack of experience in dealing with real life situations, Vivienne abandoned her husband in October of 1972. Tod beat her to the court house and was the first to file for divorce. Undeterred, Vivienne also filed and found a fighter of an attorney, who would, she mistakenly believed, take Tod for all he had. She did receive a reasonable settlement.

Free again, Vivienne purchased another Greyhound Bus ticket, this time to Los Angeles. By fabricating her education ('... of course, I graduated with a Bachelor of Arts degree from Stockton College,') and exaggerating her age and experience, she was hired by the most exclusive beauty salon on Rodeo Drive, at five-hundred dollars per week. She used her divorce settlement to purchase a three-year-old, silver BMW, trendy new clothes and accessories, then had her hair bleached 'Marilyn Monroe Blonde'. To Vivienne's mind she had 'arrived'. Indeed, she had become the proverbial 'knock-out'. And, with all her feminine wiles, she put all her energy and enthusiasm into finding 'Mister Right'.

* * *

Manny was still numb and lost in confusion. He loved Vivienne with his very being. He had given her everything -- a beautiful home and two lovely children. She didn't lack for anything. He was jolted back to the reality of the present as he was joined by two more of the club's members whom he liked and respected, both as individuals and ball players. Ike Wood and Bart Janacek, who was known as 'Lefty', due to his inability to hold even a pen in his right hand, sat either side of him on the locker room bench.

Ike spoke first. "Manny, we couldn't help hearing Burrows as you walked in. Is there anything at all that me or Lefty could help you with, or do for you?" Their concern was genuine.

Remembering a movie he had once seen about an earthquake, the still-shaken Manny relived that cinematic moment as the ground had split open and swallowed people; he wished at this very instant that the same scene would happen to him. He shook his head at his teammates. "I don't know," he said. "I just don't understand any of this."

"That's why we stepped over to see you, Manny," intoned Lefty; "would you like us to look at these papers for you?"

With head hanging down toward his knees, he blindly handed the papers to Lefty. Ike then took them, read them to himself, and handed them back to Lefty.

After a moment Ike spoke. "Manny, in this country, these documents are what the courts issue to tell people that they must appear in a court of law, on a specific date and time. They're called a summons. These were prepared by your wife's lawyer in Phoenix. It says here that the lawyer's name is Derrickson Henze... does that name mean anything to you?"

"No," Manny responded, "I've never even heard of him."

Ike continued. "Manny, your wife is seeking a divorce from you, the custody of your two children, and a lot of money for alimony and child support. My best advice would be to get yourself a lawyer, the <u>best</u> you can afford, and do it fast."

Lefty nodded approvingly.

"How much time does it say I have?" Manny asked.

"Twenty business days," Ike replied.

"Thanks, fellas," Manny said. "I really do appreciate your kindness."

As Ike and Lefty turned to go to warm up, Manny again said, "Thanks a lot, fellas."

Ike turned back and said, "Manny, let us know if there's anything we can do. I remember your wife when she was with you at spring training. I have no idea what her problem is, but then again, she's a woman, and I'm damned if I ever understood any of 'em. Anyway, we're here for you if you need us... just let us know."

Changing from his street clothes into his ball player uniform, much slower than usual, Manny realized that he was the last one still in the clubhouse.

Billy Long, the clubhouse boy, walked up to Manny and said, "Great throwin' last night, Manny. Got anything there for safe keepin' today?"

He handed Billy his billfold and wristwatch wrapped in a red bandanna. Thanking Billy, he started toward the dugout, and Billy put the valuables in the clubhouse lock box.

As he passed the cubicle used by visiting field managers as an office, he saw that Bill 'Snake' Fitch was sitting in there.. "Hi, Skip," Manny mumbled to the team's manager, as he tapped his knuckles on the glass.

"Manny, good to see you. Come on back and talk a second." Manny stepped into the cubby-hole of an office. "What's this I hear about your wife serving divorce papers on you?" Snake asked.

Numbly, Manny replied, "I really don't know. All I do know is that I talked to her on the phone last night and everything was great, then today I get some papers which Ike and Lefty say I'd better take to a good lawyer."

After a moment's thought, Snake suggested: "Tell you what, Manny, why don't you go home to Phoenix and overnight there instead of flying out with us tomorrow. You can join us in L.A. on game day, or even take an extra day if you need to. But talk to that little lady and see if the two of you can't fix it. Hell, I know what a strain domestic problems can be; I've had four of 'em with three women -- married one twice! If it doesn't work out, get a lawyer and let her go, but talk to her first."

Impressed with Snake's advice, Manny agreed to leave for Phoenix immediately after the game. He thanked Snake for his concern and added, "Don't hesitate to use me today, Skip; if you want to, I'll be ready." However, the experienced club manager's intuition told him that Manny Hernandez probably couldn't throw his best fast ball -- one that reached the plate at about ninety-five miles an hour -- past a Little Leaguer, on this day. But Snake nodded agreeably as Manny turned to make his way to the playing field.

As Manny stepped onto the playing surface at Wrigley Field, the divorce thoughts permeating his mind caused a severe gut-wrenching sensation. He felt quite nauseated. His initial thought was to run it out, as he would a leg cramp, so he headed for the outfield and began his regimen of wind sprints along the boundary wall. He sprinted from right to left field and back again several times, taking deep breaths. This exercise cleared his queasy stomach to a degree, but not his aching head. He forced the smiles in greeting the other players, but still only concentrated on the thunder inside his head.

'Why? Why? Why?' he silently questioned, with each stride. 'Phoenix, Phoenix... I've got to get to Phoenix. I've got to see and speak with Vivienne face-to-face.' Manny's thoughts continued along this vein. He was sure, in his heart, that he could calm her and straighten out this mess once he was with her. His mind continued to fill with questions that centered on, 'Why now... now, when we've finally got everything we've worked so hard to get?'

Manny lengthened his stride, breathed deeper and ran faster than he ever had. His heart rate was good, his adrenaline pumped and he was pouring with sweat, but continued to experience that same ugly gut-wrenching anxiety. He slowly let up on his stride and speed, then completed a few slower laps to cool down. Manny finally jogged over to the bull pen, grabbed a towel and wiped down his face and body. His friend and fellow countryman, Luis Guerrero, a Chicago Cub's utility infielder, walked up to the bench and sat beside him.

"Hey, Manny, you're coming over tonight for supper, aren't you?"

"Hi, Looie, huh-uh, no, I'm planning on leaving right after the game. Going back to Phoenix -- got some personal stuff to tend to."

"So I heard. Problems with that li'l lady o' yours, huh?"

Manny both liked and trusted his fellow Dominican friend. Luis was a very dark six-foot eight-inch happy-go-lucky guy with an ever-present smile. Normally Manny would have enjoyed a pre-game conversation with Luis, but today he was trapped in a mental quagmire. He wanted to talk, but chose not to give momentum to a puzzle he was convinced would be solved by the next night.

Draping his long right arm over Manny's hunched shoulders, Luis tried to comfort his friend.

"Ah, Looie, you know how women are; who knows what goes through their minds. Last night on the phone, she was fine; then today some fat, dirty guy with rotten breath hands me some court papers saying Vivienne wants a divorce."

Manny rambled on, "Looie, Snake's a great guy and he's told me to go home tonight after the game and talk to her... work things out, ya know, an' after that I can join the club again in L.A."

"Okay, okay, *mi amigo*," Luis consoled, grinning at Manny's sad face, "but my Teresa, she won't accept two no-shows." He continued, "I love my wife and she loves me, and I want to keep it that way. Things are good for Teresa and me, so the next time you guys are in Chi Town, you'd better come and eat supper and visit with us for a while."

Manny nodded his agreement and thanked his friend.

Luis grinned and started to walk away, but he turned and added, "You know, Manny, we don't know your wife very well, but if there's anything we can do to help -- well, anything for an old friend -- anything, ya know!" Manny again nodded his thanks.

In that moment, Manny pondered what Luis had insinuated about Vivienne. It was true, she had never let any of his friends get to know her; she always managed to come up with some reason or excuse to avoid the company of his friends, fellow teammates, and even his own family.

His thoughts of Vivienne became an inventory: she had only been to his home in Dominica once. Manny had forgiven her behavior by convincing himself that Vivienne was a cut above his friends and his Dominican family. After all, hadn't her social status been a large part of his reason for marrying her? It had certainly improved his image in the eyes of the North Americans with whom he lived and worked during the season. To Manny's mind, Vivienne was a beautiful, helpful, loving lady, and the fact that she was a '*gringo*' certainly enhanced her value to him as a wife. He also loved her and was still in love with her.

His inventory-taking was interrupted by big Glenn Ballenger, a handsome Caucasian outfielder whose quiet demeanor was the antithesis of his booming, explosive power with a baseball bat. "Hi, old man Manny." Glenn sat down as he greeted his teammate. "You sure are far away in thought about something."

"You mean you haven't heard the latest?" questioned Manny innocently. "My wife is suing me for divorce."

Glenn's initial smile, which exposed the high-dollar cap job on his teeth, quickly disappeared. "Well, I know the locker room was buzzing with some new gossip, but I wasn't too sure what it was all about. I'm sorry, Manny, but perhaps when you go home to Vivienne you will be able to work things out." Glenn had never married; therefore, he was unable to relate to Manny's domestic problems. Then, shrugging his big shoulders, Glenn, who abhorred gossip, diplomatically changed the subject.

"Look Manny, there's a new rookie on board. He's up from Joplin, Missouri... and really green. He's a good kid with a lot of talent, but we want to properly initiate him into the big leagues, so the boys and I ordered a huge birthday cake. We need the help of an old pro such as you. We would like you to go along with us and get his face close enough to the cake so you can shove his pale white face into it... sort of break him in right, you know?"

Remembering the same old trick being pulled on him six-and-a-half years earlier, Manny grinned boyishly. "Sure, Glenn, I'll do it... I could use a laugh about now. How about this? Just before the pre-game warm-up, I'll tell the kid the cake smells really bad and ask him to check it out; then when he's close enough, you dunk him with those two sides of beef you call hands."

"That's a great idea," chortled Glenn.

Laughing in agreement, the two ball players jogged toward the dugout.

As they approached the dugout, Snake signaled Manny to join him on the bench where he was sitting, then Snake said, "I've spoken to Mel, Manny... asked him to have you relax in the whirlpool for a while and then give you a thorough rub-down. The massage should help get you relaxed enough to where you can settle down a bit from this legal snafu." Snake had purposely taken care not to mention the 'D' word. "I want you totally relaxed, as I may need to use you later. Hell, if we can take this one and have a break-even visit to sunny California, we'll get back to St. Louis in great shape to start on the stretch run for the Division Championships. So lighten up, Manny, get yourself relaxed 'cause I'm gonna be counting on you."

The Division Championship was now a three-way race between the Cardinals, the Cubs and the Pittsburgh Pirates.

"Sounds good, Skip," Manny agreed. "So, tell me, who's the new guy Glenn's ordered the cake for?"

"Name's Woodrow Justice... goes by 'Woody'. Real nice kid, with a strong right arm. And, if he can continue up here what he's been doing downstairs, we could win it all. The old stinky cake trick should get him loosened up fast. I'm told he's a real clean-cut guy -- doesn't smoke, drink or chase. The Big Show is just the place for him." Snake was laughing as Manny returned to the locker room for the stinky cake gag and his session with Mel, the Cardinal's trainer and masseuse-extraordinaire.

Still elated by last night's victory, the players' mood in the locker room was one of joviality. Everyone was looking forward to the age-old ritualistic prank that was about to be played on the newest rookie, Woody Justice. In many ways, these men resembled a bunch of overgrown schoolboys.

Manny always looked forward to meeting a new team member, and made a point to speak with him in reassuring tones and do whatever he could to bolster his ego. As his own arrival as a rookie hadn't been the easiest, he went out of his way to help and encourage all the newcomers to the team.

After showering and pulling on a pair of shorts, Manny grabbed a sandwich from the extensive spread laid out by the club's caterer. Sandwich in hand, he made his way to the new man's locker. He ate his food and patiently waited while a reporter finished a short interview with Woodrow Justice.

"Better get used to that sort of thing, and fast," he said, extending his hand.

The rookie stood, gave Manny a firm handshake, and said with admiration, "I'm Woody Justice; you're Manuel Hernandez, aren't you?"

"Well, my friends call me Manny," he said.

"Yeah! thanks, Manny. I sure hope I'll be here for a while."

A handsome young man of twenty-four, Woody had been an outstanding college player at Cal State, Fullerton. Although his roots were in Springfield, Missouri, his high scholastic achievements and his outstanding performances on the diamond at Central High School had caught the eye of many a recruiter, but Woody chose Cal State. He was then signed and sent to the minors, and, after only two years, he was called up to the St. Louis Cardinals, when the old veteran of baseball, Augie Marido, was placed on waivers. Everybody missed Augie; however, that is the way of life in the major leagues. Now the focus was on this rookie catcher, who might be the catalyst to lead the Cardinals to a championship.

Over-awed in the presence of Manny, Woody complimented him. "I've really admired you ever since I was in college, and I'm looking forward to catching you," he stammered shyly. "Why, thanks, Woody... we've heard some great things about you, too, and I want to tell you how good it is to have you here with us on the team. You're bound to have some questions come up, so please feel free to ask me about anything."

"That's great, Mister Hernan... er, uh, I mean Manny. I really appreciate that." Embarrassed, Justice quickly added, "I'm sorry, I'm still a little amazed at being here. I'm sure no Augie Marido, but I'll give it my best."

Grinning, Manny patted his shoulder.

"I know you will, kid. Oh, by the way, in just a bit there's gonna be a cake delivered for Glenn Ballenger's birthday; have you met him yet?"

Woody shook his head, indicating that he had not met the outfielder.

"Good," Manny said, "you can meet him at his surprise birthday celebration."

"Sounds great," Justice replied with enthusiasm, having not the slightest idea that the surprise was to be on him.

Manny strolled by Glenn's locker space and winked at him, signaling that the rookie was primed for the arrival of the cake. He made his way back to his own locker and sat down.

CAUGHT STEALING

All of Manny's teammates and the staff knew that Manny always reserved a few minutes before each game to sit with his head bowed in silent prayer. His mother, Angelica, had taught him respect for the Almighty from childhood, and Manny praised the Lord long before it was popularized by television evangelists. Her influence and his Dominican upbringing had stood him in good stead through the years, and his religion had been most instrumental in developing an attitude of selflessness, humility and loyalty. As indicated by his short conversation with the rookie, Manny was able, in the face of potential emotional and financial disaster, to find time for another human being. Now he could focus on his routine of prayer. Ironically, Manny would spend every Sunday morning, regardless of where he was, watching Evangelists on television. He often mailed them a generous donation, a habit of which Vivienne was extremely critical. Manny, however, continued to donate, but was able to hide this practice from her.

While he was praying, the cake arrived, and the players started meandering by to admire it.

Having completed his pre-game prayers, Manny joined the crowd by the table supporting the cake. Each player assumed a facial expression resembling a person who had just had his nostrils assaulted by a stinky and flatulent passenger in a hot and over-crowded elevator. Each player walked away, shaking his head and holding his nose.

Manny then walked over to Woody, who was engaged in conversation with another player, and when there was a break in the conversation, Manny whispered to Woody, "I think there's something wrong with the cake; it seems to have a sour odor. Would you please go over there and really smell it and give me your opinion? It would be awful if the entire team got sick on bad cake!"

Woody, honored at being asked to help, walked over to the table, waited until he thought his movements were not being observed, and quickly bent over the cake, placing his face close enough to take a deep sniff. From behind him, Glenn Ballenger placed his huge hands on the back of Woody's head and firmly squashed his face into the 'birthday cake'.

The rookie's 'baptism' resulted in a volcanic eruption of whoops, jibes and loud laughter as the room seemed to explode on cue! Embarrassed to the bone, Woody Justice wiped cake and frosting from his eyes and nose. Before he could allow his embarrassment to turn to anger, however, all the men began grabbing his hand and congratulating him on his arrival to the Big Club.

Woody chose to believe that if his teammates hadn't liked him, they wouldn't have played this harmless, yet embarrassing, prank on him, so, after a moment, he said, "This damn joke sure demonstrates team effort; let's keep it rolling right into the World Series." The entire team laughed at Woody's apparent naiveté, knowing that until he wised up he was to be fair game for the club's practical jokers. But no one realized how prophetic the youngster's words were to become about the Series.

When the cake incident had run its course, Snake walked to the center of the clubhouse and shouted, "Listen up!", his way of calling an impromptu meeting. The players allowed the wily team manager this method of ventilating his authority. They knew he was serious, but the veteran players also knew that Snake's most serious messages were delivered one-on-one. On occasion, he'd been known to lift a man by his collar straight off his feet. Snake was old fashioned, and while the old methods of dealing physically with an errant player were long outdated, Snake would resurrect them from time to time in order to make a point.

"Fellas," Snake began, 'we started out this spring in agreement that we had the personnel on this club capable of beating everybody and takin' home all the marbles this season. We're now on the last lap, and it looks like we were right; we're two ahead of the Cubs and one behind the Pirates. Now don't get smug and think the Cubs are gonna follow their tradition of foldin'. This club we're playin' today won't fold, so we'll have ta beat 'em. But if we're gonna beat 'em, we're gonna have to wake up and stop makin' mental mishaps which could lead to us beatin' ourselves!" He paused and gave them a minute to absorb his dialogue.

"Hey guys," he continued, "winning ball games is no different than anything else in life... it all starts inside." Snake used his forefinger to point at his brain. "So, dammit, THINK! I'm not pointing to any one individual -- I'm telling all of ya. It would be nothin' short of a tragedy for us to get this close and lose! Don't beat yourselves!" He stopped for a while and looked as if he was finished, but he surprised every last man by taking a deep breath and continuing.

"About Augie, just so's you'll know, he's gone now, so I figger I can tell you. Augie came to me last week and said he wanted to be shipped. I protested, but he made a

24

good point. His knees were shot from squatting back there for sixteen years. He'd followed this Justice kid closely and knew he was ready to join us. Augie didn't want to hold the club back. They don't make 'em like him anymore. I told him we'd find a coaching spot for him next year. Anyway, when we win it all, we can show our gratitude to Augie by voting him a full share of our Series money."

At these words, the men let out unified screams of approval, not stopping to think that screaming approval now and voting approval later were two widely divergent activities.

"Finally," Snake resumed, "let's get back to fundamentals. Hit the cut-off man, back each other up, and dammit, execute, execute, execute! Pay attention, base runners, to the coaches. And, as for this ball park, remember a fly ball lost in the ivy is a ground rule double, so don't find it just to give a guy a triple -- leave it lost! Now, I know you've all met the new guy, but I want to introduce him to you all now so you can see him without any cake on his face -- Woody, meet the boys."

Still feeling slightly intimidated by the cake incident, Woody took a step forward, and raised his arm in a shy wave to his illustrious teammates. Snake clapped his hands.

"Okay guys, let's go get 'em... and don't be late to the airport in the morning." Snake's travel rule was, 'do what you want the night before, just don't miss the plane.' "Oh yeah, so's you'll know... Hernandez is going to Phoenix on personal business and will join us in the City of Angels a day later." This small additional comment was designed to let everyone know that Manny's absence had been approved and also as a reminder that the manager would bend any rule to help a player out of a jam, especially a personal jam.

After the pre-game meeting, Woody approached Manny. "This may sound dumb," he said, "but thanks for the cake joke. Until that happened, I really had the jitters. Now I've calmed down."

"I think that's the real reason we do it to rookies... sort of makes 'em feel like one of the boys," Manny volunteered. "Although it isn't likely, if you should end up catching me in the game today, let me go over some things with you now, kind of fundamental things, like Snake was talking about."

The youngster listened intently while Manny detailed his four pitches and coordinating signals. With a simple "Okay, Manny," he turned and headed to the playing field.

Manny draped himself in a towel and stepped over to the whirlpool. He immersed himself while Mel Stoll, the club trainer, was adjusting the water temperature. After half an hour, Manny climbed onto a rub-down table, and Mel went to work on Manny's muscular body. At Snake's instructions, Mel was not under any time restraints and had told his assistant to cover on the field, if he were delayed until after the game had started. He began to knead harder along Manny's shoulder, determined to work out the tense knots.

Chapter 2 -- THE AGENT - PHOENIX, ARIZONA

     The phone in attorney Sammy Snider's office was ringing off the hook. Shirley Simmons, his secretary and office manager, answered each call with a consistently courteous manner, assuring each caller that Sammy would get back to them as soon as he returned from his morning court appearances.

     Sammy Snider was a handsome, well-groomed and always immaculately dressed maverick lawyer. He was intelligent, personable and possessed an insatiable ego that demanded perpetual pursuit of money and power. When a new acquaintance would inquire about his legal specialty, Sammy's quick response was always the same, 'Making mon-ney!' And so it was. This transplanted Midwesterner had arrived in the Valley of the Sun ten years before with a new wife (his second), a new car and five-hundred dollars. Today, through what Sammy characterized as hard work and a little luck, he had a six-thousand square-foot home in the most exclusive subdivision in Arizona, two Mercedes Benz Four-Fifty SL convertibles, plus a Corvette he used as a

CAUGHT STEALING

'loaner' for friends, and a high five-figure bank account. On the surface there was little doubt that Sammy had arrived. If ever a man's ego thrived on his own grandiosity, it was Sammy's. Some joked that Sammy probably drank his own bath water!

As an attorney, he was well-respected by his contemporaries of the bench and bar. Sammy was not all show. Only a month before, he defended a well-known narcotics dealer in a high-profile trial which lasted six weeks. The defendant was acquitted, much to the chagrin of the federal, state and local law enforcement agencies involved in what was reported as a three-year investigation culminating in indictments of several major Arizona drug dealers. Many other defendants, with less competent counsel, were convicted.

When discussing fees with a client, Sammy liked to stand behind his huge desk, lower his voice to an audible whisper and say, "You'll get just as much justice as you can afford." He often quoted a renowned criminal defense attorney who was reported to have said "... after they've paid my fee, they've been punished enough."

A few years earlier, Sammy had gotten involved in doing the legal groundwork that enabled the parents of young adults who had become members of the pseudo-religious cults to have their children de-programmed. It appeared that Sammy was performing this work with little or no remuneration. In truth, Sammy was very handsomely paid. In each instance, the parents, for reasons of their own, never discussed the exorbitant sums Sammy had charged them and, of course, Sammy didn't disclose his fees to anyone. The end result was that Sammy made several hundred thousand dollars in quiet fees, while appearing to the general public as a beneficent lawyer unselfishly devoted to the reuniting of broken and grief-stricken families. Sammy played this to the hilt. His 'de-programming team' had been on every major television talk show in America, the result of which was national publicity for Sammy, both as a fine lawyer and as a good Samaritan. Sammy's public image thus portrayed him as a highly competent friend of the helpless and oppressed, while privately his motivation was little different from that of a greedy Shylock. But this public image was what had originally caused Manny Hernandez to contact Sammy and hire him as his player-agent.

In the middle of the 1979 season, Manny Hernandez was in his sixth year as a major league player. Under the master contract, a player may become a free agent after he completes six years of major league service. Thus, at the conclusion of the 1979 season, Manny was to become a free agent since, at that time, his existing contract would expire. Manny was watching the Phil Donahue Show during a televised interview with Sammy Snider. Sammy would use every available opportunity to expound on what he called 'fundamental Christianity and freedom.' Manny didn't understand terms like 'mind control' and 'de-programming', but he decided, based on what he thought he understood, that this was the lawyer he wanted to represent him in his contract negotiations as a free agent.

Manny talked it over with Vivienne and she agreed, well knowing that once she met Sammy, she could persuade Manny to abandon him if it appeared that Sammy couldn't be easily manipulated by her. From reading the paper and watching the news in Phoenix, Vivienne was aware of Sammy's legal conquests and withheld final approval until satisfied that Sammy would play her game. To assure herself of this, she met alone with Sammy before she and Manny went to meet him together. When Manny met Sammy for the first time, he was not aware, and was never made aware later, that Sammy and Vivienne had already met. In fact, that first meeting between Vivienne and Sammy had gone so well that Sammy had made a strong suggestion to her that they meet again -- and often. At that moment, Vivienne felt confident that Sammy would do her bidding regardless of any negative effects that might be suffered by Manny.

Vivienne knew after meeting Sammy that she had him in the palm of her hand. She also knew that if he ever became a reluctant player in her game, she had only to spread her legs for him, and he would obediently go along with her. Vivienne and Sammy shared a strong physical attraction; besides, such tactics had never failed for Vivienne in the past, and she was sure they wouldn't fail now. She didn't give in to Sammy's first advances, however, because she realized that such a valuable chip should not be cashed before she needed it.

Vivienne was the dominating force behind the negotiating of Manny's new contract, but publicly appeared as the loving wife and mother of the children of baseball's newest millionaire, giving all credit to Manny and Sammy.

Sammy let Vivienne run things where Manny was concerned; he never crossed her. In fact, at her urging, Manny agreed to pay Sammy a ten-percent fee for his

30

services, while unknown to Manny, Sammy agreed to funnel five percent back to Vivienne. Further, out of his five-hundred thousand dollar signing bonus, Manny, at Vivienne's suggestion, agreed to leave half of it in Sammy's special interest-bearing trust account. She convinced Manny that the two of them wouldn't be as apt to spend it if they had to go through Sammy to get it. Manny finally, but reluctantly, agreed to this arrangement. What made him give in to her was her agreement that he could send ten-thousand dollars to his parents in Santo Domingo so they could remodel their house and add some modern appliances. Vivienne disliked sending Manny's parents anything. She viewed them as ignorant animals who shouldn't mind living in squalor, and this was a major bone of contention between Manny and her. Vivienne usually won the arguments by pleading that what she and Manny had should be kept for their own children. She would remind Manny that his family obviously had gotten along fine up to now and didn't need to feed off Manny and her. She constantly prayed that Manny would not ever want his family to come to the States to live, or even to visit.

* * *

When Sammy returned to his office, he breezed past Shirley, pausing only long enough to pick up his phone messages. Shirley called to him just as he reached his office door. "Maybe you should call Vivienne Hernandez right away. She's called three times, and it sounds urgent."

Seating himself comfortably behind his desk, Sammy dialed Vivienne's number without referring to the message. Her number was permanently emblazoned in his memory. She answered on the third ring.

"Hi Viv," Sammy greeted her.

"Hi Sammy," she came back. Her voice took on a throaty tone as she continued, "The kids will be at the sitter's the rest of the day; think you could find time to drop by and see me?"

"Sure, Viv," Sammy replied, "what's goin' on?"

"Just make it about two o'clock," Vivienne replied, "and stop for a bottle of good white wine. Maybe you and I need to tie up some loose ends that we've neglected for a long time."

Sammy couldn't suppress a chuckle of surprised anticipation as he said, "Well, Viv, I could use a little afternoon delight."

"And by the way, Sammy," Vivienne continued, "park your car in my garage and come in through the kitchen; I may still be out by the pool. Oh, and don't forget to push the garage door closed behind you. We wouldn't want your car seen by prying eyes."

"Sounding better all the time," Sammy said, "but humor me; is it possible that I'm about to be blessed with something I've been strictly denied so far?"

"Now, Sammy," Vivienne purred, "if I told you, that would ruin the pleasant anxiety I hope you'll experience before you get here, but I will say this, I hope you're feeling at least a little bit... well, should I say, 'randy'?"

Sammy lowered his voice to match the conspiratorial tone of hers. "Viv, sweetie, where you're concerned, I'm always as randy as a rabbit. See you soon." He placed the phone into its cradle slowly, enjoying the budding erection which had commenced beneath his clothing.

Chapter 3 -- THE GAME

The lineup was posted on the dugout wall in the traditional fashion with the players' names listed in the order they would bat:

1.	Shand	2B
2.	Strecker	SS
3.	Marine	RF
4.	Ballenger	LF
5.	Kirkham	3B
6.	Gonzales	1B
7.	Knight	CF
8.	Justice	C
9.	McCoy	P

Woody Justice read it with trepidation, then sat down and became lost in daydreaming until Snake walked in front of him and said, "Everybody is expecting great things of you, which is good. Just remember to take it a day at a time; put one foot in front of the other, and the rest of your career will take care of itself. The only two people in the world you <u>have</u> to please is <u>you</u> and <u>me</u>. If your personal standards are high enough and you please yourself, I become satisfied automatically. When you make a mistake -- and you will -- just remember, the last guy who didn't make any, they crucified. Also, try to remember that it's different up here. Startin' now, you're in the big money game -- and that's what it's all about, no matter what anybody ever tries to tell you. We should all have fun -- but win. If we don't win, we all get to go home, one at a time, to a lunch bucket. End of lecture... now try to relax by going down to the bull pen and precisely fifteen minutes before game time, start warming up Duffy McCoy. That big Irishman used to throw so hard nobody could hold him, but now with age, he's a real artist -- finesse pitcher, you know? Get down there and talk over each of the Cub hitters. Pay attention to him and learn -- but don't go drinkin' with him unless you have a hollow leg." The rookie stepped gingerly out of the dugout and trotted to the bull pen to commence his big league career by visiting with an old pro. Snake had called Duffy an encyclopedia on enemy hitters, and Justice was ready to learn.

Thirty-eight year-old Duffy McCoy had done a little running and stretching, and was now settled on the bull pen bench signing autographs for fans who reached over the short wall behind him. As Woody approached, the big man broke into a huge smile, and he hollered out, "Everybody welcome the world champeen cake tester, Mister Woody Justice."

Woody laughed, somewhat abashed, while an alert fan who had misinterpreted Duffy's words led several other fans in a chorus of 'Happy Birthday'. Several players came over and joined in until Bob Chastain, the pitching coach, ended the fun with, "Let's get to work before I trade all of you to the Mormon Tabernacle Choir."

The singing over, Bob motioned Woody to sit between Duffy and himself. Slapping Woody on the knee, Bob began to talk. "First of all, kid, I'm glad to see you here -- we all are -- we need you to finish this job. Secondly, you're damn fortunate to be receiving ole Duffy here for your maiden assignment in the Big Show. Last, remember the words of the immortal Mark Twain, 'tis better to remain silent and let everyone think you're a fool than to open your mouth and remove all doubt.' There'll be nearly forty-thousand screaming Cub fans here today, and maybe a couple hunnert of ours. It's an old, small yard by modern standards, and before this game is started good, you'll think every damn one of 'em is inside your shirt collar. Now, Duffy, let's go over the lineup with him." Bob pulled out the Cub lineup, which read:

1.	Mosby	RF
2.	Morcardi	SS
3.	Christopher	LF
4.	Tucker	2B
5.	Cromer	3B
6.	Singer	CF
7.	Peterson	1B
8.	Noble	C
9.	Herring	P

Just looking at the names on the list made Woody feel like he was reading a sports magazine. The unreality of playing in the big leagues overwhelmed him, not for the first time. Bob continued to talk, "Any one of the first three

36

hitters can bunt well, and they have speed. Kirkham and Gonzales know that, but if they were to fall asleep and drift back, with less than two strikes on any of these guys, then holler at 'em! Don't be shy... wake 'em up! That's part of your job! You're not just a receiver here, you're a full-fledged field general, and don't forget it."

Not pausing to see if Woody was taking all this in, Bob continued. "And another thing... those first three guys are rabbits. When we played 'em at home two weeks ago, Mosby got hit by Hernandez and limped in apparent pain to first base. Hernandez thought he was really bruised bad by the way he acted, then the little son-of-a bitch stole second, and when the ball drifted into shallow center, he went to third! Cunning, that's what he was, pure cunning. Hell, I thought 'Pepper' Martin had been reincarnated."

Bob paused momentarily and gazed into the distance, as if he were seeing Pepper Martin again. Then he turned his gaze to Woody and returned to the present. "We got Morcardi out, but then Christopher squeezed Mosby home, and they beat us by that run. The first three are spray hitters -- not a lot of power -- but they can also hit bad pitches. Best way to pitch all of 'em is low and outside, but since they'll be lookin' for that, mix 'em up. That applies to the whole damn team. If Duffy shakes you off, listen to him. This old pro was here before most of us got here, and he'll probably still be here when we're gone."

Bob looked briefly at Woody, shook his head, and started in again. "Tucker, Cromer, Singer and Peterson are premier, first-class hitters. Tucker is the best 'guess' hitter in either league. I'd give anything if we had him, but when we could have had him, nobody guessed, at that stage, that he would've turned out like this. Excuse my digressing. Noble can't hit a shoulder-high fast ball, and he'll swing at 'em all day. But, as Duffy here will tell you, Mister Duffy left his live fast ball between the sheets a long time ago. So, what starts out as a Duffy shoulder-high pitch ends up in the dirt away from the guy who, hopefully, can't stop his swing and misses it by a foot.

"Again -- and I can't emphasize this enough -- they got the book on us, just like we got the book on them, but if all the intelligence that's passed around worked on everybody all the time, baseball would die from a lack of fans -- it'd get real boring. But it doesn't, and it won't, because the so-called <u>book</u> changes, day by day. The only thing that stays the same is that the team with the most runs at the end of regulation play, <u>wins</u>, and that, my young friend, is the object of all of our combined efforts and our main purpose in being here!"

"Bob," Woody interrupted, "since I don't know these hitters -- and a few others in the league -- while I'm learning, I should rely on my pitchers, isn't that right?"

"Well, yes and no," Bob answered. "Generally, you're right, especially with a guy like Duffy on the mound, but the exception to that rule will occur when a young fire-baller gets over-confident and thinks that just because he blew some guy away yesterday, or his last time out, he's gonna do it again today. It's this way, kid, up here... just because something worked yesterday doesn't mean that it's cast in stone, that it will always work. Big Leaguers don't stay in the show if they can't change and adjust. That's why

I started this conversation by stressing that you should keep you mouth shut. The flip side of that is, only open your mouth to ask an intelligent question. That's how you'll learn."

Bob looked at the rookie with something akin to pity. He smiled, patted him on the back and said, "Hey, kid, I know this is a lot we're all throwin' at you, but you'll get it down pat real soon. If you feel the need, call time and walk out there and talk to Duffy about a hitter. You learn by mistakes, and since the time for learning is now, you have to assume that you're going to make mistakes. Just don't make too many of them all at the same time, and try hard to <u>never</u> make the same one twice." Bob paused to see how Woody was taking all this talk, slapped him on the knee and stood. "Well, kid," he said, "time's run out; you've just got a couple of minutes before Duffy'll want to start his warm-up tosses. Like all good pitchers, Duffy's got his own routine, and fifteen minutes of warming up is a major part of it -- he never varies -- so I'll shut up and let you and Duffy talk."

Woody looked at Duffy, and Bob started to leave, thought better of it and sat back down. He relaxed and listened as Duffy began to speak to the young catcher. "In a word, kid, any part of playing baseball is simple -- but never easy -- especially at this level. With me, I've gone full circle, from flame-thrower to pitcher. I used to be three-fourths brawn and one-fourth brain, but now those measurements are reversed. When I throw a fast ball, for instance, it won't move like it used to, but i can thread a needle with it. My curve ball isn't a wide, sweeping one with good velocity, but it's one that seems to float up there and then acts like it fell off a table. You might say I have three speeds: slow, slower and slower yet. As they say, I can't break a pane of glass with any one of my pitches anymore, but I can destroy the magnificent timing of any hitter for the short time he faces me." Duffy scratched his head and frowned slightly.

"Now you need to know that, when you're catching me, be aware that rarely will I repeat a pitch to any one batter at the same velocity. So don't look for my slow curve to look like the last one I threw. With me, it's a game of keeping the hitters off balance. I can't dust 'em off any longer. Hell, if a guy sees one of my pitches coming at his head, he knows it's not hard enough to hurt him, so he's apt to just let it hit him and take his base. Well, that's about it, unless you have any questions."

"Just one," Woody said; "what signs shall we use?"

"Simple," Duffy replied, "one's fast, two's curve, three's fork and four's knuckle. I don't have a screw ball, and I've stopped trying to get anybody out with a slider; can't throw it hard enough. My knuckler's not bad; I just can't control it as well as I'd like to. My bread and butter is the curve at all sorts of different speeds, and having it end up wherever you're holding your glove -- and I assure you, if it's not hit, it'll end up where you show me to put it. Okay, let's get to throwin."

Bob Chastain watched as Woody and Duffy got up and moved away from each other in preparation for Duffy's warm-up tosses. 'What a study in contrasts,' he thought, as he started for the dugout. 'God, in the old days, young guys never got treated that nice. It was strictly survival of the fittest. Nowadays, it's all different; we got unions, retirement plans and baseball card shows. I wonder sometimes which way is best. Oh, well,' he thought, 'the answer's probably like everything else -- somewhere in between.' He entered the dugout and took a seat next to Snake.

Chapter 4 -- THE DOPE DEALER

In a high-rise office building along the Central corridor in Phoenix, Tino Borozi was anxiously awaiting an important telephone call. His first lieutenant, Gus Kirby, was unsuccessfully trying to keep his boss calm, which was doubly difficult because Gus was also on pins and needles.

"You know, boss," Gus offered, "I thought after Sammy Snider got you acquitted, the heat would let up for a while. Instead, we can't feel it from the Feds, but our suppliers -- especially Raphael -- start stonewalling us."

"I know," Tino sighed angrily. "But we're not out of it, just slowed down. Dammit, don't you remember, after our first year together, in 1969, when we were just getting started good and the DEA thought they'd cut our legs out from under us with that big bust in L.A.?" Before Gus could answer, Tino continued, "Well, all they did was make us mad and more determined, and look where we went after we got back on track. The big problem now that we didn't have then is one word -- money. Who'd a dreamed the Feds woulda crippled our cash position with that last bust. And now, Sammy Snider beats the damn rap, but says he's havin' a problem gettin' our money released because of red tape. I oughta 'red tape' his young ass!"

Tino was getting more worked up as he talked. He began to pace the floor and wave his arms as he continued, "I don't understand how the hell I get acquitted and they keep the money. Then Raphael stonewalls us -- but when I talked to someone at his house in Barranquilla last night, they were very cautious, almost whiny courteous, you know, and assured me he'd get back to me personally -- himself -- today. Damn, I wish the old bastard would hurry up. I'm paranoid about talking on the phone, but I think we can disguise our conversation enough for me to get all the answers I need. Hell, I just need him to give me the signal that we're starting up where we left off when I got busted."

Before Tino could continue his nervous chatter, the phone rang. "Let it ring, Boss," Gus advised, "so you don't look too anxious, and speak slow, calm down. If that old shark gets the idea we're running scared, he'll eat us alive."

"Dammit Gus, quit talkin' to me like I'm a school kid," Tino barked. He picked up the phone on the third ring.

"Hello, Tino Borozi here."

"Overseas operator calling Mister Tino Borozi, are you Mister Borozi?"

Tino answered the nasal voice affirmatively and listened as Raphael spoke in broken, accented English. "Hello, Tino, my friend, sorry I missed you last night." Actually Raphael had <u>missed</u> Tino for a month. "*Mira* Tino, I'm sorry we haven't been able to touch; you know how I am sometimes... I've just been to the hills, sort of a little rest; maybe you've needed one, too, eh?"

43

Without waiting for Tino to speak, the voice continued, "Tino, our people are afraid of industrial espionage, you know, phone bugging and such, and our trade secrets are the lifeblood of our business. What would you say to a face-to-face meeting, you know, like last time?"

Tino quickly assented, then asked, "Where?"

"I said like last time, Tino, you remember, don't you?"

"You mean you and me?" Tino answered.

"Sure, old friend, you and me... now I think you are remembering." The last time they met face to face was on an airstrip in Panama, with security provided by the Panamanian Army under the direct orders of that country's dictator, General Amoroso.

"When?" Tino asked.

"When can you be there?"

"Time is of the essence to me, Raphael," Tino replied. "What about forty-eight hours from now, at noon, Panama time?"

"Fine," Raphael agreed, "see you then. And, Tino, one more thing, congratulations on your trial victory; you must be very happy."

"Yes, sir, I am. After all, justice will out," Tino said, "but that's as it should be when an innocent is put on trial."

Through a half-muffled laugh, Raphael ended the conversation with, "See you soon; pleasant journey."

Getting to Panama was no big problem for Tino and Gus, but, as they had learned the hard way, getting there undetected <u>was</u> a problem. Obviously, commercial air travel was out of the question, which meant that excellent private aircraft and trustworthy pilots were necessary. They could arrive in Panama under tight security on what amounted to a private airstrip, but they had no such veil of security for departing the U.S. Tino had located several private airstrips and a few trustworthy pilots who, for a price, could safely fly them at low enough altitude to avoid radar. The aircraft would undoubtedly be visually picked up by the Coast Guard, but if the pilot kept his I.D. lettering disguised well enough, he could minimize their risk, as well as his own. Tino hurriedly made contact with just such a pilot as he and Gus made preparations for their journey. They were excited about getting the cocaine importing going again. Gus was elated that Raphael had finally returned the call.

"How did he sound, Boss?" Gus asked.

"Like nothing has changed," Tino replied.

"You know, as long as Raphael has been in this business, he's bound to've had his people busted before; I'd think that goes with the territory. Maybe we were worried about nothing. I just can't see him getting upset over being busted, especially when we beat it, Boss. Eh, I mean," Gus corrected himself, "you beat it, Boss."

Tino smiled and said, "You know, Gus, in this business, you never know from one day to the next when a guy, especially a big boss guy, is gonna cop an attitude. After all, Raphael don't need us like we need him. Shit, there must be a hundred guys tryin' to muscle in on our territory if they just had a source. I know in my heart of hearts that Raphael could deal us out tomorrow -- hell, he could've already done it. The only reason I don't think so is that he asked us to meet, like before. If he'd decided to drop us, he wouldn't lure us to Panama; shit, he could have us killed in our beds right here real damn fast and easy." Tino stopped and considered his own words, while Gus listened intently. "No, Gus, I think this meeting means we're still in. Funny thing is, the way he operates, he could be telling the truth about just bein' up in the hills. He does things like that; sometimes he's just tired of the world, and he disappears for a week or two right there on his ranch."

When Tino stopped momentarily, Gus jumped in. "You know, Boss, I'm sure you got this guy figured, but I think he also knows he'd have to look long and hard before he found another stand-up guy like you. And I'll tell you another thing, he has to respect the way you went to trial and won. Other men, lesser ones, might have handled it in a way that threatened Raphael and his operation. You know what I mean, not a stand-up guy like you."

Tino smiled at Gus' words, pleased that his 'second-string' showed the proper admiration for the boss. "Yes, Gus, I could've taken a guaranteed easy way out, but you and I know I'd <u>never</u> do that, just like my men would never do that to me."

"I know, Boss," Gus confirmed in a quiet voice, then hurriedly asked, "which car we takin', Boss?"

"The Chevy," Tino replied, "and while you go get it, I want to make a call."

When Gus left the room, Tino dialed Sammy Snider's office. Shirley answered and informed him in her usual courteous manner that Sammy was out. She asked if there was any message.

"Only this, Shirley; I'll be out of pocket for a day or two, but I'd like to buy his lunch about the middle of next week."

"I'll see that he gets the message, Mister Borozi. Anything else? Do you have a preference as to what day?"

"No, Shirley, nothing else, and no preference; just whatever is good for Sammy. I'll call back in a few days and see what we've got set up."

"Fine, Mister Borozi, I'll take care of it."

Tino replaced the phone and headed for the elevator.

* * *

Conversation in the car during the two-and-a-half-hour drive was dominated by Gus' obsequious compliments about how Tino handled the phone call and Tino's bragging about how Raphael obviously realized, after thinking it over, that Tino was the best in the business, and Raphael wouldn't dream of dumping him. The two kept up this line of conversation until they were both imbued with an air of overwhelming confidence.

The pilot who Tino had contacted after Raphael's call was one with whom he had a long-standing arrangement. The man kept his private plane at his own home in northern Arizona. With only a short coded notice, Tino and Gus could show up there, and he would fly them, without an officially recorded flight plan, anywhere in the hemisphere. Only after they had boarded the twin-engine plane did the pilot inquire, "Where to, gentlemen?"

"We're vacationing for a couple of days," Tino replied quietly, "take us to Hermosillo."

47

"Just give me a minute to check the map, and we'll get going." Tino's plan was for the first leg of the trip to be diversionary. By flying to Mexico, if he were being followed, he would have time to detect it. If not, he could proceed with another pre-arranged pilot and plane on the Mexican side of the Gulf and then over the Atlantic to Panama.

The trip to Hermosillo was quiet and uneventful, and the two men were soon in another plane bound for Panama, confident they had not been followed by ground radar. Even if they had, it didn't bother them, because they were sure they weren't at risk in their trip over the Atlantic. Arriving safely in Panama, they were greeted warmly by Raphael, which boosted their confidence even more. A makeshift boardroom style meeting table had been erected adjoining the runway, and they settled themselves around it. The pilot busied himself with refueling, and, other than Raphael's personal security men, the three were quite alone.

Raphael spoke: "I know your trip was tiring, but I have pressing business both here and at home; therefore, I chose to meet with you immediately so I can get on to other things." His courteous but firm tone left no doubt as to who was the dominant authority at the meeting.

"It is my desire to continue doing business with you," Raphael continued. "We shall make some necessary logistical changes because of the problems in your recent past."

Tino and Gus were proudly smiling their approval, until Raphael said, "However, it is imperative that we make some changes in the transfer of money. You will, for the time being, need to pay cash on delivery for your merchandise."

Tino's expression changed to one of dismay, and he uncharacteristically interrupted, "But, Raphael, you must know that our funds are temporarily frozen."

"Yes, I am aware of that. But you must be aware that I can't operate on receivables that shall or shall not be made available at the whim of the United States government. I urged you early on to leave your money here in Panama; it has traditionally been a safe haven for many who appreciate the anonymous banking system."

Raphael looked at Tino as if he expected a response, but Tino simply glanced down at the table. Raphael continued, "But I did not deny you the privilege of ignoring that advice, which led to your present situation. So, at this juncture, I no longer care where you deposit your funds, but the funds required for me to do business with you shall be paid on delivery, or else we have nothing further to discuss."

"Look, Raphael, we apologize for not following your advice," Tino pleaded, "but the simple fact is, we haven't sought other cash sources because we're supremely confident that our funds will be returned to us."

"I share your optimism, but my business isn't geared to run itself on mere expectancies. This point, Tino, in case you haven't understood, is no longer negotiable. I like you; I want to continue doing business with you, but it must be on terms of cash on delivery."

Gus looked at Tino in disbelief. Tino's own expression registered pain, but, after a moment, changed to resignation as he quietly asked, "When will you be ready to deliver?"

"One week from today."

"Has the price changed?"

"Yes," Raphael replied quickly, "in your favor. If you will accept delivery right here, I'm prepared to offer you a price of twenty thousand a kilo, if you will take no less than a quarter-million dollars worth at a time."

Tino's expression reflected approval. "I'll agree to that, but it will take me a few days to make my financial arrangements."

"How many days, Tino?"

Tino knew that when Raphael pinned him down, he had better have an answer. He considered a moment, then replied, "One week. In one week, Gus will be here with two-hundred and fifty-thousand dollars."

"Very well, then," Raphael said with a smile. "One week from today, the merchandise will be here ready to be transferred to your aircraft. By the way, for the time being, Tino, I'll take care of the General's requirements to allow us secured free access to his country. At an appropriate time in the future, I'll expect you to be kind enough to share this burden with me."

"Done," Tino replied.

The meeting over, the three men exchanged pleasantries about the weather in Panama and parted company. The return trip to Phoenix was noticeably less light-hearted than the trip to Panama had been. At one point, Gus remarked in a sad tone, "Sum bitch, Boss, I didn't expect that; what a shocker, but I'm sure you'll think of something."

"Yeah, sure, Gus, I'm sure I'll think of something."

* * *

Immediately upon arrival in Phoenix, Tino made a phone call to Sammy Snider's office. Shirley informed him that Sammy was gone for the day, but advised him that she had set the luncheon for the following noon, if Tino agreed. After assuring Shirley that the time was agreeable, Tino replaced the phone and turned to Gus. "You remember the fee deal Sammy made with me?"

Gus thought a moment, then when the light bulb connected in his head, he blurted, "You mean the fifty thousand up front and fifty thousand if he won?"

"Yeah," Tino replied, "that just might be the key to our getting the money we need for our celebrated but a little-too-slick-for-his-own-good lawyer friend."

Gus scratched his head in questioning perplexity as he said, "But I don't understand, Boss."

"That, Gus, is why I'm 'Boss' and you're not. But, by this time tomorrow, I predict we'll have all the money we need."

Gus' interest was really piqued. "Come on, Boss," he pleaded, "I'm dying to know what you're up to." With childlike seriousness, he added, "I promise I won't tell."

Tino smiled at him. "I think I'll take you to lunch with me and Mister Sammy Snider tomorrow just to let you watch the show; it should be very entertaining for you."

"Please, Boss," Gus begged, "just give me a hint."

"I don't want to spoil the show for you. Rest assured that, once again, Tino Borozi is going to save our bacon by pulling a rabbit out of Sammy Snider's hat with a trick that nobody -- especially Sammy -- dreamed I'd do."

In spite of Gus' pleading curiosity, Tino refused to share what he had in mind, but he continued to reassure Gus that their money problems would soon be over.

Chapter 5 -- THE TRYST

Sammy Snider hurriedly finished looking over his messages and headed out of his office, stopping only long enough to speak briefly to Shirley. "Set up the lunch with Borozi when he calls back and call the escrow company to confirm that they've recorded everything from my real estate closing."

Shirley was taking shorthand notes as Sammy spoke and didn't look up until he reached the door, when she inquired, "Gone for the day?"

"Yeah," Sammy replied as he continued out the door. Shirley had been with Sammy since he opened his office in Phoenix. She had a sixth sense that was pretty accurate when it came to her boss. She was also prudent; if she could avoid any knowledge of his personal activities, she did just that. Shirley knew instinctively that mere idle curiosity could only place her firmly in a no-win situation. Sammy didn't make sexual advances toward her, and she didn't pry into his personal life. Consequently, Shirley was the envy of every law office in town. She received regular offers of employment from attorneys attempting to pirate her away from Sammy. She just as regularly refused them; Sammy treated her very well, financially and otherwise. She was even granted days off or vacation time just for the asking. He was the best in town to work for, as far as Shirley was concerned.

* * *

Sammy Snider wheeled his sport convertible out of the parking garage and around to Jefferson Avenue, then struck out toward Scottsdale. He was feeling very pleased with himself. His thoughts were whirling so quickly that it was almost as if he had spoken aloud. 'Just think, I've got what amounts to a five percent interest in a millionaire ball player who has a gorgeous wife who's just invited me over to fuck her.'

As he slowed for a corner, he couldn't resist laughing aloud, which caused a pedestrian waiting for the light to look at him. He allowed his thoughts to continue: 'If that's not enough, I've got a special trust account in my bank, under my signature, that's a quarter of a million and growing.'

The thought of money always delighted Sammy, but just now it was difficult to separate the excitement of money from the sexual excitement caused by Vivienne's phone call. There was no denying the pulsation between his legs. It crossed his mind that, unless he did something about it, he was liable to go off before he reached his destination. Again he laughed out loud.

'This Hernandez guy could be an annuity for me,' his thoughts continued, 'and I could eventually parlay his action into a full-time job -- an easy one at that. He goes away for six months a year to play ball, and I get paid handsomely, while I'm porkin' his foxy old lady. This is a deal that most men only dream about.'

Sammy almost giggled. 'I wondered how long she could hold out before she had to have me.'

He reached Curry Road, turned left in order to hit Scottsdale Road, continued to Thomas and turned back west. The Hernandez home was on a side street cul-de-sac just off Thomas Road, with lots of privacy.

Spotting a liquor store, Sammy pulled in and purchased two bottles of the best available California white wine. He then continued on to the Hernandez home, pulling into the open garage. He could see the pool as he drove in, and Vivienne wasn't there. Following her instructions, he went in through the connecting door and pushed the automatic door control. He listened to the slow grinding as the garage door slowly shut.

Sammy strolled through the kitchen and into a long hallway without a sign of Vivienne's presence. As he neared the master bedroom, he could hear the shower running in the adjoining bath. The bathroom was open, so he stuck his head in and quietly announced, "Viv, I'm here."

"Come on in and join me," she responded.

"Give me a minute, and I'll be right there." He was carrying the wine bottles, so he turned and headed toward the kitchen on a dead run. He quickly placed ice in a bucket he found on the counter, stuck a bottle of wine in the ice and returned quickly to the bedroom. He tore at his clothes, hopping on one foot to remove the final sock and literally jumped into the shower, thumping the shower door with his knuckles as he entered. Vivienne was soaping a bristled back

brush and invited him to turn around. As she slowly
scrubbed his back, she reached around him with her free
hand and began to fondle his genitals. By now, Sammy was,
as the saying goes, so hard a cat couldn't scratch him.
Vivienne was behind him, on one knee, scrubbing his back
and rubbing his dick, all with a rhythmic eroticism that was
driving him crazy. She dropped the brush, put her hand on
his butt and pushed. He responded by turning around, and
she slid his penis into her mouth and continued the rhythm,
sucking and flicking his penis with her tongue. Sammy
couldn't control himself, and he started to climax, but
Vivienne kept right on sucking. Sammy attempted to muffle
his scream of delight. As he relaxed toward her, Vivienne
slid her body up his and began to kiss him, pushing her
tongue around his mouth. He withdrew from the kiss and
began to apologize for his premature ejaculation. Vivienne
just smiled at him.

"Don't worry about it," she said, "we'll do it again,
slowly, in a little bit. First, let's dry off and have some wine,
then that beautiful root can perform between my legs, where
I'm itching for it."

They took turns toweling each other off, then Sammy
slipped on his shorts and went to get the ice bucket and wine,
assuring Vivienne that he'd be right back. Sammy thought
he'd died and gone to heaven. His wildest anticipation had
already been exceeded, and his sexual appetite was
temporarily satiated. But he knew he would be able to get
another erection in about fifteen minutes and he didn't want
to put his clothes on, so he hurried back to Vivienne. When
he re-entered the bedroom, she was lying across the bed, her

nudity only partially covered by a bath towel. Sammy poured each of them a glass of wine and sat on the side of the bed. Vivienne sat up and Sammy watched the shift of her breasts, thinking that she still looked very seductive. She began to scratch his back with her long fingernails. Sammy couldn't resist asking if the nails were her own.

"I'm an all-natural woman, Sammy," Vivienne said. Sammy could hear the smile in her voice. She moved her nails in a circular motion around his back. "Sammy," she almost purred, "I need a small favor."

Without inquiring what it might be, Sammy replied, "Anything you want, Viv, you know I'd do anything for you."

Vivienne had been confident of Sammy's cooperation, but she was delighted by his quick agreement, and she started to explain her plan. "I've been to Henze, my attorney, and started divorce proceedings. The papers will be served while the Cardinals are in Chicago -- they may have been served already. When he gets the papers, I'm sure he'll be very confused. I'm sure that at some point early in his confusion, he'll contact you, because he doesn't know any other lawyer; besides, Manny totally trusts and respects you."

She had his full attention and, as Sammy looked at her questioningly, she continued, "When he does contact you, I want you to tell him that I did it in a fit of misplaced anger. Say it any way you want to, but impress on him that I'm not going through with it. If he asks you to represent him, tell him you can't because you have represented both of us in the past. Tell him that to represent one of us against the other would be a glaring conflict of interest and highly unethical."

Vivienne smiled and patted Sammy's arm. "Oh, he won't understand any of that language, but, coming from you, he'll accept it. Now Sammy," she added seriously, "it's extremely important that when you conclude this conversation, Manny is completely at ease with the situation, so he won't go out looking for another lawyer. He'll contact me, and I'll tell him the same thing about just being a little miffed. I'll tell him to forget it, because I'm not going through with it anyway."

Sammy sipped his wine and asked in a puzzled tone, "Then, are you dropping the divorce action?"

"No, Sammy, I intend to get a default judgment against him after he fails to answer my petition."

Sammy raised his eyebrows. "Then why --?"

"Because, honey," she answered before he could finish, "we want him to finish the season in a good frame of mind, so he'll continue pitching well. You know, Sammy," she continued, in a tone she sometimes used when explaining something to her children, "the Cardinals could win it all this year. If they do, I'll see that you get your cut of Manny's playoff and World Series money, even though your contract doesn't include that." She stroked his chin with one finger. "Vivienne will see that you aren't penalized by your oversight, but, of course, I'll expect you to split it with me, as usual."

She stood up, letting the towel drop completely. Sammy was momentarily distracted by her nakedness. Her next words reclaimed his attention. "You know, Sammy, I'm going to end up with everything, including custody of the kids. When I do, I want you back in the picture as my legal counsel and business advisor. But, just so you know where my heart is, I'm aware that you dipped into our special trust account so you could close your big real estate deal a few weeks ago. I've made it a point to monitor the account regularly since it was set up."

Sammy sat expressionless as his feelings of lust were overridden by his fear of losing his law license.

"Oh, Sammy, I'm sure you intended to replace the funds before we called for them. Anyway, don't worry... I won't tell Manny, and, more importantly, I won't tell the Bar. I hear they're rather touchy about such things. That's how most lawyers lose their licenses."

The words 'misappropriation of funds' echoed in Sammy's head. He breathed a sigh of relief when she said she wasn't going to expose him to the Bar, and he began to speak quickly. "Viv, I'm only going to need that money for a short time, and I'll put it back in the account. I just meant to --"

Vivienne interrupted him, "I'm sure you will, Sammy, and I trust you. So much so that my lips are sealed. But you'll honor my wish about the divorce petition, won't you?"

"Sure, Viv," he said, "it's as good as done."

Vivienne climbed back onto the bed and ran her hand between his legs. "Poor baby, it's gone to sleep on me; let me see if I can't wake it up."

They finished the wine, and, as predicted, Vivienne again aroused Sammy. They spent the afternoon rising to the peak of sexual pleasure. Before Sammy left, they had explored every inch of each other's bodies and arrived at that peak four times, the last time in the swimming pool.

Sammy drove home to his wife and kids, comfortable with the thought that he had dodged an ethical bullet, and pleased with the expanded relationship with Vivienne. He liked the idea that when Vivienne did end up with all Manny's cash -- and he had no doubt that she would -- he would have personal access to that cash. That meant more real estate deals, with Vivienne as his financial backer, as well as his fantastic sexual partner.

"God," Sammy said aloud, "if more women came on to their husbands like she came on to me, the divorce rate in this country would evaporate."

Sammy's willingness to engage in deceit for a price was now only equaled by his concupiscence.

Vivienne took another shower and lay down to take a nap before retrieving the kids from the baby-sitter. She dozed off thinking, 'So far, so good; not bad for a poor little girl from Medford, Oregon.'

Chapter 6 -- MANNY COMES THROUGH - AGAIN

Mel Stoll was vigorously rubbing Manny's back when he noticed a six-inch scar running diagonally from left to right.

"Hey, Manny, I've never noticed this before," he said as he traced it with his finger, "it looks pretty old."

"Yeah, Mel, it happened when I was a kid. You might say the day that happened was the day I got started in baseball."

"Tell me about it," Mel urged.

"Not now," Manny replied; "right now, I feel like relaxing, and you're doing a good job of helping me."

"Okay, but some day, when you feel like it, I'd sure like to hear that story -- don't forget."

"I won't," Manny assured him. Mel continued with the back rub as Manny relaxed on the table. Manny was almost ready to drift into a light sleep when Mel remembered something he was supposed to tell him. "Say, Manny, one of those lady sports reporter types sat down in the hotel bar last night and bought me a drink. Seems she's doing a special report on Latin baseball guys. Said she'd do almost anything

61

to get to meet you and interview you for her story. What do you think; can you take a few minutes to talk with her before we leave town?"

Mel could feel Manny tense momentarily, then relax again. "I really don't want to this trip, Mel," Manny said, "but I'll be glad to, the next time we're in town. Tell her I'll do it, but not right now, okay?"

"Sure, Manny, but we won't be back in town this season, so she'll have to wait 'til next year. Oh well, she really seemed like a nice gal... pretty, too, and by putting it off, I'll get to see more of her. She's really nice, not just another pushy broad who beats ya over the head with her press credentials."

"Okay, fine, Mel, I'll be glad to." Manny closed the subject as the soothing touch of Mel's fingers began to have the effect that Snake had intended. Manny once again started to doze off.

* * *

Woody Justice got his first major league hit when he led off the sixth inning of a scoreless game with a double. Duffy McCoy sacrificed him to third with what should have been the leading run. With an 'O' and two count, Charlie Shand hit a ground ball to the right side. Snake had flashed the signal to his third base coach, 'Tennessee' Jim Walker, for Woody to run on contact, meaning if Charlie hit the ball on the ground to the right side, Woody should be off and running at the crack of the bat. Tennessee Jim, to avoid any confusion on the rookie's part, even whispered the instruction in Billy's ear as Jerry Herring, the opposing pitcher, was off the mound fingering the resin bag. Everyone in the Big Show knew that little Charlie Shand was a fierce competitor, and with two strikes on him, he was as dangerous as a wounded water buffalo. The crowd sensed that, with this pitcher's duel, the rookie running at third base could score the only run they would see that day.

Tension filled the air as Charlie dug in and fouled off two straight pitches that might have been called balls, but little Charlie was wisely guarding the plate and not taking the chance of getting called out on strikes on a close pitch. Snake, without looking at Bob, who was seated next to him, said, "That ornery son-of-a-bitch, he hasn't wasted a pitch yet. That Herring's a barrel of guts and then some. I'll betcha Charlie's up to the task; watch him bounce one to second and score the rookie."

"Yeah, Snake," Bob agreed, "and the way Duffy's throwin' today, that's about all we'll need to win this one."

"Is Duffy okay, Bob?" Snake snapped.

"Far as I know."

Snake was momentarily relieved because Duffy was prone to develop a recurring blister on his middle finger if he threw more than one hundred and ten pitches. Somebody always kept a careful count on Duffy's number of pitches. Today that 'somebody' was Tony Jackson, a pinch-hitter utility player. Snake glanced down the bench at Duffy and Tony and asked, "Where's Duffy on pitches?"

"Ninety-five, Skip," Tony answered.

"I don't mean miles per hour; I mean numbers," Snake shot back. Everyone enjoyed a tension-breaking laugh. They all knew that Duffy hadn't had that kind of velocity in at least ten years.

Herring threw Charlie a fast ball on the outside corner and low. Charlie measured it with the millisecond reaction time of a veteran major leaguer and swung the bat with a motion of wrist-snapping synchronicity which brought bat to ball with a resounding crack. The ball left the bat and bounded on the ground as if it had eyes toward a point too far right of the first baseman for him to make a play.

Woody had clearly understood Coach Walker's whispered instruction and kept mentally repeating to himself, 'Run on contact.' When the ball left Charlie's bat, it looked at first like it was clearly headed for right field, at least from Woody's perspective, along the third base line. Woody started to run, but not with authority. By the time the ball was beautifully fielded by the Cub second baseman, moving to his left, he had a play on Woody at the plate. When Woody saw this, he shifted gears and started to run hard.

Tucker's throw to the plate, made on the dead run, beat Woody by three feet because of Woody's original hesitation. Woody slid into home, but by that time, his slide was to no avail. Noble tagged Woody and stepped aside, saying, "Welcome to Chicago, kid; there's lotsa fun in Lincoln Park, where you'll probably be playin' tomorrow!" Woody ignored Noble's words, knowing that a response would only aggravate his situation.

Woody was flustered as he dusted the dirt from his uniform and walked back to the dugout. Forty-thousand fans, as Bob had told him a little over an hour before, were under his collar. He made his way to that part of the dugout where his gear was lying and was starting to put on his shin guards, when someone put a hand on his shoulder. "Skip

64

wants you." Woody didn't even see who said it, but he quickly picked up his mask and chest protector and started walking toward Snake, who was sitting at the other end of the dugout.

'A man's 'last mile' walk to the electric chair would be easier than this,' he thought as he passed in front of his silent teammates. 'What more could happen to me today?' he wondered. 'First, I get my stupid face shoved into a cake, and now I fuck up with the lead run.' By the time he arrived at where Snake was sitting, Woody fully expected to have the man break into a rage, criticizing his monumental failure to execute a simple running procedure, then hand him his pink slip back to Springfield, or out the door. What he had just done, Woody thought, could conceivably be the beginning of the Cardinals' failure to win the division. His heart was pounding; sweat was popping out on his forehead, and it had little to do with temperature, exercise or humidity. Without saying anything, Snake motioned for Woody to sit down. Woody felt more inclined to show Snake how he really could run -- straight to the shower and out of there.

Woody sat down and Snake put his big long arm around Woody's back and gave him a half-hug by gently pulling on him and then letting go. He put his arm back in his own lap and said, "Damn, Woody, I haven't seen a catcher make such a beautiful slide in thirty years. Some day, that slide will win a ball game for us, probably many ball games. I really appreciate your demonstrating it for us." Woody was mystified by Snake's attitude, which lay somewhere between sarcasm and forgiveness.

Snake continued. "You're a smart boy, Woody, so remember the lesson you learned here a minute ago, and don't let guilt eat you alive. I know Noble said something to you as he tagged you. Just remember, that son-of-a-bitch has struck out twice today, so he's not exactly made himself a moving force in this ball game.

Woody was listening to everything Snake was saying, but he still had trouble holding his head up. Snake continued. "Now look, kid; what separates you from the guys you left in Springfield is the ability to get up one more time than you get knocked down. Forget the shame, shock and self-condemnation, and get on with the business of winning. One more thing, let's have dinner tonight and a few drinks."

"Okay, Skip," Woody agreed, forgetting that he was not a drinking man. This overpowering feeling of relief would have caused him to agree to anything just then. Later, he could deal with going out with his new manager, while trying to abstain from alcohol.

Strecker made the third out with a routine fly ball, and the Cardinals trotted back onto the field with the ball game still in a scoreless tie. Snake turned to Bob and told him to go check on Manny. Bob informed him that Mel had reported that Manny was sound asleep on the training table.

"Bob, if Manny was on, he could close this thing and pick up a win, if we could do a little scoring. I hadn't intended to use him; now, I'm wondering if it wouldn't be best for all of us if I did." When Bob didn't reply, Snake pushed him for an answer.

"You think this damn divorce thing has ruined his concentration? Hell, he'd have more chance of surviving a German concentration camp than pitching against these damn Cubs with his mind on family problems."

"Snake, let's get him ready." Bob assumed his most serious expression. "For my part, Hernandez is a helluva horse. That damn wife of his must be nuts, but that's none of my business. They say the reason he's been with so many different clubs is his wife."

Snake looked at Bob as if he expected more, so Bob continued. "I know it doesn't sound like I'm answering your question, but he has been with a lot of clubs, and if she is the reason, then he's probably learned to roll with the punches. Besides, if she isn't gonna drop this thing, then we got to learn to operate with him in a fucked-up frame of mind anyway, so we might as well get started; he's gonna be here awhile. We might as well get used to him and his troubles. You know, the front office don't pay a guy the kind of money he's getting and then ship him. Face it, Snake, he's ours now to live with, warts and all."

"I've never had it put to me quite that way, Bob," Snake replied, "but go wake him up and tell him we need him. I'm sure Duffy's close to blister time, although I'm real pleased with the way he's held out. Our old junk dealer has been a real credit to us today."

Bob slid off the bench and strolled to the dressing room. Just like Mel had reported, Manny was dead to the world on the training table. All the excitement and stress must have worn him out, Bob thought, as he tapped Manny gently on the shoulder. He tapped him twice more, moving back after each touch, knowing that some guys come up swinging when aroused from a sound sleep. Manny opened his eyes and blinked a few times before seeing Bob.

"Oh, hi, Coach, I must've fallen asleep."

"That's what we wanted you to do, Manny, but Snake wanted me to come and see how you were feeling. Do you feel up to pitchin' today?" Manny sat up, yawned and blinked some more before answering.

"Sure thing, Bob; I'm okay. That nap sure felt good. I'll take a leak and get dressed out and be right there." Manny was pleased with the way Snake and Bob -- and everybody else, except Baxter Burrows -- had treated him since the divorce summons had sent him into a state of confusion. Almost as an afterthought, Manny asked, "How we doing? Is Duffy okay, still in there?"

"Yeah, Manny," Bob answered, "but it's about blister time, and we're in a scoreless tie, so you could pick up a win."

"I'd rather get a save and Duffy get a win, but I'll be right out and start loosening up."

By the time Manny arrived in the dugout, the Cubs had runners on first and second, with one out. Snake was on the mound conferring with Duffy, while Woody Justice listened. Snake summoned the home plate umpire to the mound. Nobody had been warming up in the Cardinal bull pen, and the Cub fans were bewildered by this sudden parley called by Snake. The umpire, Bob Murphy, walked briskly to the mound.

"Murph, my man here has a blister that's broken and bleeding," Snake informed him. "Can I be allowed unlimited warm-up for Hernandez?"

Murphy motioned for Duffy to turn his hand over so he could get a better look at the broken blister on top of Duffy's big middle finger. "Don't hold that thing up, McCoy, or forty-thousand people will think you're given' me the bird, and I'll have to boot you." They all laughed. Murphy was known for his sense of humor. In spite of the fact he did make mistakes, everybody liked him. At least he was consistent. Murphy agreed to Snake's suggestion, but, as they walked away, he asked, in a voice only Snake could hear, "You suppose bringing Hernandez in will be good therapy for his old lady's doin's?"

Snake laughed; he and Murphy had long been friendly enemies. After signaling Hernandez to come to the mound and start warming up, he walked to the third base line with Murphy.

"What do you think of my rookie catcher, Murph?" Snake inquired.

"He's okay, Snake; I like anybody who doesn't give me an unearned ration of their shit. The sooner everybody realizes that it's a live-and-let-live world and we've all got our jobs to do, the better I'll like it." He grinned at Snake. "Even you've mellowed with age, and we're both still here, so that's sayin' something." The two commiserated over Hernandez' domestic problems and then parted, not wanting the fans, especially the ones in Chicago, to get the wrong impression of their little visit. As Murphy started to walk away, he said, "Scowl at me, Snake; I'd hate for anyone to think I was letting you off easy."

Hernandez signaled Woody to meet him halfway between the mound and home plate. "Let's run through the signals again, Woody," he said; "one's fast, two's curve, three's change and four, if we want it, is fork. Just stick to the first three. My curve's a hard slider, like I told you before. Don't be afraid to call time and talk. I know these Cub hitters pretty well, so if I shake you off, don't get your feelings hurt. We need to win this one."

'Get my feelings hurt,' Woody thought as he trotted back to home plate; 'I never expected to hear phrases like that up <u>here</u>. Hernandez must be one sensitive dude.'

The first hitter facing Manny was Phil Christopher. He had a lifetime three-hundred average, which was better than that with men on base. Manny threw him two sliders, a change and a fast ball. Responding to Woody's signal, Manny threw him another change on a two-two count, and Christopher knocked it off the wall, scoring two runs. Christopher 'died' on second as Manny routinely got Tucker and Cromer on fly balls.

The Cardinals scored runs in the seventh, eighth and ninth and entered the Cubs' last at bat ahead by one run.

Before taking the field for the last of the ninth, Snake motioned Manny and Woody over for a message. Manny could anticipate, word for word, before they were out of Snake's mouth.

"Look, fellas, just throw strikes, back to basics, high and tight, low and outside, just throw strikes."

"Okay, Skip," Manny said, and Woody nodded his assent.

Manny warmed up and motioned with his glove hand for Woody to throw the last warm-up pitch down to second before facing Singer, Peterson and Noble.

Singer singled sharply on a three and one fast ball. Manny worked Peterson to three and two before getting him to hit into a double play. The crowd was going wild, not the least bit subdued by Manny's heroics.

The big catcher stepped in, and Manny dusted him off with the first pitch. He collected himself, dusting the dirt from his uniform pants and stood in to face Manny once more. "Ball," shouted Murphy, after observing Manny's fast ball go too far outside. With the count at two balls and no strikes, Noble stepped out of the box, tapped his spikes with his bat and said to Woody, "You guys afraid to give me something to hit?"

Recalling what Snake had said to him earlier, Woody said nothing and squatted down to give Manny the signal for the next pitch. It was a slider, slider and two called strikes. Now Noble not only stepped out of the batter's box, he turned and walked a few feet away, trying to maintain his concentration. Noble stepped back into the batter's box, and Woody signaled Manny for a fast ball. Manny shook it off. Woody gave the two-finger-down signal for Manny to throw another slider. Manny shook it off. Woody signaled for the fork ball and knuckle ball, and Manny continued shaking his head from side to side. The crowd started to boo their displeasure with Manny, as if Manny were afraid to throw the big catcher anything. Woody reluctantly signaled for the change. He didn't want Noble to sit on it like Christopher had done when he knocked in two runs.

Manny deliberately stepped off the mound and pinched the resin bag. He would step up for another sign from Woody, but, hopefully, Manny thought, Woody got his message and would give him the change first. Woody did, and Manny, to the screaming crowd's approval, shook his head 'yes'.

The crowd was on their feet as Manny pumped, gave his patented high leg kick and let the ball go toward the plate with a lot less velocity than his body machinations were telegraphing. Noble swung through the ball's path long before it got there. Murphy cried, "You're out!" As Noble was righting himself from the unbalanced, corkscrew position he had ended up in, Woody deliberately said, in his most sarcastic tone, "See you in Lincoln Park," and he walked off.

All the fellows gathered around Manny for a high five as he made his way to the dugout. The thought of going to Phoenix started gnawing at his guts again, but for a little while, he intended not to show it and to join the victory celebration. Again in the clubhouse, the team came over to shake Manny's hand or give him a congratulatory slap on the shoulder. Most of the players truly admired Manny's willingness and ability to set aside his personal problems and focus on the team and the game. Once more, Snake gave his familiar "Listen up," salutation, and the din lowered so he could be heard.

"Fellas," he started, "in accordance with the Commissioner's directive, this locker room shall be open in fifteen minutes to reporters -- male and female. So get decent to receive the ladies, and guys, please watch your language. Also, we leave O'Hare at ten in the morning. The bus leaves the hotel at nine. See you later, me and this great rookie catcher have a steak waiting for us." Snake was open about taking Woody to supper, because he knew the older guys would get a kick out of remembering what they had gone through when they first joined the club.

Glenn Ballenger, Ike Wood and Manny showered and ended up on stools in front of Manny's locker. Ike smiled and asked Manny if he knew how their manager, Billy Joe Fitch, acquired the nickname 'Snake'. When Manny shook his head, Glenn said, "It seems that when the skipper couldn't hold his own in a barroom fight, he would get a 'pier six' brawl started and then slither away, like a snake, unscathed, leaving whoever was with him to kill or be killed, while he became an observer from a safe vantage point.

"Oh, you mean that tonight, if the rookie isn't careful, he'll be the Snake's latest unsuspecting victim?"

"You got it," Glenn said, and Ike nodded agreement.

"Then that poor guy's day of fireworks has just gotten started good." Manny laughed, but they stopped discussing Snake's off-field antics as Woody walked by.

"Hey, Woody," Ike barked, "great game, kid."

Woody smiled humbly and said, "I guess it's easy to look good when you've got two guys like Manny and Duffy out there." They all slapped him on the shoulder and let him go. As he walked away, Ike shouted, "Be careful of pretty young female reporters, Woody, especially if they're single."

Manny was thinking about what Mel had said to him earlier, and he looked at Glenn and asked, "You know anything about a reporter named Kari Robins?"

"Not much," Glenn answered, "but she'd have to either have a bad case of penis envy or be a nutso women's libber to want to have a job talking to a roomful of horny ball players with nothing but towels around 'em. From what I hear, we could get fined for saying anything to her that could be called abusive. I try to steer around these reporter dames unless they just corner me, and then I'm real careful about what I say and how I act."

"I see," Manny said, thinking that the best course for him would be to hurry out of there before Miss Sports Reporter cornered him. He dressed in street clothes and, as was his habit, he prepared his second, and last, meal of the day from the spread provided in the locker room. By doing this, he could save his per-diem provided by the ball club and send it to his parents in the Dominican. Vivienne knew nothing about it, and so he didn't have to listen to her bitter criticism of his financial aid to his parents.

Kari Robins approached him as he sat down to eat. Before he was fully aware of her presence, she said, "Manny Hernandez, I'm Kari Robins with the sports section of the *Beacon*; I'm very pleased to meet you." Manny had a mouthful of food and pointed to it as if to suggest that he couldn't speak for a moment.

"Sure," the attractive lady said, "did Mel Stoll tell you I want to interview you?"

Manny nodded his head, then, with his mouth clear, he said, "How do you do, Miss Robins." She interrupted

74

him and asked that he use her first name. "I told Mel that I'd be willing to talk with you, but I'd rather do it the next time we're in town."

"I don't have that much time, Manny. Let me explain while you go on eating."

Manny agreed. He was impressed by the young woman's appearance, and as she talked, he was thinking that if he weren't happily married, he would like to get better acquainted with this lady. He was also impressed by the lady's dignity in a roomful of half-naked jocks.

"Manny, there are six-hundred and fifty major league players; about fifteen percent of them are foreign born," Kari started, "mostly Latin nationals. I'm doing an in-depth report on the Latin players. As you know, most of the Latin players come from your home country, the Dominican Republic; the rest are from Puerto Rico and Venezuela, with a few from places like Nicaragua or Panama. You being a well-known and popular Dominican, I thought that if you would cooperate with me, it would be good for you and your country, as well as for me and my paper. What do you think?"

Manny was so taken by this woman's beauty and personality that his defensive walls became evanescent.

"How long would it take us, Kari?"

"Not over two or three hours," she answered quickly. "I've taken the time to outline what I need, and basically, it boils down to your home life as a child and young adult, school experience, how you got started in baseball, minor league experiences and how you got to the show, how you like it, with maybe a little bit of what you plan to do after baseball. That's about it. I do hope you'll work with me. Frankly, this could be very important to my career."

Though Kari didn't realize it, at this point, Manny was amply persuaded to help her in any way he could. "Tell you what, Kari," he said, "why don't you give me a ride back to the hotel, stop and let me pick up some soda pop and we'll start right now on your story."

She was thrilled that this had been so easy and told Manny that she would talk to Woody Justice while he finished eating.

Her visit with Woody concluded, Kari excused herself and left the clubhouse with Manny. Woody looked at Mel Stoll and said, "I'd give anything to be going out tonight with that pretty thing. Some guys have all the luck."

"Don't let it fool you, Woody," Mel said. "You've still got a chance with her. Manny is simply accommodating her with an interview to help her out. I guarantee you that's all that'll happen; he's as monogamous as they come." Mel shook his head in amazement. "That's why his being sued for divorce has everybody puzzled; that guy wouldn't touch a strange piece of tail with your dick. If he was any other way, maybe the girls wouldn't give him a tumble, I don't know. But I do know he's true-blue to his old lady. I just don't understand her wanting to get rid of a guy like him. I guess that's what makes life so interesting." He shrugged and turned to face Woody directly. "As for you, that gal won't be taken out of circulation on Manny's account, so if you like her, go after her."

"Maybe I'll do just that," Woody answered. "I know one thing... I like it just fine in the big league. No more

Springfield for me, and I sure like these big league lady reporters." Mel laughed at Woody's refreshing innocence.

Chapter 7 -- THE INTERVIEW - PART 1 - IN CHICAGO

Kari and Manny went to the Pyramid Hotel where
the Cardinals were staying in Chicago. She perceived an
uneasiness in Manny which she couldn't account for. He was
polite enough, and for her part, she surprised herself with
how at ease she felt with him. It occurred to her that maybe
she had agreed too quickly to go to a man's hotel room when
she had met him scarcely an hour earlier. Yet, Manny was so
easy-going and unaggressive that it had not entered her mind
to be on guard. After all, she thought, would a man planning
anything indecent have you stop for soda pop to take to a
hotel room? By the time they reached the lobby of the hotel,
she had worked through the question of her safety and had no
worries about it.

They were stopped several times before reaching the
elevator by people seeking autographs and offering
accolades.

She had noticed the sheaf of legal-sized papers he
had under his arm, but other than a reporter's natural
curiosity, she didn't give them much thought. Manny
unlocked his door and politely let her enter first. She was

unexpectedly surprised by the neatness of his quarters. Manny put the papers on a table and told her to make herself comfortable while he went for ice.

When he left the room, she knew she'd have ample time to satisfy her curiosity about the legal papers, so she picked them up and started to read them. She got as far as the second sheet, which was underneath the summons and saw the style of the case:

IN THE SUPERIOR COURT OF THE STATE OF
ARIZONA
MARICOPA COUNTY
PETITION FOR DIVORCE

Vivienne Ann Wilson Hernandez)
)
vs.) Case No. DR17572902
)
Manuel Hernandez)

Now comes the Petitioner, Vivienne Ann Wilson Hernandez, and for her Petition for Divorce against Manuel Hernandez, states, alleges and avers as follows:

Kari could hear Manny nearing the open door, so she replaced the papers just as Manny had placed them and took a chair across the room by the window.

Manny fixed both of them a soft drink on ice and sat opposite Kari at the table. She was trying hard to mask her feelings of curiosity about the divorce petition. She quickly, and wisely, decided to go on about the interview, hoping that the discussion might develop a lead-in to the subject. If Manny didn't bring it up, she couldn't, without risking

Manny's ire. Reading the papers was an invasion of his privacy, not unlike opening someone's mail. True, she thought, a reporter may have a wide license to conduct an inquiry, but there was no way she was going to risk jeopardizing this scoop by exposing her bad manners.

The phone rang, startling her, but providing a break which allowed her to compose her thoughts once more. It was Luis Guerrero, once again letting Manny know that he and his wife were behind him if he needed them. Manny thanked him. Kari could not understand much of the conversation, because Manny spoke to Luis in Spanish, just so she wouldn't understand what they were talking about. He did not intend to tell this lady reporter anything about his domestic problems.

"I'm sorry, Kari," Manny apologized after closing the phone conversation. "Now, where do you want to start?"

She had taken her notepad and pen out of her purse. Still sensing that Manny was ill at ease, and now understanding why, she said, "First, I want to compliment you on the neat way you keep your room. I haven't spent any time in ball players' hotel rooms, but I have two younger brothers, and I'm pleasantly surprised at the uncluttered way this room looks."

Her compliment caught Manny off guard. He smiled and said, "I owe so much to my parents, especially my mother. Maybe that's who I should start telling you about."

Kari heard him in disbelief; a millionaire ball player being sued for divorce, and he wanted to talk about his mother? She saw the look on his face and quickly said, "Sure, Manny, start with your mother."

"Have you ever been to Dominica, Kari?"

"No, tell me about it."

"When I was a very small boy, just a baby, I wasn't expected to live. I didn't have any particular ailment or disease, except malnutrition, which made me very sickly, and threatened my life. Since I had several brothers and sisters, my father urged my mother to go ahead and permit me to die. My mother firmly refused and devoted her every spare moment to helping me, her infant son, to live. She baked extra bread and sold it and did anything else she could do to make a little extra money to buy medicine for me. I believe my mother would have suffered any hardship necessary to keep me alive."

Kari was furiously taking notes. "Because I was so puny," Manny continued, "I did not go to the sugar cane fields with my father and brothers. You see, in the Dominican Republic, when I was growing up, a boy was considered a man when he was able to swing a machete all day in the cane fields. Usually a boy can do that by age eight. That's why people in poverty-stricken countries like mine are so thrilled when a boy is born; they know that soon he can support himself and maybe other family members, like his sisters." He looked directly at her and said, "It makes for strong family loyalties, do you understand?"

"Yes," she said quietly. She produced a cassette recorder from her purse and placed it on the table in front of Manny. She didn't want to miss anything of what he was saying and she knew that she wouldn't be able to keep up by taking notes. Manny nodded his approval and continued talking.

"So, since I was too puny for the fields, I went to school with my sisters. After school each day, I did house chores -- girl's work. I didn't enjoy being made fun of by the kids at school, and I would respond by fighting; I don't remember winning a single fight as a child. Then, when I was about ten, I got very ill. My family didn't think much about it at first, because I had always been sickly. My father was a shift foreman in the fields; he had an excellent work record, and the company allowed our family to go to the company infirmary. My mother took me there, and the doctor examined me very thoroughly, then asked my mother to leave me overnight for more tests. I protested, but she agreed to leave me. This was the first time in my life that I had been away from home after dark."

Kari sat quietly and waited for him to continue.

"That night, the doctor came in and sat down to talk with me. He said that he could help me, but that I would have to cooperate with him completely. I was very frightened; my mother had to return home for the evening chores, and I was all alone in that room in the infirmary and really, really scared."

"I apologize for interrupting you, Manny, but don't you have hospitals in your country?"

"Not as you are used to," he replied; "in fact, the company infirmaries are abundantly better equipped than any public hospital in Dominica. That's why I could never hold it against my father for urging my mother to let me die as an infant; it's quite common and socially acceptable there."

Kari shook her head in disbelief as Manny continued. "The doctor brought a very nice lady with him;

he referred to her as his nurse, but she wasn't trained as a nurse is in the United States. He told me that she would wake me regularly during the night and give me some fluid. He said that if I swallowed this, I would feel much better by the next afternoon. He left, and the nurse lady made me feel much more at ease. He still hadn't told me what was wrong with me, and the nurse didn't either.

"About lunch time the next day, Mother came to see me. I was beginning to feel really sick at my stomach. My mother tried to comfort me, but I felt like I'd have to warm up to die."

"Did they ever find out what was wrong with you?"

"Yeah," Manny quietly replied. "Suddenly, I started to vomit violently. At first, I thought I wasn't going to be able to stop." He stopped and looked at her questioningly. "Have you figured out what was wrong with me yet?"

"No," she said, "I haven't the foggiest."

"I was regurgitating worms."

Kari's expression reflected pain as she said, "My God, Manny."

He could tell that she believed him, even though she was shocked. "You see, Kari, in my homeland, many of the simplest creature comforts that North Americans take for granted are considered luxuries. Like shoes -- very few children have footwear while they're growing up. So it's common for them to contract various parasites which infiltrate their intestinal system by entering through their feet. I've never said it publicly, but I intend to use part of the money I earn from baseball to at least start working on the common health problems of the youth of my country."

What Kari had originally perceived as a little above average, but routine, interview had become a storytelling session that had her spellbound. She was full of questions, but refused to stop and ask them, afraid that she would break Manny's rhythm. But she did risk asking, "Manny, have you ever told anyone else about this?"

"Only my wife; why do you ask?"

"Simply because it's so incredibly interesting that I can't understand why it hasn't been written about before."

"That's quite simple, my friend, the general public doesn't like to hear about poverty, hunger and disease. They want to hear about home runs, no-hitters and touchdowns. The Latins don't play football, as you know it, so baseball becomes their one-way ticket out of their ghettos." Manny paused and laughed. "I was amazed at the riots in L.A. when the newsmen referred to those areas as ghettos. Any one of those places would look like the Waldorf next to the house I was raised in with a family of eight. It's only been the last few years that we had indoor toilets.

"When Trujillo was President, he would make occasional visits to our village and pick out young virgins to have brought to him for his sexual amusement. Everybody wanted their sister or daughter to be chosen, because, in return for her spending a week at his palace, her family would get enough money to buy shoes, or other things, to last a long time." He paused and looked at Kari. "Are such stories beyond your belief, Kari?"

She shook her head and checked the tape recorder, not wanting to miss a word.

"Maybe you are beginning to understand why baseball means so much to us when we're growing up," he continued. "I understand that once boxing was seen as a way for a youngster in the U.S. to get himself and his family out of poverty. In Dominica, every young man plays baseball if he's able to walk. There are baseball fields everywhere. And when a Dominican player makes it to the big league in the U.S., he is expected to return and play winter ball in Dominica. If he comes home to live for the winter and doesn't play baseball, his neighbors will stone his house and break all his windows. He gets the message real fast."

"What about equipment?"

"When players come home, they carry as much equipment as they can and give it away to the youngsters who are still at home. Most families do well just to survive, so equipment is not in the budget. Some of the major league clubs are starting to have clinics or camps that run all year at home, so lots of kids get equipment that way. When I was growing up, I was usually lucky enough to hustle equipment off U.S. players who came down for winter ball. There's lots of fellows coming down there now just to stay in shape over the winter. Anyway, when I go home now, I take all the bats, balls and gloves that I can carry and give them to the kids."

Kari got up to replenish her drink, and Manny did the same. After getting ice and pouring her drink, she returned to her seat and said, "Manny, it's really amazing to me that this story has never been told."

"I know," he said, "but now it will be."

"You can bet on that, I promise you. You said before that you had told your wife about this... is she not Dominican?"

"No. I met her five years ago when I was playing for the Phoenix Giants. You see, I was signed by the Giants and actually came up through their farm system. I came to the Cards last fall through free agency."

"How many clubs have you played for?"

"Four."

"Which ones?"

"San Francisco, Detroit, Pittsburgh and St. Louis, but only San Francisco's minor league system."

Kari guided the subject back to Manny's wife, hoping she could get him to open up about the divorce. "Where is your wife now, Manny?"

"In our home in Phoenix. Would you like to see pictures of our children?" Upon hearing that she would, Manny proudly pulled pictures of his son, Joseph, and his daughter, Marie, from his wallet. Admiring the pictures, Kari asked, "Do they spend much time in Dominica?" For the first time since Kari had been with him, Manny became noticeably defensive.

"Not exactly; that is, well, no, they don't." He stopped there, unwilling to enlarge on his answer, and Kari was discreet enough to not to force the issue. Uncomfortable with his awkward silence, Kari changed the subject enough to get Manny back on the track of his early life.

"It must make you feel wonderful to be able to give your children an upbringing without the hardships you faced."

86

"Yes, it does," Manny answered, brightening a bit. "But I wouldn't trade my past life for any other. You see, I believe that we all have to go through such things to get where we are today. For all the hardships a Latino has in growing up, he is a better human being as a man. If I had grown up having never been hungry or sick, and gone to college with a car to drive and money to spend, I don't think I'd have nearly the appreciation for what I have gained. Kari, I get on my knees every morning and night and give thanks for my blessings. Somehow, without my past, I don't think I'd have this attitude."

Kari agreed and then asked, "Manny, do you think the Latinos are treated any differently by the owners -- the baseball club owners -- than the North American players are?"

"Absolutely," Manny answered. "When you start your working life at age eight cutting sugar cane for fifty cents a day, by the time you're old enough to play baseball for a living -- and sometimes that's as young as fifteen -- all you care about is getting that machete out of your hand. The money is a very secondary consideration. I knew a shortstop, Kari, who was on a major league roster for nine years and never made over thirty-four thousand dollars a year. Once in a while, he got up enough nerve to ask for a raise. When he did, they would always answer him the same way: did he want his contract renewed at the same pay level, or did he want a plane ticket back to the cane fields. Put in those terms, a decision in their favor came quickly. He finally got an agent, but was still in real fear of being released. With the agent, he got a hundred thousand a year during his last three years in baseball, with a forty-thousand-dollar signing bonus."

"So what you're saying, Manny," she broke in, "is that even though salary levels are breaking new records all the time, the Latinos are still at the bottom of the pecking order."

"That's right," he replied, pleased that she caught on so quickly. "Kari, when we come over here to play ball, we don't have a 'green card' or a permanent work permit. The U.S. government will only give us a temporary visa that expires seventy-two hours after our playing season is over, or when we're released, whichever comes first. Unless a club owner, or someone with a lot of political pull gets involved actively, it's next to impossible to get a permanent work permit."

"What I hear you saying is, the owners have tremendous leverage against your people in contract negotiations because of your tenuous citizenship status," Kari commented.

"You got it. Just compare my last salary negotiation, as a free agent, with any comparable U.S. player, any of them, not just pitchers, and you'll see that I make at least fifty percent less than the least paid of them."

"Does this anger you?"

"No," he replied, "anger is not the right word. I'd rather call it frustrating."

"Can you enlarge on that?"

"Sure, but do you mind if I digress and give you a little history lesson?"

"Not at all." She smiled and looked at her watch.

Noticing her action, Manny apologized. "I'm afraid I'm getting a little far afield. Perhaps we should go back to question and answer."

"Not at all," she replied, "it's just that I have a date tonight and... would you let me use your phone?"

"Sure, just dial nine to get outside. Do you want privacy? I'll just go get some more ice."

Manny left the room, and Kari made a quick call, excusing herself from her prior commitment. When he re-entered the room, she said, Mister Manny Hernandez, you're quite a guy. You come into Chicago and almost single-handedly overpower the Cubs for two straight days, then sit down with a stranger and start telling a life story that would probably make a best seller. Yet, I find you so warm, thoughtful and humble."

Manny stopped her, and with quiet modesty, said, "Like I said, Kari, I've got a lot to be grateful for. Okay, ready for the history lesson?"

"I'm all ears."

"When Christopher Columbus, as your people put it, discovered America," he began, "he didn't land here, he landed in what he called Hispaniola; today it is called Santo Domingo, the capital of the Dominican Republic. Columbus brought black slaves with him from Africa. What he encountered were natives quite like what you call Indians. Columbus was, of course, Italian, (representing Spain). This is very important, Kari, to your complete understanding of the Dominican mentality, which is important to your article, if you are to accurately depict the Dominican baseball player."

"Go on," she urged.

"The African slaves and Caucasian crew members all intermingled with the native Indians and each other. You see, nobody explained racial prejudice to these people, so they didn't learn it. The result is that today the Dominican Republic is a society of interracial foundation where probably -- and I'm not exact on this - a fourth are white or black, and three-fourths are of mixed blood, like me. That's why I have Afro hair, fair skin and green eyes. I'm what old southerners in the U.S. call a 'high yellow', like Lena Horne. On the other hand, anywhere in the U.S. I'm considered black, or Negro, and subject to all the racial prejudice that goes with it. So, when I enter business negotiations, although your constitution says otherwise, the hard, cold facts are that there is no place in this country where such prejudice, even unsaid, is not felt."

"Don't you think you're exaggerating it, Manny?" Kari asked.

"Let me tell you this, then you decide. I came to your country unable to speak your language and was assigned to a minor league club down south that had one other Spanish-speaking player and no interpreter. By necessity, we ate most of our meals in restaurants. The only way we could order a meal was by walking around and looking at what others were having and pointing to it. We learned to say words like 'hamburger' and 'coke' real fast. Consider that, along with going into places that wouldn't serve us because we were, in their eyes, of an inferior race. Before you say anything, let me say this: things have improved tremendously, but they're a long way from equal. Are you beginning to get the full picture?"

"I think so, Manny. What you're saying is that you aren't brought up in Dominica under any pressure attendant to racial prejudice. When you or your contemporaries come over here to play ball, what you have to contend with in terms of culture shock is compounded by the racial prejudice against you, plus the language barrier."

"That's right," Manny replied, "and I hope you understand that I really am not angry... but, as I said, it is very frustrating."

"So how does this affect you on the field, Manny, or does it?"

"The one-word answer to that is very, very seldom. The real problem isn't on the field, but that's a whole different subject, which I doubt we'll have time to address now. What I do want to get across is that Latin players undergo infinitely more hardships to make it to the major leagues than native U.S. players do. The old fashioned minor league system of U.S. baseball doesn't exist anymore; it's been almost completely replaced by college baseball. The emphasis in your country is on persuading your youth to go to college. In my country, the emphasis is on getting a job, becoming self-supporting, as quickly as possible. With a college education, or even part of one, a North American guy can always get a job -- a good one -- if he wants one badly enough. Not us; it's back to the cane fields. I know a thousand guys that would love a job just driving your garbage trucks. You're a society of 'haves', but we're not envious or jealous; we just want a shot, a chance, and once we get it, we don't take it lightly."

"Well," Kari sighed, "this interview has really turned into an eye opener for me. I guess we take a great deal for granted, and I know the average person here has no idea what your people go through just to survive."

"Kari, keep this in perspective. I sure don't want to come off here as some ungrateful Latino who is feeling sorry for himself, when quite the opposite is true."

"You're not, Manny, and I won't present you that way in my article, that is actually starting to shape up more like a book entitled 'The Manny Hernandez Story'." Manny smiled and gave a shrug at her suggestion.

"I guess the reason I was willing to talk with you was to find out if you were interested in hearing the truth and if you'd write it that way."

"An emphatic yes, Manny, to both your questions."

"Kari, time is getting away from us; I don't mind continuing a little longer, but I really should stop and make a plane reservation."

"Sure," she said, "go ahead." She knew that reservations were made by road managers for traveling ball clubs, so she accurately surmised that Manny was doing this for personal reasons. She further assumed that it had something, or everything, to do with the papers she'd surreptitiously glanced at earlier in the evening.

"Manny, while you're doing that, could I use your bathroom?"

"Sure, go right ahead."

As she entered the bathroom, Manny sat down on the bed and picked up the phone. While he was making reservations for Phoenix, she was touching up her make-up and lost in thought. She had met a hundred of these guys, but something about this one was different; she couldn't put her finger on it. She found him handsome, intelligent, obviously self-taught and very... well, he was warm, courteous and considerate. 'If only he were single,' she thought, 'story of my life. Wait, would I marry a 'mixed blood', as he puts it? Interesting question. Could I deal with the prejudices I've grown up learning -- as he so adroitly pointed out? I'm sure I could with this guy, and if he's involved in a divorce, maybe he will be single before long. Oh, Kari,' she chastised herself, 'to get involved with him now would just add more complications to the ones he already has. That wouldn't be fair at all; he's such a nice guy.'

She could hear him say something on the phone, and then he raised his voice to speak to her. "Kari, could you give me a ride to O'Hare about midnight?"

Without hesitation, she replied, "Sure."

He was hanging up the phone as she re-entered the room. He began to look over some notes he had made from his phone conversation. She glided over and sat down next to him, ostensibly to see his notes and discuss what time he needed to be at O'Hare. Her real intention was just to see how it felt to sit next to him, up close. She found out she liked it.

"I'll be glad to take you, Manny; what time is your plane?"

"Three a.m.," he said, making no effort to avoid her closeness.

"Could I ask you a personal question?" she inquired, "without offending you?"

"That depends on the question," he answered wisely.

"Why aren't you traveling with the club? Is there some emergency that I could help you with?"

Manny was finding Kari very disarming -- her beauty, her warmth, her attitude and especially since she came over and sat so close to him on his bed. Manny sensed that this was no ordinary woman. He thought he recognized class and dignity. 'Just like Vivienne,' he thought. The thought of living without Vivienne hadn't crossed his mind, but it was beginning to creep in now, just a little bit.

"Have you ever had a problem," Manny began cryptically, "that so perplexed you that you didn't want to discuss it, for fear of giving it more inertia than it deserved, yet you wanted to get it out in the open with someone you trust, so maybe you could find a solution, or a way to deal with it?"

Reaching over to take his hand, Kari said, "You haven't known me very long. Let me say a few things before I even try to answer your question." Manny made no move to avoid her holding his hand, which pleased her.

"You see, Manny, I was orphaned as a very young child. My parents were simultaneously killed in an automobile wreck. I was young, five years old, but I remember going to live with relatives. None of my parents' relatives had the money to keep me over two years at the most, so I got shuffled around a lot. As a result, I didn't make friends in school because I didn't want the grief I went through when I left them. I concentrated my energy on school work, much like you concentrated yours on baseball. My ambition revolved around writing. When I graduated high school, from the seventh school that I'd attended since losing my parents, I had high enough grades to get a college scholarship. I used that to get a degree in Journalism from the finest journalism school in the country, University of Missouri, Columbia. After several interviews, I was finally hired by the *Beacon*.

"When I told you that I grew up with brothers, the truth is, I grew up in a total of eight households containing twenty of the male sex, all totaled."

She stopped and looked at him to see if what she said had made an impression. Manny squeezed her hand a little tighter.

"So, you see, our backgrounds aren't that much different. Oh, I grew up with far more of the creature comforts than you did, but we have shared many of the same emotional stresses. And I don't know what your problem is, but I do feel a closeness with you, just from visiting over the last five hours."

She smiled as he patted her hand. "By the way," she said, "I'm not holding your hand to come on to you, but as an expression of that closeness, and in what I hope is the beginning of a lasting friendship."

Manny turned toward her and put his arm around her and held her closely. Then he quietly whispered in her ear. "Kari, I really do like you; the thing is, I'm married, and I want to stay that way. But I have to tell you, and I'm not coming on to you either, I really like you very, very much and would consider it a privilege to be your friend."

He paused and hugged her tightly, then, still whispering, he said, "I guess you would gladly have suffered worms or other childhood hardships, if you could have kept your parents. Don't answer; I know the answer. Remember what I said about going through life's hardships to get where we are today? I'm sorry you had to undergo all that emotional pain, but I'm very glad that you're here with me now."

Kari started to speak just as they both seemed to lose balance and lie down across the bed, still in each other's arms.

"Manny," she said, "I have respect for you and your marriage. If someone had told me this afternoon that I would end up like this, I would have told them they were crazy. I really want this closeness and your friendship, but I'm not a home wrecker. On the contrary, how can I help you preserve your marriage?" Her last statement was sincere, but spoken half-heartedly. She found herself fascinated by this hours-old relationship, but having divided emotions, because she truly wanted him to be happy in his marriage. They were both enjoying where they were at the moment, but each was experiencing pangs of conscience about being there.

"Look, Kari, I think I know how you feel. Could we do this... could you come to see me in St. Louis after the road trip to L.A.? After I get back to St. Louis, I'll have a better understanding of what's going on in my marriage. The truth is, I talked to my wife last night, and she was fine. Today, at the ball park, I was handed divorce papers by a process server. That's why I've been so ill at ease and bound up inside.

"I may be guilty of a lot of sins, Kari, but I'm true to my wife, and I'm sure she's true to me. I adore my kids. In fact, I finally have my life where I want it. That's why I don't have the most remote idea why she is suing me. The papers are over there on the table; feel free to look at them if you want."

Kari had to stop herself from saying, 'I already did.' And she felt quite ashamed for being so sneaky.

"Manny, I have the utmost respect for you, and I am your friend. What I want, first, is to preserve anything that makes you happy. We should both be thankful for this new friendship we've just fallen into. Frankly, I'd go anywhere to renew it, even St. Louis," she chortled, "the home of the Cub-Busters."

He joined in her laughter and they both sat up simultaneously. Manny handed her the divorce papers and headed for the bathroom. Kari looked at the papers more carefully now, but her head was preoccupied with the romantic rush she was enjoying.

Manny stood in the bathroom, his back up against the door. He reached over and flushed the stool to make some noise. While on the bed a moment earlier, he knew his own feelings well enough to know that if he didn't do something fast, he would kiss Kari. Now he wondered what to do next; even in his marriage, he had never known the romantic feelings that he was having at this moment. He told himself that these feelings needed to be tempered by reason and good judgment, and he felt that Kari would do the same.

He opened the bathroom door slowly and returned to the room. Kari had replaced the divorce papers and was once more sitting on the bed. She looked at him and asked straight-forwardly, "Are you feeling what I'm feeling?"

Manny's green eyes looked straight at her as he joined her on the bed. "Until I was a grown man, I'd never heard the words 'body chemistry', and not until now have I had an understanding of what those words mean."

She whispered, "Me, too." They embraced and once more fell across the width of the bed. They lay there for what seemed like a long, long time, just holding and stroking each other's hair.

Finally, Manny spoke: "I have to get ready to go, or I'm going to miss the plane. Do you still want to drive me to O'Hare, or are you too tired?"

"Right now, I'd drive you all the way to Phoenix just to be close to you that much longer."

"Good," he said, "just let me pack my things, and we'll be on our way." They got up, not having yet kissed each other, but each clearly in touch with the other's feelings.

Kari thought, 'You are insane; you can't be falling in love with a married Latin ball player that you just met!' But she couldn't deny the feeling, and, knowing no other way to describe it, she decided to wait and see what happened. One thing she knew, for sure, she did not want to lose this lovely, thoughtful man. She would take him any way she could get him. She might not ever be his wife, or even his lover, but she was determined to be his special friend.

Manny finished packing, and they went to the lobby. As he was checking out, Woody Justice walked in the front door looking totally disheveled. Kari saw him first, but waited until he saw her before she spoke.

"Hi, Woody, big night on the town?"

"Not exactly, Miss Robins. I really don't think I'd better say much, you being a reporter and all."

"Come on, Woody, I don't wear my reporter hat all the time; tell me."

Woody carefully explained how he had started the evening over a steak with Billy Fitch, and after dinner his manager had invited him to go bar hopping for a little fun. "So far, so good," Woody said, "then we ended up in a singles bar -- I thought. Snake had really taken me to a gay bar full of drag queens. Before I realized that the beautiful fluff I was makin' out with was really a guy, Snake had started a fight."

Kari was trying hard to keep a straight face while Woody related the evening's events. When Woody went to Snake's defense, the wigs flew off and so did a lot of other things, revealing, to Woody's consternation, that he was in the middle of a war involving big, strong homosexuals who obviously enjoyed fighting as much as they enjoyed dressing up as girls. Woody told how when the dust had cleared, Snake was nowhere to be found.

By the time Woody had finished his story, some of his teammates, who had been standing around listening, could no longer contain themselves. The same laughter Woody remembered from earlier in the locker room was now repeated in the hotel lobby at nearly one o'clock in the morning.

Manny finished checking out and walked over to Woody and Kari just as the laughter reached its peak. "Woody, what are you up to now" he asked. By the tone of Manny's voice, Woody was sure that Manny already knew the answer.

Ike Wood confirmed Woody's suspicions by saying, "We've had someone posted, watching for Snake to come in all night. When he did, we all started gathering to wait for you. We knew if you survived you wouldn't be far behind." Now Woody was really embarrassed, especially so because all of this was being bared in front of Kari, whom he had so wanted to impress. He'd impressed her all right, one-hundred and eighty degrees away from what he had intended.

Kari looked at him standing there so innocent, pitiful and put upon and said, "Woody, the boys wouldn't joke you if they didn't love you. Don't worry about it."

Woody thought her words were nice, but not enough to salve his wounded pride. Then Kari reached over and kissed Woody on the cheek and whispered, "You're going to be a great one, Woody. I'm looking forward to reporting your career for a long time."

Woody was so pleased by what she'd said that he didn't hear the laughter any more as he made his way to the elevator. Manny and Kari went out the front door.

On the way to O'Hare, Kari broke the silence. "Manny, forgive me if my conduct back there in your room caused you more problems. I certainly didn't intend things to happen this way when I asked you for the interview."

Manny hesitated, to make sure that she was through speaking, then he said, "Kari, please don't apologize. What

100

happened was unplanned and sincere. The situation I find myself in is this -- what do I have, and do I want what I have? I'm being sued for divorce, and since I got the papers, I've convinced myself that she doesn't want it, but maybe she does. If she does, I'll let her have it and go on with my life, maybe with you. If she doesn't want a divorce, I'll stay with her and love you forever and hope that we can stay close. In any event, I want you to come to St. Louis to finish the interview and we can have some more time together there. Does any of this make any sense?"

Kari shook her head slowly and said, "I think so."

"Oh, Kari," he said, "there's so much more to tell you about me. You know, I was deeply hurt by racial prejudice when I first came to play ball in this country. I was totally unaware of it, so when it started happening, I didn't know what was going on. As it turned out, I handled it pretty well, by the grace of God and the help of an old black woman named Rennie Parker. She cooked in the boarding house I stayed at in Mobile, Alabama. Rennie saw what was happening when I talked about it at the house. She lovingly sat me down and gave me a lengthy explanation about the plight of the black man in the United States since before your Civil War. The great thing about having her explain it was that this loving old Christian woman harbored no resentment for anyone. I made up my mind right there and then that I wasn't going to live under those conditions. I couldn't and keep my sanity. I knew one young Dominican pitcher who came up to a club late one season and helped them win the pennant and was declared the Most Valuable Player in the World Series that year. But immediately thereafter, he suffered a nervous breakdown, caused by just what we're talking about -- culture shock, topped by racial prejudice."

"What happened to him, Manny?"

"Oh, his club isolated him for the winter in a private psychiatric hospital and traded him during spring training without disclosing to anyone what had happened. He had a relapse, of course, and was released and sent back to Dominica. It was a thousand wonders that he wasn't sent back in a pine box."

Kari concentrated on driving the familiar streets of Chicago, unwilling to say anything that might break this flow of his. She was beginning to worry about his silence, when he spoke again. Looking out the window he said in a voice so soft she had to strain to hear, "I've never told anyone this, Kari, but I married Vivienne not because I loved her, but because she was white, and attractive to the point that when I walked into a room with her, you could see the heads turn to look at her."

He shifted in the car seat and said to Kari, "Marrying her represented my grand and final acceptance into the White Man's World. I figured when I won her that my racial problems were over. After that, when the kids came, I thought I grew to love her; at any rate, I won't abandon her or the kids; I'm just not made that way."

He sighed and shifted back to the window. "Anyway, the kids are my Achilles heel, so to speak. I could give Vivienne up much easier than I could them. It constantly grieves me that Vivienne won't let me take them to see my family in Dominica. My mother doesn't let on, but

I know it causes her sorrow to have two grandchildren that she's never been permitted to see."

"That's why you changed the subject so fast earlier when I asked you if they'd ever been to Dominica, isn't it?"

"Yes," he replied, "but now I'm not holding anything back."

They were nearing the airport, and he spoke quickly. "I'm on the horns of a dilemma, Kari, and I want you to bear with me. Can you do it?"

"I'll try, Manny. God knows, emotional strain is nothing new to me. I'm quick to add, however, that I've never had it manifested in me like this."

"That's good enough for me," he said, as they reached the entrance to O'Hare.

"Which airline?" she asked. He told her, and she continued down the long entrance lane.

"Just pull up to the baggage unloading area and drop me off. You don't need to park and walk in with me; in fact, I don't want you walking back to your car alone at this hour.

"There's not much traffic. We could be together for a few more minutes before I have to go -- if you want to," he added.

She found a parking spot and pulled into the three-minute unloading zone in front of TWA. She turned off the engine and lights, then slid from behind the steering wheel into Manny's outstretched arms. He hugged her tightly and whispered, "I realize that racial prejudice isn't my problem, Kari. What's important is how I conduct my life, not how others conduct theirs. If God intends it, we will be together, and if we are, I just want you to know that it won't be because of your outside color, but because of your inside color. I hope you feel the same way."

"I do, Manny," she whispered, and they kissed for the first time. Manny could feel her nipples stiffen up under her blouse. He realized that parts of his own body were also growing stiff. When they released each other, he said, "I don't know any other way to say it, Kari; I know that regardless of how things turn out, I love you now and I always will. For the first time in my life, I feel complete, and I'm simply overjoyed by it."

Kari laughed as she said, "God, we must sound so corny, Manny." Then her voice turned serious again and she reached for his hand. "I've waited a long time to find you, and I'm willing to wait some more. Whatever takes place with you and Vivienne in Phoenix, nothing can change the way I feel right now."

A parking officer tapped lightly on the car window and said, "Let's move along, kids; you'll get me in trouble if I let you sit here and neck." They laughed, kissed again as if it might be their last, then Manny got out, pulled his luggage from the car and walked into the airport. Kari's eyes never left his retreating figure until she could no longer see him.

Chapter 8 -- THE LUNCHEON

'Aunt Polly' Pollard had operated a restaurant in downtown Phoenix for as long as anyone cared to remember. She knew all of her customers by their first names, and when she wasn't in her kitchen conjuring up a new entree, she was passing among the tables in the dining room making sure that everyone enjoyed their meal.

Polly's life was quite a story. She had been married to a member of an old Arizona land and cattle family, and when her husband died, she was left financially well off. She never remarried, but remained happy as everybody's 'maven'.

Sammy Snider liked to arrive early enough to visit with her before his luncheon appointments, which also ensured him a choice table. When Sammy walked in, Polly was in the kitchen, so he just continued on his way, only pausing to say "Hi," to the maitre d'.

Aunt Polly saw him as he came through the kitchen door and rushed over to give him a big hug. She snapped her fingers at the nearest waiter and said, "Beefeater rocks for the visiting royalty, and I mean <u>now</u>." Polly could see, by

Sammy's expression, that she had succeeded in massaging his ego.

"And what brings the King of the Courtroom to this fair damsel's nest?" Polly bellowed.

"Why to woo the damsel, what else?" Sammy responded in kind. The waiter handed him his drink as the kitchen help roared their laughing approval of the friendly exchange.

"And after you woo me, I suppose you'll want my best table."

"A fair exchange, if the damsel is willing," Sammy replied.

Polly summoned her maitre d'. He had anticipated what would happen and showed Sammy back to the dining room, seating him at a table for four in a prime corner of the huge room.

Sammy had just ordered his second martini when Tino and Gus Kirby came in. He had been watching for them and gave the maitre d' the high sign. He ushered the two of them to Sammy's table.

"Nice to see you, Sammy," Tino said, "bet you don't have time to answer all the calls for new business you get from the publicity of winning my case."

"Why, Tino, it looks like I'll have to hire a bunch of new help and move to larger quarters." They all laughed.

Tino turned serious. "Sammy," he said, "I've missed several good deals because my money is still tied up. Are you making any progress on getting the government to release it?"

"Not really, Tino," Sammy answered, "and I know that's not what you want to hear, but I called the D.A.'s office before coming down here. All he'd say was that he's working on it. The problem, as I'm sure you know, is that there were several convictions arising out of this one big bust. The government argues that they can't separate the ownership of the money; they don't know of a method to divide it according to who got convicted and who got acquitted. Since you were one of the fortunate few, they've taken the position that you should be happy that you beat the rap and just forget the money."

Tino started to sputter, and Sammy cut him off before he could get loud. "I know that's not any consolation to you, but that's what I'm up against. I don't want to sue for it, because they would require testimony. I don't think you would enjoy being interrogated under oath by a U.S. District Attorney." Sammy let him think about that for a minute, then said, "Tino, I'd really love to get your money back, but I'm not willing to risk your freedom to go after it."

"I appreciate that, Sammy," Tino said, "but I do have a business to run, and that takes money. I'm just sitting around on my ass watching good deals go by because the damn government has my seed money tied up."

"What, you don't have any credit, as long as you've been in this business?"

"Not anymore." They both knew what he meant without it being said -- the bust had eliminated his ability to get credit.

"Look, Sammy," Tino spoke carefully. "You know how I feel about you. Why, I even went along with that fee deal you cooked up without saying a word, when you and I both know it's totally unethical for a criminal defense attorney to enter a contingent fee agreement in a criminal case. I not only made the agreement, I paid you the other fifty thousand when we won."

Sammy's eyes narrowed. His mind was racing. This was the second time in two days that a client had thrown the ethical book at him. "Tino, tell me right now, are you threatening to take that to the State Bar?" he demanded.

"Hell, no," Tino snapped; "I'm just pointing out that, as your friend, I won't. Now, as my friend, you should get your priorities straight and get busy and recapture my money!"

"Okay," Sammy said, as he settled down. His mind was working furiously to come up with an alternative to Tino's cash problem that also could inure to his own benefit.

"Tell me, Tino," Sammy questioned, "these deals you're missing out on, is there enough profit in them for an outside investor?"

Tino had to struggle to keep from laughing. The greedy bastard had finally taken the bait, but Tino didn't want to appear too anxious.

"Could be, Sammy. You know, it all depends."

"On what?"

"Well, Sammy, first and most important in such an arrangement, is how trustworthy the proposed partner is. Secondly, such a person should not get involved unless they're in for the long haul. Third, they have to be acceptable to me personally; that is, I need to know that we can work well together. Does that help you?"

Sammy smiled and settled back in his chair. He looked around the restaurant and signaled the waiter to refill their drinks. He was thinking that he had secretly wanted some of this big asshole's action for a long time; so here was his chance. He didn't want to lose it by acting too anxious. If he set the hook now, he could reel him in later.

Gus broke the silence by speaking for the first time. "Gentlemen, I think I hear a deal being born."

"Maybe you're right, Gus," Sammy said. "Look, Tino, as you know, I represent several people who have money. Some of them are quite willing to trust me with it with no questions asked; others trust me, but want a full disclosure of what I'm doing with it. New clients show up all the time. Maybe I could get one of them to go along with me, but before I can decide who to go to with it, I have to know some basics. Let's start with you telling me how much, for how long?"

"Right now," Tino began, "I have a proposition that just presented itself. There is, let us say, seven-hundred and fifty-thousand dollars worth of merchandise, at street wholesale, that is waiting for me to pick up for two-hundred and fifty-thousand dollars." Tino was doing some quick calculating in his head as he was talking. He knew Raphael's cocaine could be cut enough to triple in volume and still be quite potent. He also knew the kilos, after being cut, would bring at least fifteen-thousand dollars more per kilo than he was paying for the nearly pure stuff. This latter profit would remain secret, for himself.

"Three-hundred percent is a damn good margin, Tino," Sammy said; "what kind of a time frame are we talking about?"

"Sammy, this thing has no limits. That's why I just told you I want someone for the long haul. If your investor will stay with us for, say, three months, then we can double our money at a minimum of twice a month, pay them in full at the end, and all three of us have enough money that none of us would have to work for the rest of our lives."

Gus just sat there smiling. He'd seen Tino run this scam so many times he practically had it memorized. He couldn't curb his silent amusement. 'Jeez', he thought, 'how can this big-time lawyer be so stupid? Once he gives Tino the money, it's gone forever. I wonder if he thinks he can sue Tino and get it back when Tino dumps him. I won't live long enough to understand how what appears to be such intelligent people all of a sudden get so dumb. Who in the name of Jesus would trust a dope dealer, let alone a big-time criminal lawyer? Greed, greed, greed, the motive that beats everybody over the head with the mallet of ignorance.' Gus thought he had heard that last line from some movie.

While he was engrossed in thought, Tino and Sammy were fashioning the beginnings of a new alliance. "Looky here, Sammy," Tino went on, "how long would it take you to find that kind of money? Don't bullshit me... for once in your life, give me a straight answer."

Sammy ignored Tino's reference to his usual method of speaking much, but saying little. "At the most, four days, but there's one catch; the person I have in mind may want a meeting, and knowing you as I do, you would like to know her."

This reference to a female as their proposed financial partner piqued Tino's interest even more, but he was trying hard to hide this obvious pleasure from Sammy. "Sammy, you of all people should know that, as much as I love the ladies, I operate with as few, uh, witnesses as possible. I don't need people who might be able to implicate me if the pressure is on."

Sammy understood Tino's reluctance. "What about this, Tino... let me arrange a meeting in my office for you to see the lady and judge for yourself."

"No, no," Tino barked, "that's like saying, 'little boy, you can take the puppy home, but if you don't like it, you can bring it back.' Damn it, Sammy, pussy is my weakness, and you know it."

As Sammy threw back his head to laugh, he detected a presence out of the corner of his eye. He turned his head and found Manny Hernandez standing at his shoulder. The laughter died in his throat. Sammy didn't know that Manny had just walked up to him; at first, he feared that Manny might have overheard part of the conversation, but he realized that Gus wouldn't have allowed that to happen. Before Manny had a chance to greet him, Sammy jumped up, stuck out his hand and said, "Hi ya, Manny. Gee, this is a pleasant surprise... how are you?"

"Fine, thank you, Sammy," Manny replied. Then, as an afterthought, he added, "Well, not so fine, really. I apologize for interfering with your lunch, but I really need to speak to you."

Sammy was caught quite off guard. Vivienne hadn't warned him that Manny might actually show up. A phone call was one thing, but face to face in his favorite restaurant was another. He wondered if Manny had talked to Vivienne, but he couldn't very well ask.

Before Manny could speak again, Sammy motioned for the maitre d' to bring another chair, arranged with the waiter to bring him a club soda, and turned to Tino and Gus. He proudly announced, "Gentlemen, meet Manny Hernandez." He spoke loudly enough for many others to hear. Sports hero that he was, Manny still possessed a childlike humility and did not enjoy being made a spectacle of in public. Many public figures relished the attention, but not Manny Hernandez. Very politely he said, "Excuse me, gentlemen, I didn't catch your names." He hadn't heard the names because Sammy hadn't said them. Sammy tried to gloss over Tino's and Gus' identities.

"I'm sorry, Manny," he said, "these are two of my sometime golfing pals. You know me, I'm always looking for a patsy, and both of these guys have a fat pocketbook and a fast backswing."

Sammy's attempt to avoid introductions failed miserably when his humor went right over Manny's head. Determined to be polite, and not realizing Sammy's exercise in diversion, Manny put his large hand in front of Tino and said, "You are?"

Tino shook his hand and replied in a small voice, "Tino Borozi, and my friend, Gus Kirby."

His social etiquette taken care of, Manny turned back to Sammy. "Again, I apologize, but when I told Shirley that it was an emergency, she told me where I could find you."

"No apology necessary," Sammy assured him. Regardless of his complicity in what Vivienne was cooking up for her husband, Sammy was still afraid of telegraphing his guilt to Manny. He had always heard, 'you can't cheat an honest man,' and he surely didn't want to tear up his own playhouse by unconsciously giving away his involvement with this man's wife. No courtroom histrionics had ever taxed his ability to think as fast as he was called on to do now. "When did you get into town?" he asked.

"About an hour ago. I got a day off to come home. There's something I need to ask you about; it shouldn't take too long."

Tino looked at Gus and said, "I think we can excuse ourselves for a few minutes, Gus. Come on, let's see who's in the bar."

Gus was a big baseball fan, but was not previously aware of Sammy's connection to Manny. He got up reluctantly to follow Tino. When they were a few feet away, he said excitedly, "Tino, do you realize who that Hernandez guy is? He just signed for a million bucks a year to pitch for the Cardinals." Tino didn't break step, but he changed his course and headed for the main entrance.

"No, I didn't recognize him. Let's go outside and have a smoke; this Sammy thing is getting more interesting all the time."

Once outside the restaurant, where Tino felt more comfortable talking, he asked, "Now, what's this again about the big beaner being some heavy-duty ball player?"

Gus gestured excitedly toward the restaurant door. "Boss, that beaner, as you put it, gets a cool million bucks a year to throw a baseball. His right arm is like having a key to Fort Knox."

"Yeah, and obviously Sammy is somehow in with him. What do you think he's doin' with Sammy, Gus?"

"I don't know, but I just like what the guy makes for a week's work."

"Let's see," Tino was thinking aloud. "Sammy said he could get the quarter-mil from a dame; that lets the ball player out. Shit, no millionaire ball player is gonna have any truck with us anyway. Besides, being a beaner, he could go home, wherever that is, and get better connected in fifteen minutes than we could in a lifetime."

"But he wouldn't, Boss. He's probably so straight he squeaks." Even low-lifes have their heroes, and Gus liked the idea of Manny Hernandez being one of the good guys.

Inside the restaurant, Sammy had looked over the divorce papers and was listening to Manny's explanation.

"So you see, Sammy, you are the only lawyer I know, so I decided to come to you before I did anything. I was awake all night on the airplane, praying to God for some answers, and the best answer I got was to come to you first."

"Manny, the only thing I can tell you is the only thing I know. Although I don't do divorce work, I know the first thing an attorney tells a divorce client is to empty the bank accounts. Vivienne hasn't said anything to me about the quarter-million the two of you have in my special trust account. That suggests to me that she did this on the spur of the moment, maybe in a fit of anger; you know how women get, but I'd say she doesn't intend to go through with it." Sammy watched Manny's face and lied in his most sincere courtroom voice. "Honestly, she's never given me the slightest hint that she was going to do this. I don't talk to her often, but, for something as serious as this, I think she should have said something to alert me. After all, I am the custodial trustee of a lot of money that belongs to the two of you."

"You don't have any idea what reason she'd have to do this to me?" Manny pleaded, almost in tears.

"No, I don't, Manny. And please don't think I'm taking it lightly, but I just don't think she's serious. Are you telling me that you haven't spoken to her since you got the papers?"

"That's right; I haven't really had the time or known what to say. I thought I needed advice first."

"Tell you what, Manny," Sammy said, "here come Tino and Gus. I know Gus is a big baseball fan. Why don't you give me those papers, and you visit with them a minute while I go try to reach Vivienne by phone?"

"Sammy, I can't tell you how much I appreciate your help; I'll be forever grateful." Sammy patted his arm and excused himself as Tino and Gus rejoined Manny at the table.

Vivienne's telephone rang several times before she picked it up and said "Hello?"

"Viv, this is Sammy...."

115

Before he could continue, she interrupted him, "You mean the handsome lawyer with the absolutely divine pleasure equipment?"

"Wait a minute, Viv," Sammy implored, "Manny's in town, and he's here with me now at Aunt Polly's."

There was a short silence. Vivienne was amused by the urgency in Sammy's voice. "Not to worry, sweet Sammy. What has he said, and what have you told him?"

"I told him what you said to tell him, dammit." Sammy was finding her cavalier attitude less than humorous. "Wait," Sammy corrected himself, "I told him I didn't think you were serious because you hadn't emptied the special trust account. Now listen, this is important. I also told him that you had not mentioned this divorce thing to me, ever. When you talk to him, back me up on that, Viv, do you understand?"

"Sure, Sammy, and I will. So what does he want to do?"

"I don't know; what do you want him to do?"

There was a long silence while Vivienne thought about it. Finally she spoke. "Okay, maybe this will work out even better. You tell him that I'm extremely sorry for what I've done and that I can't wait to see him. Then you see that he comes right on out here. I don't want him to get a wild hair up his ass and go see another lawyer... that would blow my plan sky-high."

"All right, Viv, I'll do it. But I can't stay on this phone much longer, or he might get suspicious. I know, I'll tell him you've been crying your heart out over doing this to him, and you couldn't talk until I got you calmed down."

116

"Good," Vivienne agreed.

In spite of Sammy's anxiety over keeping Manny waiting too long, he couldn't resist mentioning the possible money scheme. "Oh, Viv," he said in an excited tone, "as soon as your husband leaves town, I've got a gilt-edged money-making deal to talk to you about. It's tailor-made for the two of us to get filthy rich quick, and I know you'll go for it."

"First things first," she answered him, "and I don't want to sound like I'm doing your thinking for you, Sammy, but if you could find a way to keep those papers, we'd have a built-in way of knowing right away if he ever went to another lawyer. If he does, the guy would call you and ask for the papers, wouldn't he?"

"Yeah, I guess he would. Good thinking, Viv; I'll do it." He said his good-byes, promised to get back to her soon and returned to the table.

Gus had been absolutely fawning over Manny. Sammy joined the group just as Gus asked Manny to explain how he knew just what pitch would cause Noble to strike out in yesterday's Cub game. Gus, who had watched the game on television, had already told Manny how Scottsdale was a hotbed of Cub fans. Manny was flattered that Gus had rooted for the Cards and was happy to explain the pitch.

"See, Gus, I had a rookie catcher in his first game. The book on Noble said to throw him a shoulder-high fast ball -- tight. I knew that he knew what our scouts had told us and he would be looking for it. Instead, after shaking off the sign for what the book said, I threw him one high and tight, but at about three-quarter speed. Had he delayed his swing for even another half second, he would have hit it so far out of there that they'd still be looking for it. As it was, I had his timing off, and he missed it." In order not to appear boastful, Manny quickly added, "Noble's a fine player; it was just my turn to get him. I'm sure someday he'll get even and take me deep."

Sammy took advantage of the lull in conversation to speak to Manny. "I'm sorry I took so long. Vivienne is quite remorseful, very sorry she did this to you. She's been leaving messages for you all day at the hotel in L.A. She's crying her eyes out, and she really wants to see you right now. Women, who can figure them?"

"I don't know how to thank you," Manny said with great relief. "I guess I'll go on out there now."

"Not before I get your autograph, big guy," Gus squealed. Manny signed autographs for Gus and Tino and a few other well-wishers in the restaurant, then departed to see Vivienne.

After the commotion over Manny subsided, Tino said, "Back to business, Sammy. You say you have a hot prospect for the quarter-mil in the person of a rich female?"

"Who is about to become a lot richer," Sammy smiled as he answered.

"Anything to do with the beaner?" Tino asked.

Sammy cut him off. "You handle your end, and I'll handle mine, and the right hand doesn't have to know what the left hand is doing as long as we both deliver, right?"

"Right," Tino agreed.

At first mention, Tino didn't want to meet Sammy's proposed source of money, but while he and Gus were away

118

from the table, he changed his mind. He figured once the chosen individual was committed to participate, he could persuade them to join him in squeezing Sammy out. Then he'd squeeze them out. No muss, no fuss, just business as usual.

"Tell you what, Sammy. You set up the meet, just like you'd introduce me to your banker; no hidden ball tricks. Introduce me to this money broad so she's cold, doesn't know what's coming, and then just sit back and watch me work -- uninterrupted."

"Suits me," Sammy said, "let's get going. I'll go back to the office and put a call in for her. I may not get to her right away; she's a busy one." Sammy wanted to give himself some time because he wasn't sure how long Manny would be in Phoenix. "I know I'll be able to catch her by this weekend, so why don't we try to meet in my office no later than Tuesday afternoon?"

"Fine with me, Sammy," Tino answered, as they prepared to depart the restaurant.

"God, Boss, just think," Gus said, "we got to meet Manny Hernandez." But it was the rest of the afternoon's business that Tino Borozi was pleased with. He had even felt generous enough to pick up the check.

Chapter 9 -- THE RECONCILIATION

Vivienne Wilson Hernandez' life had been one great exercise in dissimulation, and her marriage to Manny had not changed this at all; on the contrary, it had stimulated it. She was born of an alcoholic construction worker and a neurotic mother. Her father would get drunk and beat up her mother, then start on her. Despite this, she worked hard in high school, graduated with honors and left home to go to cosmetology school in San Francisco. It was there that she blossomed, became a blonde and finally got to eat the right meals regularly enough to fill out her attractive figure. This bottle-blonde with the bombshell figure had tried out unsuccessfully for the Forty-Niner's Cheerleader Squad, which, as far as anyone knew, represented her last defeat.

As a result of that experience, she started dating football players, but none of national prominence. Her sexual education came fast. Her reputation among those she partied with was legend, and her interpretation of safe sex meant to keep the bedroom door more securely locked. She'd had two abortions before she met Manny. But she observed early on that mistress to the taxi-squad was a one-way ticket to nowhere.

When she decided to switch to baseball players, she started hanging around the bar at the Mark Hopkins, where visiting ball clubs usually stayed. She went on a few dates with Benito Salazar, a Dominican shortstop from Manny's home town, who played for Montreal. Benito had introduced her to Manny five years before, and when he did, he told her that Manny was destined to do great things in baseball. It had been four-and-a-half years since she came to Scottsdale during spring training to live with Manny. The Giants held camps at Casa Grande and Phoenix, so she and Manny shared an apartment in Scottsdale.

It was her intense research during that spring training that revealed to her the inflated value of good pitchers and thus Manny's tremendous financial potential as a ball player, especially when he became a free agent.

Manny's treatment of Vivienne was exactly opposite of what she had experienced at home or while dating football players in San Francisco. Her attitude toward all men, however, had been cast in stone long before she met and married Manny Hernandez. Men, to Vivienne, were as much a utility as a toilet or a tire iron. Her mind had long been made up that she would tolerate them, at best, to attain her goal -- in a word, money.

When she was living with Manny before their marriage, she lied and told him she was pregnant. When he reacted happily and said he would marry her, she waited a few days, lied again and said she had miscarried. But she knew that not only would Manny marry her, that she could persuade him to do anything she wanted. He truly was putty in her hands. He never questioned her when she would criticize owners or managers, or even teammates of the clubs he had been affiliated with. This devotion to Vivienne was an extension of Manny's love and devotion to his mother. His total commitment to Vivienne, and later to the children, was clearly similar to the deep love he held for his family in Dominica.

When Manny was faced with returning home after the regular season, four years ago, it was Vivienne who came to his rescue by agreeing to marry him, thereby insulating him from deportation. Manny had been unaware of such a law and credited Vivienne with great intelligence. He came to rely on her totally. His problem was that he exaggerated his own limitations as well as her intellect. She was the reason that he had bounced around to four ball clubs since she came into his life. Highly capable front office men had come off second best more times than not in confrontations with 'Missis Manny', as the clubs dubbed her.

Jack Hogan, who owned the Cardinals, had let it be known that she would never buffalo him, and, to date, she hadn't tried. Actually, in Vivienne's mind, she didn't need to; after all, they were paying Manny a million a year. Vivienne had seen to it that his checks were mailed to her in Phoenix. Manny didn't mind; he wanted her to handle the money anyway.

Their first child, Joseph, proved to her that her two abortions had not destroyed her ability to conceive, carry and birth a baby. The second pregnancy, almost on the heels of the first, was an unplanned accident. Vivienne decided to go through with the pregnancy just to increase her support payments when she pulled off her grand plan. So Marie arrived and completed the ideal family picture. Except for one thing -- Vivienne certainly had not married for love. She learned while in San Francisco that she could marry more money in fifteen minutes than she could earn in a lifetime, so the concept of love, or what little she knew of it, was thrown out, never to be considered. Now, this veritable vixen of a woman awaited her next victim, her husband, baseball's newest millionaire. He was unknowingly following the trap line she had methodically put out for him, and at the moment it lead him to the threshold of his own home.

She heard the doorbell but made him ring it again before she opened the door and flung herself at him, holding on for dear life. She managed to squeeze a few tears, as she said, "Oh, Manny, dear Manny, please, <u>please</u> forgive me! I don't know what made me do it, but I'm dreadfully sorry. Please say you forgive me."

Manny lifted her off her feet, kicked the door shut, carried her to the couch and returned her embrace.

"I really don't know why I did it," she continued to whine, "I just get so lonely sometimes, and then I get angry at baseball for separating us, but I know it's our livelihood. Honey, you must be dead on your feet. How long can you stay? I'm so glad you're home. I missed you so much. Please forgive me. I love you so much." Vivienne was wound up like an eight-day clock. The machine gun staccato of her words made it impossible for Manny to get a word in edgewise, so he just sat and let her sputter.

Finally, Manny interrupted her, "Where are the kids?" he asked.

"When Sammy called," she explained, "I took them to the sitter's so we could be alone."

"Let's go get them." At this moment, Manny was truly more interested in seeing his children than he was in listening to Vivienne's tearful pleading. She picked up on this sentiment and changed her act to one of seduction. She pulled Manny close to her on the couch and began rubbing gently up and down the fly of his trousers. He was tired, but responded quickly, as she knew he would. She got up and pulled him behind her into the same bed where she had seduced Sammy the day before. She started to unbutton his shirt and pants; he assisted in their mutual disrobing and crawled on top of her to fill her with his maleness.

There was no denying one thing -- for all the many men Vivienne had lured to her bed, Manny was the most capable of satisfying her. She didn't question how he accomplished it, but she was never able to make him climax before she did. Usually she had experienced two or three back-arching thrills before his first. Sex with Manny was the best, but sex with Manny was not an expression of love; it was a distraction -- another weapon in her arsenal of deceit.

They took a swim, naked, then showered and dressed to go get the kids. While Manny showered, Vivienne raced into the kitchen and hid the empty wine bottles left from Sammy's visit. She didn't usually drink around Manny because he didn't drink.

He hadn't even thought to question her about the divorce petition; he was once again being lulled into a trance of false security. She smiled smugly.

The children were excited by their father's surprise visit. They squealed and hugged and kissed him, and he returned their affection lavishly. On the way home, they picked up some steaks and Manny did what he enjoyed most -- charcoaled next to the pool, in the company of his children. The children loved the pool, and Vivienne had taken them to swimming lessons, which greatly reduced the fear of tragedy they both had when they bought the house. That was another thing Manny admired about his wife -- she appeared to share his devotion to the children and the family unit.

For a few precious hours, Manny had been spared the awful gnawing in his stomach that he had lived with since receiving the divorce papers. There was still a point, however, that he wanted to clear up. "Sweetheart," he said quietly, "if you did this thing in anger, I accept it and forgive you. But don't you have to do something to stop it?"

"No," Vivienne quickly assured him; "the way the law is in this country, just because you start something in court doesn't mean that it automatically happens. You see, dear, if I don't follow up on it, it dies; the court routinely throws it out. But, my love, I promise to call Mister Henze's office in the morning and instruct him to dismiss it."

"Must I do anything," Manny asked, "about the papers I got?"

"No," she answered; "by the way, where are they?"

"I left them with Sammy, sweetheart; actually, he's the only lawyer I know." Vivienne was thrilled that, so far, her plan was working perfectly.

"That's good, darling," she cooed; "the one thing I didn't want you to do was waste money hiring some lawyer, when I don't intend to go through with this mess." Vivienne appeared properly contrite, and she knew she had handled the situation to Manny's satisfaction, so she deftly changed the subject.

"Do you realize, dear, that if you play in the World Series this year, the share for you and the kids could be as much as a hundred-thousand dollars?"

Manny took great personal pleasure in any reference to things he might do for the benefit of his little ones. "That's another thing I love about you," he said, "you are always planning ahead for the sake of our kids -- you are so unselfish. I haven't heard anybody mention it, but you know the player's share is based on the first four games' attendance. It would make a big difference if we played in a larger stadium like New York as opposed to a smaller one like Boston. Anyway, it will be a substantial amount of money, I'm sure."

"Other than Sammy's percentage," she said, "we'll just set that aside for the kids."

"Fine," he answered, "but we have to win it first; then we'll worry about the money."

"To be sure, my love," she said, "but you're doing so well, I just <u>know</u> we're going to the Series."

His lack of comment about paying Sammy assured her that he had accepted it. She was particularly satisfied with her ability to have her own way with not the slightest argument from Manny.

They put the kids to bed and retired early. Manny had not given much thought to Kari. He had been so wrought up before coming home and talking to Vivienne that the end result was complete exhaustion, which followed relief from worry.

The next morning, Vivienne brewed fresh coffee and took it to Manny in the bedroom. This little act of thoughtfulness pleased Manny very much. He sipped his coffee, then made love to the mother of his children. As he lay on top of her, she whispered what he loved to hear: "That's such a nice fit, my love, please don't ever leave me."

The satisfying of Manny, sexually, bolstered the restored confidence he had in their relationship. The contradiction of Vivienne's actions of the last few days had escaped his scrutiny. Her meretriciousness was safely outside his range of vision or understanding. She kept all of her bases covered with sensuous deceit, veiled in an exaggerated pretense of her devoted motherhood. Manny padded off to the shower, a happy man.

Out of Manny's earshot, Vivienne was able to reach Sammy by telephone. She kept him on the phone until Manny got out of the shower, then she said, "Manny, step in here, I want you to hear this. I have Mister Henze on the phone." Clad in a bath towel, Manny followed her beckoning voice like some mechanical wind-up doll. As he stood there, dripping wet, he heard her say, "That's right, Mister Henze, "I'm very sorry to have troubled you, but I absolutely and unconditionally want you to drop the divorce action I filed last week. I'm sorry to have taken up your time, but I'll gladly pay you for it."

At a break in her words, Sammy said, "Great, Viv. When Manny leaves town, get back to me. I have a meeting set up for you in my office on Tuesday afternoon. Be there without fail; this is your chance for a small-risk, big-bucks profit deal. Call me if you have any questions, but be there."

Vivienne responded to Sammy's words by saying, "That's fine, Mister Henze, I will, and I'm sure he'll appreciate it," giving Manny the impression that her lawyer was sending Manny his best wishes.

It would have been out of character for Manny to question the way Vivienne conducted this charade. She was supremely confident that Manny would accept what she was doing without any questions and that he would soon forget about it. Manny was not given to more than superficial questioning of her motives, and he was never given to resentment or revenge. His loving wife had righted her mistake.

Manny dressed and started repacking his things. Vivienne noticed his packing and renewed her act. "You don't have to leave so soon, do you, Lovey?"

"I really should," he said, "I can get there in time to suit up for tonight's game. That way, I won't have missed a game to come home. After all, Bill Fitch was nice enough to let me do it, so the least I can do is show him my gratitude by not taking unfair advantage of his generosity."

"Oh, Manny," she sighed, "just when we were having so much fun being together again." Not wanting to overplay what she was pleased in having accomplished, she added, "I do understand, Darling, it's just that the kids and I miss you so much."

Manny held her close and kissed her. "I know," he said, "and I miss all of you, very much." He pulled back from the embrace and held her by the arms. "You'll promise me, won't you, that everything is settled now with this divorce thing." She nodded as he continued, "And I don't have to give it any more thought?"

"Yes, Manny, I promise." She kissed him again, long and hard. Satisfied, he patted her and said, "Don't wake the kids; they'll just be upset that we have to say good-bye; just tell them that Daddy loves them and I'll be home soon, will you do that for me, Vivienne?"

"I tell them that every night when we say our prayers." Once again, she had pleased Manny by her answer.

Manny made his reservation and left in a taxi-cab. He settled back for the ride, completely at ease in the false security his wife had bathed him in during his short time at home. Notwithstanding the comforting belief that his family life in Scottsdale was securely intact, Manny could repress, but not deny, the feelings he had experienced with Kari in Chicago. He was sure that Kari would understand; he had been completely straightforward and honest with her.

'I'll see her in St. Louis,' he thought, 'and make it right with her. The last thing in this world I want is to hurt her.'

The last thing Vivienne had told him was that she would telephone ahead to inform the hotel in L.A. that he would be checking in and to disregard the messages she had left for him, the messages that he had no way of knowing were never left in the first place.

He boarded his flight for Los Angeles, but not without being cornered for autographs. His presence in the Phoenix airport ignited a commotion among loyal fans. They were so insistent to have his attention that security posted two large male flight attendants at his boarding station to keep the fans from following Manny right into the tunnel. Once seated in the plane, Manny felt at the height of his glory. He had devoted fans; his wife was paving the way for his arrival in L.A., and things felt good. He had no suspicion whatsoever that his Cinderella world was on the verge of collapsing around his shoulders.

Chapter 10 -- THE L.A. SERIES

Arriving in L.A. unencumbered by more than his shaving kit and carry-on bag, Manny left the plane and strode directly through L.A.X. to the cab stand. He had learned from previous encounters with L.A. cab drivers never to engage a cab without first asking about the fare to his destination. He was headed downtown to the Biltmore Hotel, his favorite L.A. quarters, due to Andy Martin, the always congenial Biltmore manager. Manny anticipated games with the Dodgers because it gave him a chance to stay at the Biltmore and because the massive Latin-speaking population of L.A. made him feel comfortable, almost like visiting home.

After settling with the driver on a reasonable fare, Manny sat back and enjoyed the short ride to the hotel. The Biltmore desk personnel recognized him and handed him a phone message with his room key. He read the message while they completed the short check-in procedure.

'I love you more than life
itself; no words can express
my joy from your short

visit. I miss you and the
children miss you. I can
hardly wait to see you when
the season's over.

All our love,

Viv'

Noticing Manny's broad smile, one of the clerks
asked, "Good news, Manny? Are they giving you a raise,
already?"

"No raise yet," Manny replied. "Maybe after we
beat the Dodgers." Manny enjoyed the good-natured
laughter and kidding from the staff, but he knew full well
that everyone present was familiar with the contents of his
memo. He was also aware that they were all Dodger fans,
except when he was playing against their team. Manny was
popular with the hotel workers; many of the Latin workers
brought their children to meet him, and his reaction to the
kids was never disappointing. Once, when Manny had
arrived a day early, he made arrangements to give some of
the children a tour of Dodger Stadium. They still talked
about '*Señor* Manny' playing ball with their kids 'right down
on the real field'. Manny loved the *jovans* and enjoyed their
presence as much as they enjoyed his.

The ball club had already departed for Dodger
Stadium, so Manny couldn't linger to visit as he usually did.
He headed for his room to drop off his belongings. A
bellman getting off the elevator greeted him. "Manny, glad

you're here again. If you need anything, speak up; we're at your service."

"I appreciate that, and actually there is something," Manny replied, "I need a cab to the stadium; I'm running late. If you could get one for me, that would help me out. I'll be right back down."

"It's as good as done, Manny." The bellman never broke stride.

In the room, Manny took a minute to reread the message from Vivienne. His eyes filled with tears as he dropped to his knees in a prayer of thanksgiving for what he considered a joyful resolution of the nightmare which had started in Chicago. With little time to linger, he bounced to his feet, crossed himself in the traditional Latin fashion and hurried to his waiting cab. The driver was an aspiring actor and had driven Manny several times before. Hearing the man tell of his struggle, as he always did, Manny was reminded of his own early days in professional baseball. His success was encouraging to the young driver, and the two felt a comfortable familiarity. Knowing Manny to be a good listener, the driver launched into a tale of his latest experience in his film career.

"Hey, Manny, since I last saw you, I won a fairly good part in a movie." The young man shifted his eyes from the street traffic to Manny's face in the rear-view mirror and back again as he talked, a habit that had made Manny somewhat uneasy in the past.

"Yeah," he continued, unaware of Manny's discomfort with his driving habit, "they had me sign a contract calling for minimum, you know, just scale, but they promised there would be more money when the movie was released." He continued to glance back at Manny as he continued. "So, guess what... the producer never tried to release it because he made so much money on some of his other projects, he just left this one in the can and used it as a tax loss. Did you ever hear of such a thing? Instead of being my big movie break, it ended up as part of his big tax break!"

Manny was earnestly trying to concentrate on the man's story, but the darting movements of the taxi were making him uneasy. The grimace on Manny's face did not deter the young man from finishing his conversation. Fortunately, they arrived at the stadium almost as he finished speaking. Manny was spared the need to comment. The driver moved quickly to open the back door for Manny. Manny handed him a twenty and waved his hand for him to keep the change. As the two men called their good-byes and wished each other luck, Manny headed into the player's entrance, this time stopping to speak with no one.

Manny's appearance in the Cardinal clubhouse was a pleasant surprise. Big Glenn Ballenger, walking around in a jock strap and undershirt, was the first to shout a greeting. Every man on the ball club had hoped Manny would return confident and happy, with personal problems resolved. His huge smile seemed to indicate that their wishes had been favorably answered. The entire club, including the trainers and the clubhouse personnel, surrounded him for a high-five or a handshake. Snake let the tumult subside, gave Manny a hug and signaled him to follow into Snake's makeshift office. Closing the door behind him, Manny sat and looked

Snake in the eye. Before Snake could say anything, tears of relief began to well up in Manny's eyes.

"Things turned out okay at home, huh, Manny?"

Manny nodded as he struggled to regain his composure. "I could hardly believe it, Skip," he said in a broken voice. "It was like the whole thing had just been a bad dream that went away when I woke up." Clearing his voice, he continued, "I walked in the house, she threw her arms around me and apologized. She said she was just lonely and angry. Why, she even had me listen to her telling her lawyer to drop the whole thing."

"What do you mean, 'listen'? Were you on an extension?"

"No, I wasn't, but I heard what she told him."

Snake, while not as confident as Manny, let the subject drop. Obviously, Manny was convinced that his marital problems were over; but Snake would reserve his judgment.

"Well, Manny, we're almost as happy as you are," Snake said, "and to have you in L.A., in this frame of mind is just what this ball club needs. Our prayers are answered." It was uncharacteristic of Snake to use words such as 'prayers', but he did when dealing with Manny; he was sure that someday, he would be struck by lightning.

An impromptu meeting was called so Snake could make sure everyone knew Manny's good news before the game started.

"Gentlemen, as I told you in Chicago, these are critical times, with respect to our chances to make the playoffs and the series. Manny's good new is our good news. Matter of fact, I think it's a sign that we're all in for a run of good luck. You know, old Snake would love to win 'em all, but truth is, bein's we're on the road and in Chavez Ravine, I'd be happy as a pig in slop to get out of here with an even break. Stay awake and we will." The meeting ended on a wave of enthusiasm.

Woody Justice approached Manny just as they prepared to head for the playing field. Awkwardly, he began to speak: "Manny, I don't know how to put this, but, you see, I'd like to, if you don't mind, that is, I mean, I want to take Kari, that reporter lady, out. That is, well, you know, I just wouldn't even ask her if you're still interested in her, that is... aw, dammit, I never can explain myself in situations like this!"

Manny quickly came to his rescue. "Woody, I hope Kari and I will always be the best of friends; however, my children and their mother are the most important people in my life." Subconsciously, Manny had placed his children before Vivienne in order of importance -- not even calling Vivienne his wife, but rather, the mother of his children. The Freudian slip did not escape Woody's attention.

"Kari commenced an interview with me as part of a piece she is doing on Latin ball players in the U.S.," Manny continued; "she is to be in St. Louis when we return, to conclude the interview. If you want, you can ask her out then."

Woody pretended not to notice that Manny was speaking with obviously controlled emotion. "Okay, but again, only if it's okay with you, I'll do just that."

Manny was becoming slightly irritated with Woody's persistence in seeking his permission to take Kari out, but he recalled the usual deference that polite young players show older veterans in such matters and decided to put the conversation to rest. "Woody, personally, I think the two of you would get along great together. My only interest in Kari is her lasting friendship, and if I can help advance her career with this project on Latin players, I'll be glad to do so. For your part, I encourage you to ask her out in St. Louis, and in furtherance of that, I'll give you her office phone number when we get back to the hotel. You can call her before we leave L.A." Having spoken the words, an emptiness swept over Manny. It was as if Kari had been listening, then walked away. He understood the feeling, but chose not to dwell on it. He smiled, slapped Woody on the back, and said, "Now that the matter is settled, let's go play ball." But neither man truly felt that the matter of Manny and Kari was 'settled'.

When the clubhouse was empty, Snake quietly placed a call to Jack Hogan, the Cardinals' owner in St. Louis. As soon as Jack was on the line, Snake started to speak. "Boss, Manny's back with us, here in L.A. He's really snowed by the way his old lady treated him in Phoenix. He says she passed it off as done in a fit of anger and that he heard her tell her lawyer to drop it. I asked him if he was on the an extension line so's he could actually hear her lawyer's voice, and he said no, but he's convinced that that's what took place. For my part, I don't like the sound of this thing one bit; and I don't think it'll take long for the other shoe to drop. There's something goin' on here that just don't add up to me. And I'd bet my hat, ass and shoes that it has something to do with the possibility of her getting her hands on his playoff and World Series money!"

Snake's general distrust of Manny's reason for a good mood was shared by Jack Hogan. "I'll see what I can find out, Snake," he said. "In the meantime, having Manny in a good frame of mind couldn't have come at a better time. Congratulations on having the presence of mind to send him home. Right now, we've done all we can do. We both like this guy, and, though age and experience tell us otherwise, at least, on the surface, everything's fine, and our chances of making the playoffs just went up about a thousand percent."

Snake agreed, and the conversation ended with both men cautiously glad of the most recent turn in the married life of their star pitcher.

Dodger Stadium, like Wrigley Field, is usually filled with rabid hometown fans during any series of games with a contender. Notwithstanding the quality of their player personnel, the Dodgers were always given a slight edge because of their fan support, and the Dodger fans were 'up' for the Cardinal series. They now accepted the fact their club was out of the Western Division race, but assumed the role of the spoilers for any visiting team that was a contender. Such calls as 'boo-birds' were being heard from the stands. Relieved of the usual pressures that surrounded a contender, the Dodgers could loosen up and enjoy themselves, a luxury a contender seldom, if ever, got to experience. Ed Stroud, the Dodger manager, spoke fluent Spanish and could always be counted on to chide opposing Latino players in their native tongue. If a player had unusual facial features, as he came to bat, he would hear such calls as *'frente cheevo'* or *'naris grande'*. Although intended in good fun, there was no question that being called 'goat face' or 'big nose' could easily distract a player from his best effort.

The word was out in the baseball community about Manny's 'problem', but the community of sports reporters had respectfully opted to exclude it from the daily bill of fare, especially now that the problem seemed to have died of its own inertia. In any case, the four-game series gave them enough to write about. The opening Friday night game was a 'Kid's Night' promotion, and the stadium was overrun with balloons, clowns and miniature uniforms. The press and the visiting teams always joked about the promotions at Dodger Stadium; the general attitude was 'So, what are they doing this week?' But the Dodger publicity staff knew that gimmicks to entertain the fans and their families resulted in higher attendance, which translated into larger profits.

Friday night's game started well for the Cardinals -- Ballenger hit one deep into center field that seemed to take the Dodger outfielders by surprise. He managed to make it all the way to third base before they got the ball back into play. It was easy for Woody to knock him in, even though he got himself thrown out at second. Unfortunately, that was the only run scored; the Dodgers tightened up, but didn't manage to score, and didn't allow the Cardinals any further glory. The one-zero Cardinals' victory pleased Snake.

By Saturday's game, the Dodgers were ready. They were determined not to be caught looking around again. Nevertheless, at the seventh inning stretch, the Cardinals led, three-two. During the eighth inning, however, the picture changed. The Dodgers scored two runs, one right after the other, off errors in the field. Snake was irate, but the Cards couldn't regain the advantage, and the game ended, Dodgers four, Cardinals three.

Sunday's double-header looked like it wasn't going to be a great day for the Cardinals; the first game went to the Dodgers by two. Manny had seen limited action in the series, because the starting rotation had pitched well, but, by the beginning of the second game of the double, Snake wanted Manny in there. Snake had given all his usual 'pep' talks and had even pulled out his 'shame-on-you' tone, but it had no more effect than the 'what-the-hell-is-going-on-here' had. It was time for Manny, and he didn't disappoint anyone. The second game went to the Cardinals with a score of five-three.

Overall, Snake was pleased with the series in Dodgertown, and his joy was compounded by the fact that, while his club had lost two, the Pirates had lost three, so when the series opened in St. Louis the following Tuesday, the Pirates and Cards would be virtually tied for first place, with the Cards only down by a half game.

* * *

Woody Justice had obtained Kari's phone number from Manny and placed a call to her in Chicago. The receptionist assured him that, although Kari was absent from the office, she would give her the message. Woody went to bed on Saturday night doubly disappointed -- they had lost the game, and Kari hadn't called. Sunday morning, a sleepy Woody was awakened by the insistent ringing of the telephone. It was Kari; she apologized for calling so early, but explained that she thought the team would leave after the game and head directly for the airport. Her tone was alert and cheerful as she made small talk, giving Woody a chance to wake up.

"So, Woody, I bet you're anxious about today's games, huh? Is Snake just having a fit about yesterday? But Friday night was good, wasn't it?"

Woody muttered a sleepy "Yeah." He wasn't sure what he had replied to, but Kari went on with the talking.

I hope Snake hasn't gotten you into any more forays in the gay bars." She chuckled.

Woody, fully awake now, answered her good-natured kidding politely. "No, ma'am, this young catcher has had all of Mister Snake's nightlife he can use in this lifetime." They both laughed.

"I'm glad you called, Woody," Kari said, "anything in particular on your mind?"

"Yeah, there is, Miss Robins," Woody answered quickly. "I understand you're coming to St. Louis to finish your interview of Manny and, well, I was just wondering if I could take you to supper or something' while you're there?"

Kari knew instantly that Woody must have discussed her forthcoming trip to St. Louis with Manny, because he was the only Cardinal player who knew of it. She was careful to mask her inquietude and continued the conversation.

"Woody, I appreciate your thoughtfulness, but at this moment, I don't know how long the interview will last, or if I'll have any time to stay around after it's over. I guess the best answer I could give you now is to wait and see how things go in St. Louis." Kari was pleased with herself for ducking the question. She also was pleased because she thought she had successfully concealed what was an increasingly overwhelming feeling of sadness.

"Miss Robins, I got your phone number from Manny and told him that I wanted to ask you out," Woody continued. "Manny thought we'd really enjoy each other's company. I don't think he'd have given me your number if he didn't think we'd have a good time."

Woody's information was intended to put Kari at ease, but it had the instant effect of deepening her personal sorrow. Her mind was racing with the possibilities of what could have happened in Phoenix. Whatever had taken place while Manny was at home would determine if she had any potential future with Manny. Right now, she knew only that Manny had not called and Woody <u>had</u> called, after obtaining her number from Manny. Until Woody told her that Manny had given him the number, she had assumed that he got the *Beacon* listing from information and simply left a message at the switchboard. Knowing that Manny gave him the number, with the knowledge that Woody planned to ask her out, put things in a different light. Apparently, Manny was giving his assent to Woody's request for a date and added his encouragement. Kari's hopes that Manny's visit in Phoenix might clear the way for a permanent, perhaps lifetime, relationship with him were now dashed. Her grief was deepened by the fact she was getting what felt like bad news second-handed. She was a bit angry that Manny was insensitive enough to allow Woody to call her before he talked to her himself.

Woody continued to prattle on innocently while Kari thought about the situation. Certainly, if nothing else, her life experience had given her the ability to deal with reality. Collecting herself, she decided to change her response to Woody's request for a dinner date. Ignoring what he was saying about a bad play in Saturday's game, she interrupted him. "I'll tell you what, Woody, I should be able to get into St. Louis tonight. I'll stay at the Park Plaza. You tell Manny to come to the Park Plaza at ten Monday morning. If Manny will do that, I know I can finish the interview on Monday by six in the evening. That will give me time to freshen up, and you and I can go out about eight. How does that sound to you?"

Woody's slight observation of Kari's voice fluctuation was forgotten in his haste to reply. "Great, Miss Robins, I can hardly wait."

"Good," Kari answered, "but you have to do me a couple of favors. First, please call me Kari, and secondly, you have to make sure that Manny gets to the hotel by ten on Monday. I have to return to Chicago early on Tuesday, or I can't make my deadlines."

With childlike elation, Woody assured her that Manny would be on time, even if he had to take him there personally. After hanging up the phone, Woody sat up in bed and let out a happy shout, "Yippee, she's going out with me!"

Kari, alone in her apartment, was glad that the conversation had been by phone and not where anyone could see the tears cascading down her cheeks. She sobbed openly,

143

grateful that she did not have to go to the office on this Sunday.

Kari Robins' feelings for Manny Hernandez had only intensified during their short separation. She tried to tell herself that she truly did not know this man well enough to love him, and certainly not well enough to feel such intense pain at his apparent decision to remain married.

Unknown to Kari, Manny was telling himself much the same thing. His feelings for this woman reporter were unacceptable to him and unexplainable. He knew only that he had met this woman, and in a very short time he had come to undeniably love her more than any person he had ever known -- except his children. Manny's love for his children had to tip the scales in favor of staying with Vivienne. Manny's conscience, and therefore his best judgment, declared it sinful to reject his wife, which would affect his children, just because he felt so strongly about another woman.

His desire to protect his children and secure their family unity prevented him from expressing his feelings for Kari, even to her. He had intentionally avoided calling Kari to explain what he thought was a reconciliation with his wife. His reasoning was simple and vintage Manny -- he refused to hide behind a telephone when he did speak to Kari. The right and honorable way to handle this matter was in person. After all, this was of paramount importance, and he sensed that he was about to hurt Kari by his actions. Manny had resolved within his own mind that he was doing the right thing for all concerned -- his wife, his children and Kari. His family intact, he could help Kari further her career by seeing that she got the interview she wanted. As her friend, he would do anything else he could do to assure her a happy life. He had been honest with Kari about the fact that his family came first.

Forces were in motion. Woody was thrilled with the thought of getting to St. Louis and taking Kari out, but unaware that his conversation with her had left her crushed. Manny was reluctantly ready to stay with his wife because of the children, yet aware of the deep feelings for Kari, while completely unaware of Kari's reactions to Woody's phone call. The ball club was doing well -- Snake and Jack were happy, although neither of them were convinced of the sincerity of Vivienne. However, neither the club's ownership nor the management deemed it prudent to meddle in a star player's personal affairs, even when the franchise and Cardinals' chances of a championship rode on his strong right arm.

Of all the principals involved in Manny's life, only one had a devious plan and was really working on it -- Vivienne Hernandez. Her efforts, so far, had assured her of the desired outcome.

Chapter 11 -- THE INVESTMENT

Tuesday morning, shortly after eleven o'clock, found Vivienne in Sammy Snider's office awaiting his return from a routine court appearance. When Sammy arrived at the office, he informed Shirley that he was taking Vivienne to lunch at Aunt Polly's, but that he would be back for his two o'clock appointment. He requested that Shirley not put through any calls before three-thirty, thinking that the meeting between Tino, Vivienne and himself would be concluded by that time. Both Sammy and Shirley understood that such a request was always subject to Shirley's contrary judgment.

The short trip to Aunt Polly's was uneventful; Vivienne admired Sammy's Mercedes convertible and made small talk, reluctant to begin any serious discussion until after they were settled over lunch. Entering the restaurant through the kitchen, Sammy introduced Vivienne, by first name only, to Polly.

"Now, look at you," Polly said, feigning jealousy, "you told me long ago that I was the love of your life. Then you appear with another woman. What am I gonna do!"

Vivienne joined in the joke, attempting to match Polly's humor. "Oh, I knew there was some floozy named Polly in Sammy's life. I just had to come and meet the competition." As the silly banter continued, Polly showed Sammy and Vivienne to his usual table. Over cocktails, Vivienne was the first to speak.

"Let's get to it, Sammy. What's this mortal cinch of a profit scheme you referred to on the phone the other day?"

Sammy sat a moment in thought, fingering the top of his martini glass. "Viv, I wouldn't lead you down any path that I wouldn't walk with you. Problem is, at this moment, I don't personally have the wherewithal to do it -- but you do." Vivienne looked skeptical as Sammy continued. "There's a businessman coming to my office this afternoon who needs an infusion of capital into his business on a short-term basis. If you see fit to allow the use of your trust account, I can personally assure you of a quick and generous profit."

"How generous?"

"Let's just say that how much you make is in direct proportion to how much you want to invest. For instance, for the use of the whole two-hundred and fifty-thousand, for say, sixty days, I'm sure you would be repaid the two-fifty plus a hundred-thousand, or, you could allow this man the use of the money for a year and receive a hundred grand every two months during that year and then get your two-fifty back."

Vivienne was sitting quietly, but her mind was spinning. Talk of money always excited her. She thought she liked what she heard, but she wanted to hear a bit more.

"What security do I have, Sammy? Where's the assurance that this man can perform as you indicate?"

147

Sammy met her eyes as he said, "The best security I can give you is me. As far as you're concerned, for all intents and purposes, the borrower is me. That way, if anything should go wrong, I'll just pay you back myself; I'm sure you know that I have the ability to do so. As for the legal structuring, I'll prepare an interest bearing promissory note which the man will sign, and I'll co-sign as a guarantor."

Vivienne sipped her cocktail as she considered her next question. "Sammy, is it a fair question to ask what kind of business the man's in, or are my instincts correct that this man recently was acquitted in a jury trial for trafficking in drugs?"

Sammy's answer was deliberate. "Viv, let's face it... I could try to dance you, but we both know you'd see right through it. Sure, the guy's a dope dealer. But the stuff isn't bought here, and it isn't sold here. Let's just say that he's in the business of importing, and what he imports is for the recreational use of wealthy doctors, lawyers and business people on the east coast." Sammy knew that if Vivienne didn't excuse herself now, then she was in. Vivienne thought she wanted in, but she was controlling her greed by forming a few more questions. She was determined that, if she played, she would control as much of the transaction as possible. If it was to be her money that was used, she intended to let everyone involved understand that she wasn't another air-headed fluff who'd just stopped by to let the boys use her body, or her bankroll -- not without her own ground rules.

"Look, Sammy, you need two-hundred and fifty grand, and I have the money. Considering the nature of the deal, why do I need you?" She placed a finger on Sammy's lips to prevent him from speaking. "Before you answer, let me say that I've always liked you, and you've always kept your word with me. But let's speculate, God forbid, that you up and die an untimely death, then where does that leave me? I'm not a Rhode's scholar, but I'm smart enough to know that I can't sue anybody to enforce a promissory note that represents funds that everybody knows are going for a dope deal." Vivienne was pleased with herself for speaking up to Sammy, and she still wasn't ready to allow him to speak. She continued, "Sammy, there's dope deals everywhere; I sure don't need you to put me into one. If your guy is so good and so reliable, why doesn't he already have his own money?" Vivienne already knew all the answers to her questions. This street-smart woman knew better than to even continue this conversation, and she wouldn't have, except for one motivating factor -- her greed. Finally she sat back and signaled Sammy to speak.

"Vivienne, you're right," he said; "you don't need me, or anyone, unless, and only unless, you might want a buffer. Someone between you and the 'operator' to protect your interest and shield you from the damage, should any heat come down. That's it. Yes, you could lose all the two-fifty, or you could make a tidy profit. So, do you want in or not?"

Sammy's attempt to force her to answer was frustrated. Vivienne just wrinkled her brow as if perplexed by the premature ultimatum. "I'll make that decision after we have our two o'clock meeting. In the meantime, let's enjoy lunch. By the way, big boy, are you going to brief me on your conversation with Manny last week?"

"Little enough to tell. He gave me the divorce papers you served on him in Chicago and hasn't called to get them back, nor has any other lawyer called and asked me to forward them to him. It appears that, whatever took place between the two of you satisfied him." He smiled. "I <u>know</u> you can satisfy any man. What's going on there with you and lawyer Henze?"

Vivienne displayed a smug smile. "In another three weeks, more or less, I can default Manny if he makes no appearance to answer my Petition for Divorce; you understand that. It doesn't look like he will, so I'll go before a judge and get whatever I ask for. I don't expect Manny to get a lawyer and file an answer, so, very soon, everything will be mine, including custody of the kids. Naturally, I'm open to your suggestions about how to handle my investments. You're a smart man, and a clever lawyer; I just want to be sure that someone out there who may be smarter than both of us doesn't rob us."

"Believe me, Viv, I share your concern," Sammy replied, "but look at it like this: the guy has his money presently tied up by Uncle Sam; he's desperate to locate new funds while I work to free up the funds that were confiscated. If he doesn't come up with something fast, I know enough about the nature of his business to venture a well-informed guess that his sources will dry up. If we rescue him, it just doesn't make good business sense that he'd try to screw us, simply because he not only needs us now, he may need us in the future. That's how I see it. As far as your divorce deal, well, that's just too glaring a conflict of interest for me to even give the appearance that I was involved. As for the papers themselves, I could satisfy an inquiry by saying that I was merely holding them while awaiting instructions from Manny. That's true, but I'm sure you know that no one could ever find out that you had disclosed anything to me about what you intended to do. If the Arizona Bar could prove that I <u>did</u> know your intentions, it could come back on me for silently standing by, instead of urging Manny to seek other counsel."

"I understand, Sammy, kind of like they'd frown on you for dipping into our trust account, right?" Vivienne laughed aloud at the look on Sammy's face.

"You've got me where you want me," Sammy acknowledged.

"No," Vivienne replied. She slid her hand under the table and placed it flat against his fly. "Where I want you," she said, "is at my house with some wine after we meet with your friend."

"Agreed," Sammy answered quickly. He rotated his lower body in response to the pressure of her hand. Throughout lunch, Sammy felt an additional anxiety to get the business meeting taken care of. The meal finished, they made a quick pass back through the kitchen to compliment the Lady Pollard on a fine meal, then headed for Sammy's office.

Quite by coincidence, Sammy pulled into the parking garage beside Tino and Gus. The four made their way to Sammy's office sans introductions. Sammy wasn't about to risk mentioning any names until they were comfortably seated in his office. It was impossible to guarantee an absence of unwelcome ears in a parking garage. Sammy did not want news of this meeting to reach anyone, innocently or not.

As a preface to the introductions, in typical lawyer-like fashion, Sammy felt constrained to make an opening statement. "I have brought you folks together," he began, "because as clients of mine, I am aware of your business needs and interests. I hope this meeting ends with a resolution to join together and further your mutual business interests. And, if agreeable, to permit me to help in any way I can, beyond these introductions, to enhance the business profits of each of you. Likewise, I hope that I might realize an adequate, but not immodest remuneration." Sammy finally introduced everyone, by first name only.

Despite his occupation, Tino was a charming man when dealing with the opposite sex. He'd long known that women who were outside the loop of his dark and dingy world were sometimes fascinated with him and sought his company. A psychologist had once told him that many people were drawn to the 'hoodlum' element for reasons they couldn't explain. Tino immediately sensed that Vivienne was his kind of woman; he was confident of his ability to lure Vivienne into his net. He was also aware that such confidence could lead to his over-selling himself and result in driving his 'mark' out of range. So he was making a concerted effort during the meeting to speak when spoken to and to look very professional and businesslike.

Vivienne was drawn willingly to Tino's game. She found the atmosphere congenial -- she liked this rugged man, and as Tino suspected, she was intrigued by his 'business'. In a matter of moments, the four were engaged in friendly small talk. A stranger overhearing the conversation would swear that this was four old friends.

Vivienne began the business end of the conversation because she wanted to impress on Tino that she was more than a pretty face. "Tino, I am willing to listen to your deal, but I need to be convinced of two things before I agree to help you." She paused to give him a chance to interject. When he did not, she continued, "First, I must consider your ability to repay, and second -- quite frankly -- I don't want to end up in jail. If you can satisfy me on those two points and offer a large enough share of the profits, I believe we can do business."

Sammy took the opportunity presented by Tino's slight hesitation to repeat what he had told Vivienne at lunch about entering the deal as a co-signer, or guarantor of the loan. When he paused, Tino spoke. "As you are probably already aware, Vivienne, I am a victim of the federal government's confiscation of a large amount of my cash. Sammy tells me that I have a good chance of recovering more than enough to pay back your loan. Assuming that to be true, I would gladly assign to you all of those proceeds as security for the proposed amount. If all else fails, I consider Sammy's willingness to participate as a co-maker more than enough to secure your position. I haven't asked him, but if the price was right, Sammy might even give you a second mortgage position on his recent real estate acquisition."

An expression of obvious surprise crossed Sammy's face, and he spoke up quickly. "I hadn't thought about that, but following Tino's lead, I'd say it's a good idea. I'll do it, if the price is right. Now, since we're speaking of price, let's, for a moment, assume we all agree on Vivienne advancing the needed funds and address the question of pay-back and remuneration. Tino, what is your idea of profit-sharing for Vivienne and me?"

Tino's posturing was not unlike the C.E.O. of a big-board corporation. "Well, Sammy," he began, "in my view, the profit share should be in proportion to the risk. Since Vivienne and I obviously shall have the largest risks, we should enjoy the largest profit." Tino tried not to let Vivienne see that he was taking notice of her nods of approval. Sammy noticed this with mixed feelings, and he was pleased that Vivienne was appearing to telegraph her willingness to participate, but he disliked being relegated to a minority share of the profits. He settled his doubts by concluding that this deal had a lot of perks besides money.

"Be specific, Tino," Vivienne said, in a near demanding tone.

"Sure. If you're willing to loan me the use, right away, of two-hundred and fifty-thousand dollars, I'll simultaneously give you an irrevocable assignment of all funds returned to me that were confiscated by the federal government. No strings -- you get it all, and Sammy can answer your questions about how much it should be and when you can expect to get it. Understand clearly, lady, that's a clean bonus. Then, if Sammy will give you a second mortgage position on his latest real estate acquisition to further secure you, I'll do this. I'll give you a hundred grand, and Sammy fifty grand every three months for one year. Over the following three months -- that is, the thirteenth, fourteenth and fifteenth months from the day you fund me --

I'll pay your initial two-hundred and fifty back, plus a hundred-fifty thousand to you and Sammy. Count it up, lady. You get four-hundred thousand in twelve; Sammy gets two-hundred thousand. In the first quarter of the second year, you get your two-hundred-fifty back, plus a hundred, and Sammy gets fifty more. In the meantime, you get all the money the government returns to me, plus you get a second position on that city block of a strip center that Sammy just bought on Indian School Road in Scottsdale. Is that specific enough for you?"

Vivienne was impressed. Tino had spoken firmly and sounded as sincere as an altar boy. Vivienne was ready; she wanted to accept before Tino changed his mind, but she was trying not to seem too anxious. She looked at Sammy and asked, "Speaking frankly, Sammy, what are the real chances of recovering Tino's confiscated money? I mean, exactly how much, and in what time frame?"

Sammy shifted his weight in the high-backed chair, a sure sign that he was about to try his best to make everyone happy by avoiding the truth and substituting subterfuge. "It's like this, Vivienne," he began, "Tino was out a lot of money, and the government isn't inclined to return any of it, especially since the jury handed him his freedom. But, over the next six months to a year, I'd say I can get at least three-hundred thousand back. I could draw the assignment so the funds are sent in care of my trust account, then give them to you, Viv. I think three-hundred thousand is the very minimum we'll recover."

Sammy's relaxed use of a shortened version of Vivienne's name did not go unnoticed by Tino. He spoke up, again in a quiet and confident tone. "How does it all sound so far, Vivienne?"

"Frankly, Tino, I'm sure there's something I've overlooked, but if Sammy's willing, on the terms you've just outlined, I'll do it."

Tino gave her a winning smile, extremely pleased with himself. "Well, Sammy," he said, "I guess it's up to you."

Looking thoughtfully at Vivienne, Sammy said quietly, "Let's do it. I'll have the papers ready, and we can make the exchange on Friday night here in my office." Glancing at each individual, he asked, "anyone have any questions?"

"Just one," Vivienne said, "what about your wife's signature on the second mortgage?"

"Not a problem," Sammy replied. "I own the Scottsdale property in a corporation name, so her signature isn't required."

After agreeing to meet on Friday afternoon for the closing, Tino and Gus departed. Vivienne immediately moved into Sammy's arms, gently running her fingers along the back of his neck as she congratulated him on the deal. Within moments, Sammy suggested that they head for Vivienne's house to continue the celebration. They chattered all the way to her Valley home, delighted with the way they had handled the mighty Tino. Sammy made a quick stop for a bottle of white wine, but it was temporarily forgotten by the time they reached the front door. Vivienne began kissing Sammy and guiding him toward the bedroom; pieces of clothing littering the floor, making a path through each room.

After the lovemaking, Vivienne reminded Sammy of the wine, and they relaxed with chilled glasses. "God, Sammy," Vivienne said, "I don't know which excites me more, the thought of all that money or you."

Sammy pretended to be hurt by her remark. "Why, Viv, I can't believe you'd even have to think about it."

"You're right," she answered, "no question about it; it's the money." They both laughed, and Sammy slowly and deliberately began teasing her nipples, beginning a second round of sexual activity.

Their sexual appetite temporarily satiated and the greed on hold, Sammy drove Vivienne back downtown to her car and went home to his wife and kids. He offered the usual lame excuse for getting in late, went to bed and slept soundly, convinced that he had just butchered the fattest financial hog of his career.

Vivienne wasn't home to get the call Manny made to her. She had to pick up Marie and Joseph from the sitter. Manny wasn't disturbed by the unanswered ringing of the phone; as usual, he assumed that she had taken the children out for ice cream.

* * *

Friday afternoon found Vivienne, Sammy and Tino in Sammy's office, as arranged. After cheerful greetings all around, Vivienne spoke. "Tino, do you remember me telling you that I was sure there was something I was forgetting to ask?" Tino merely nodded. "I guess it's curiosity more than anything else," she continued, "but how can you make money after paying out so much for the cost of your seed money?"

157

Before answering her, Tino requested that Shirley bring a pitcher of water and three glasses. He waited until she delivered the water and left the room, then he took the three previously set cups of coffee and placed them near the water glasses. He poured about one-fourth of the coffee into each empty water glass, then he added water from the pitcher to bring each glass half full of weakened coffee. Finally, he spoke. "Let us say, Vivienne, that the product we're dealing in is coffee. It is a well-known fact that in South America they prepare coffee for their own consumption far stronger than we do here in North America. Therefore, they serve it in smaller cups and drink it in lesser quantities than us. If we were served coffee in the strength that they prefer, we would doubtless add water to make it more palatable to our tastes, thereby increasing the volume. Where I make my money is by increasing the volume without making the end product too weak. You see, if my raw product weren't cut with something, it would be lethal. The people I distribute it to are likely to cut it again, so it's important that I don't cut it too severely the first round. That's a part of your answer; the rest is in rapid turnover. I'll turn the money two-and-a-half times a month. Maybe that sounds like a lot, but if you consider my cost of operation, you will actually end up making as much as I do, and if I have a problem and have to lay out legal fees, your share will exceed mine. In your position, you shouldn't ever need to pay legal fees. Still, I make enough, and eventually, I'll be debt-free; then I'll make more."

He stopped talking, pausing to see if Vivienne had any further questions. When she said nothing, he began to speak again, his tone now changed to one of dead earnestness. "There's one thing I want to emphasize before we conclude this deal," he said; "<u>always</u> communicate with me through Sammy. I have no reservations about telling you how to reach me, but please don't call me. Call Sammy and have him reach me. You must understand that, with modern technological advances in voice recording and such, it simply isn't safe to be communicating directly with one another. Sammy and I contrived methods of dealing with these problems long ago. So if you feel the need to talk with me, do it through Sammy." Tino smiled as he handed Vivienne a small card with his phone number on it, a phone number she had just been expressly forbidden to use.

The afternoon's business concluded, Vivienne left the office with Sammy. She had received a valid second mortgage position in her name, together with a promissory note signed by Tino and Sammy. Tino had received a cashier's check for two-hundred and fifty-thousand dollars, which he knew he would have no trouble converting to cash in a friendly Florida bank. Unknown to Vivienne, while the meeting was taking place, Gus had delivered a shoe box to Shirley with instructions to give it to Sammy as soon as he was alone. The shoe box contained twenty-five-thousand dollars in cash.

Sammy was actually feeling a bit guilty about the way he had been treating the mother of his children. He wanted to get home and salve his conscience, but he couldn't resist taking time to enjoy a swim with Vivienne. The swim led to an hour of sex and conversation dwelling on their mutual admiration and financial conquest. Reluctant to depart such decadent pleasures, Sammy finally had to excuse himself. He hurried back to the office, stopping only long enough to pick up the shoe box and call his wife, advising her to secure a baby-sitter for the evening. When he arrived home, he withdrew a thousand dollars from the box, gave it to his wife and informed her that he was taking her out to dinner. She was pacified by the patently phony gesture of largesse.

Vivienne was home to receive Manny's call from St. Louis. She and the children took turns talking to 'daddy', and when Manny recradled the phone, he audibly whispered his prayers of thanks for the blessings he enjoyed.

The children in bed, Vivienne located the leftover wine and settled down to late-night TV. Proud of her day's activities, she drank herself to sleep. Occasionally, her thoughts turned to how nice it might be to end up married to a prominent lawyer.

Chapter 12 -- THE INTERVIEW - PART TWO

Woody Justice arrived at Manny's apartment at eight Monday morning to take him to breakfast. Usually, Manny slept in on his days off, but Woody had told him that he must be in Kari's room by ten, and breakfast prior to the appointment was Woody's way of assuring that Manny would be on time. They were having breakfast at the Park Plaza, another assurance to Woody that Manny would be with Kari by ten. Besides, Woody loved the food at the Park Plaza and looked forward to a big breakfast cooked to order. Manny ordered only coffee and toast. Manny had not questioned Woody concerning his telephone conversation with Kari.

Both men were surprised when, just as their breakfast was served, Kari walked in and joined them. Her attitude was more businesslike than friendly, especially toward Manny. She masked her feelings by putting on her reporter's face and expressing a desire to complete her business with Manny as soon as possible. Manny, having no clue concerning the hurt caused by Woody's phone call, passed off her cool manner as her needing to conclude the interview as professionally and as quickly as possible. She still seemed cheerful, if somewhat distant.

Once Woody's breakfast was finished, he excused himself, saying, "I'll pick you up for supper at eight, Kari, if that's still okay?"

"That'll be fine, Woody," she replied softly. I'll see you then."

Listening to Kari and Woody planning their evening gave Manny an uncomfortable feeling that he did not like, but his decision was made, and he knew he must stick with it. Smiling, he called 'good-bye' to Woody and followed Kari to her room. The short trip was made in chilly silence.

Kari had set up a work area with chairs on either end, so she and Manny would have the length of the table between them. The obvious act of dividing the two was not lost on Manny, but he pretended not to notice. Seating herself at one end of the table, Kari started her recorder, picked up a pen and began the interview.

"Manny, when we were talking in Chicago, you alluded to some childhood events that led you into baseball... do you remember?" Her voice was all business and lacked the warm tones she used during the Chicago talks.

Manny tried to ignore his discomfort with Kari's chilly reception of him; he didn't understand how she could have been so loving in Chicago and so cold and indifferent now, but in deference to the interview, he began to answer her.

"When I was about twelve years old, I was still skinny, but had been throwing a baseball every day when I wasn't helping my mother. One day I was walking to the

162

store on an errand for mom, and some fellows came from behind me along the road driving in a flatbed truck. The road was narrow, and I don't know whether it was accidental or on purpose, but the driver came very close to me, and one of the men kicked me as they went by. The force of his kick knocked me down, and I cut my back on the sharp rocks as I fell. The men on the truck were laughing loudly at what had occurred. Quickly I got up and hurled a rock at them. It hit one of them squarely in the head, and he fell off the truck bed onto the dirt road like a dead rabbit. I thought I'd surely killed him, so I ran away. The other men left their fallen friend and chased me. When I was out of their sight, and also out of breath, I crashed through the unlocked door of a small house. There was a man sitting alone, eating; I asked for protection. Without question, he motioned me to another room and continued his meal.

"Soon the men from the truck knocked on his door. They were going from house to house looking for me. The man hiding me allowed them to push open his door, and he listened to their story. In the adjoining room, I was scared senseless, sure that he'd turn me over to them when he heard that I'd caused harm to one of their workers. Instead, after hearing them out, he assured them that he had neither seen nor heard anyone, and the men left, satisfied that I must be hiding somewhere else.

"Ironically, that man was the San Francisco Giants' bird-dog scout in Dominica. He was a good friend of the well-known Giants' scout, Jack Skidmore, and his name is Alfred Munoz, but everybody calls him 'Rooster'. They say there are two things Munoz loves -- baseball and cock fighting, from which comes the nickname. Anyway, when the angry men departed, Rooster told me that any boy of my small stature and young age who could throw a rock that hard and accurately, just might have the makings of a big league baseball pitcher. It was an exciting thing to hear, even before I knew how important this man was. He let me stay in his house until he was sure that my pursuers had given up the chase. I never heard anything about the man I hit with the rock, so I was sure that I hadn't killed him, but I'll bet he refrained from kicking boys as they walked down the road."

Manny had become caught up in the story of meeting Rooster, and temporarily, Kari's attitude was unnoticed. He continued with his tale. "The next time I saw Rooster, he and Jack Skidmore came to a place where a bunch of us kids played baseball every day. He and Jack just sat there on the ground talking to each other and taking notes. Rooster had a stop watch, and Jack had a radar gun, but those things were unfamiliar at that time to fifteen-year-old Dominican kids.

"When we quit playing, Rooster summoned me over, and, to my surprise, called me by name. 'Manny,' he said, 'meet *Señor* Jack Skidmore. He's a scout with the Giants and has signed many of our players to go to the United States. He'd like to talk to your parents about maybe you going there, too.'

"To tell the truth, Kari, I was dumbstruck. We visited a little while longer, and the two men went home with me." He paused momentarily and smiled at the memory of that first meeting between his parents, Rooster and Jack.

Still smiling, he continued in a soft voice. "My parents were almost as excited as I was, and they agreed that in a year or so they would permit me to sign with the Giants if Rooster and Jack still wanted me. I didn't realize it at the time, but Rooster and Jack would have signed me then, except they wanted me to gain some weight first. They gave my mother money for extra food. They knew it would be used for food for the whole family; so, in effect, the entire family was already beginning to prosper from my good fortune. In a small way, I felt that this was making up for all those years when I was sickly and couldn't join them to work in the fields. Rooster explained to my mother about altering my diet with more protein. You see, most low-income Dominican families like ours eat only one meal, of chicken, rice and beans, each day, and they are grateful to have that. In our case, with Jack's money, there was more chicken, rice and beans, but I was also introduced to goat's milk, hamburger and beefsteak. My brothers and sisters didn't like the milk and steak, even though it was there if they wanted it. I was happy beyond belief that I might be able to play baseball, and that, in the process, I could help my family." Once again, Manny paused, looked quietly at Kari, and asked if this was what she wanted for her article.

Kari had been vicariously carried to Dominica and was caught up in the surroundings of the youthful Manny. Realizing that he had asked a question, she snapped from her daydream and answered affirmatively. As Manny continued, she relaxed and allowed herself to return to the story of his homeland. "During my sixteenth year," Manny said, "I gained forty pounds. The new diet amazingly changed my physique and strength. At Rooster's urging, I began to run several miles every day to strengthen my legs. Most people have no idea of it, but a pitcher's legs will give out long before his arm. By the time I was seventeen, I could throw a baseball over a hundred miles an hour for the sixty feet-six inches between a pitcher's mound and home plate. It was easy and natural for me, no big strain. The strength I had envied in others was now also mine.

"During the winter of my seventeenth year, Rooster came again to see my parents, and this time, he brought a minor league contract. It called for me to go to Class A minor league baseball in the Carolinas at six-hundred dollars a month for six months, including spring training in Arizona. Rooster said I'd like Arizona because of the many Spanish-speaking people there. I didn't realize it then, but he purposely didn't mention that <u>nobody</u> spoke Spanish in the Carolinas. My parents and I signed the contract, and I soon found myself a few miles out of Phoenix, Arizona, at the Giants' Casa Grande spring training minor league facility.

"It could have been a million miles from Phoenix, because we never got to go there anyway. I did get to meet some big league players, though, because they would occasionally play us in intersquad games. That was always a thrill. I was so green it must have been funny for them to watch me, much less face me during play. Once, during an intersquad game, a minor league coach called time-out and walked out to the mound to instruct me, in very understandable Spanish, to dust off, or knock down, the batter, who was a very well-known big league player. The hitter well knew what was going on, and he just grinned.

"I didn't realize it then, but I was being tested for several things, not the least of which was whether or not I could follow simple instructions. My head told me 'no', but my heart said 'yes', so I did exactly as instructed and I threw so hard the batter couldn't get out of the way, and I hit him. My first reaction was to do what I'd done years before when I hit the fellow in the truck bed with a rock. Fortunately, I didn't run, and more fortunately, the player didn't get mad. At that moment, I felt like I was where I belonged and started developing a calmness of attitude that I hope I never lose."

Suddenly Manny stopped talking and looked at Kari. As she averted his glance, he blurted out what was on his mind. "Kari," he said, "when I went to Phoenix, my wife told me that she had filed the divorce papers in anger -- misplaced anger -- and I listened while she told her lawyer to drop the case."

Without thinking, Kari shot back, "Is that why you gave Woody my number and encouraged him to call and ask me out? Did you think hearing from him, and not from you, would make me feel better?"

Manny was disturbed by the sarcastic tone of Kari's voice. He sat in silence, just looking at her. Kari was fighting back tears, and Manny realized that a new dimension had been added to his plight. To his utter surprise and dismay, he knew that he was the one who had added it.

Kari lost the battle against her emotions, and the tears were streaming down her cheeks. She was determined to return to business and get the story for her article. Certainly she had originally planned this St. Louis trip for a reason beyond just work, but, since that had changed, the need to leave with a completed interview had become paramount. She attempted to take control of the moment and regain her personal dignity.

"Look, Manny, please don't cause me to make more of a fool of myself than I already have. I simply should not have been so presumptuous and foolish as to think that you and I had a future together. Eventually -- though not at this moment, or for a while -- I'll come to realize that what is happening is really best for me and you and your family in Phoenix. I don't know what got into me to think I had any right to you for the rest of our lives, anyway."

She paused as the tears threatened to return full force. Manny looked like he might say something, but, to prevent that, she held up her hand and spoke through the trickle of tears. "Wait," she said forcefully, "I do know, so I might as well say it. I can't explain it, and I won't try, but I fell in love with you in Chicago. I've read about that happening to other people, and it happened to me, and I wallowed in it. It was the furthest thing from my mind; I don't believe in love at first sight, but it was love, and, God, how I enjoyed it!" Her voice caught in a little sob, and she breathed deeply before continuing. "When we parted, I became even more sure of the legitimacy of my feelings. I've never in my entire life been given to infatuation; that just told me that I really was in love with you." She hurried on before he could interrupt. "When I returned Woody's call in L.A., and he told me you'd given him my number and encouraged him to call me, I was suddenly flung from a mountain of emotional highs to a valley of emotional hurts. Now, before you say anything, Manny, let me say I absolutely had no right to expect you to go home and set your family life asunder, just because I had fallen in love with you. We're both mature adults, and I know that my 'I wants' pale in comparison to the best situation for your children."

Neither Kari nor Manny, both carried by the intensity of their personal conversation, realized that the tape recorder was preserving every word. Kari's last reference had given Manny an opportunity to break into her speech. "First, Kari," he interjected firmly, "let me set you straight on my encouragement of Woody to call you; nothing could be farther from the truth, at least, from the truth of my intentions. It doesn't matter what Woody thinks I said, he was pressing me to give him your number -- I gave it to him to shut him up. I did not encourage him."

Kari held her arms firmly at her sides, refusing to look at him. Manny moved to her; taking her hand, he gently led her to the bed and pulled her down beside him, wrapping her in his arms. He stroked her hair for a moment, letting her tears flow over his shirt front. After a moment, he began to speak, barely above a whisper. "For what it's worth, Kari, I'm in love with you, too. More in love with you than I am with my own wife. When I explain, you'll understand and believe me. The problem is... that there's more to be considered here than just you and me, and even Vivienne. I can't deny my children. I would leave them the victims of a broken home and a fatherless existence. I could never be happy again -- even with you, the woman I love."

They simultaneously sat upright and both were now crying, then Manny spoke first. "Kari, I must not hurt you any deeper. Please believe me when I say I love you. Also, know that I shall, the rest of my life, consider you a close friend and do anything on earth to help you, anywhere, any time. Understand very clearly that if my children were as yet unborn, my most fulfilling life's wish would be to have them with you." With that, Manny just hung his head and openly wept.

Kari was speechless. Manny had said it all -- for both of them. She at once knew not only how he felt about her; she knew that her interpretation of what Woody had said over the phone was not only in error, but one-hundred and eighty degrees off the mark. They both had very mixed feelings. They wanted each other more than they wanted their next breaths, but the honor and respect of each for the best interests of Manny's children controlled their moments now.

"You warned me, Manny," she said, "I just chose to ignore it because of the way I felt toward you. Know this, *Señor* Manny, a piece of my heart shall always be with you."

Manny interjected, "Kari, you are, as we say in Spanish, my *amigo de corizón*, friend of the heart." Manny then smiled through his tears, returned to his chair and continued his story. "As a young man who couldn't speak English, my earliest years in the U.S. were pure hell, and the main reason was because of the color of my skin."

He continued, "As I told you in Chicago, racial prejudice does not exist in Dominica. Here, even though I'm more a dark to tan than I am black, I'm still not white. You can phrase this thought any way you wish, but I'll guarantee that you'll never be able to accurately convey the feeling a young, non-white, non-English-speaking man has when the

170

people he's attempting to live among reject him for no reason except that he's not white.

"Another huge problem was obtaining a meal when I wasn't where I could fix it myself. Most of the time, I would just walk around and look at what people were eating and point out to the waitress what I wanted to order. You see, fledgling minor league ball players in those days who couldn't speak English were not given an interpreter. Some fellows ended up having nervous breakdowns. Remember, most of us came from very strong family backgrounds. Suddenly we're far away from home with no family in a country where we don't speak the language and are surrounded by white people who just plain didn't like us because we were not white. That's why, to this day, the Latin players always hang together. When we play away from home, we always eat at least once in the homes of the Latinos who play on the team we've traveled to play."

Manny went on, "I commenced to study English and watch a lot of TV. I really enjoyed the 'Perry Mason' shows, so my conversational English sometimes sounded lawyer-like. If I spent a lot of time watching televangelists, my words would take on a 'churchy' twinge. Can you imagine how people would laugh at my early use of English when I got crossed up between Perry Mason and Jimmy Swaggert?

"Now comes the part I really want you to pay close attention to because it will give you the most insight into why I find myself in the marriage I'm in today." He paused with a sigh, then continued, "Disillusioned by racial prejudice and driven by a desire to raise me and my Dominican family out of their financial squalor, I decided on two goals, and they were, to make the Big League and marry a gringo lady.

"When I first came up with the Giants, the major league minimum salary was twelve-thousand and five-hundred dollars. That was more money than my father and brothers had ever collectively made in five years, but I was still black, and, by U.S. standards, 'inferior'.

"I met Vivienne in San Francisco, and we went everywhere together with no noticeable prejudice. I didn't realize it then, but San Francisco is a sophisticated city with an atmosphere unlike the southern towns I had played in. In other words, Vivienne may not have ever gone out with me in the Carolinas, but I'll never know the answer to that one.

"Soon," he continued, "she moved in with me. We lived together for three years before we got married. During our time together, she has been very faithful to me and has been an immeasurably good factor in everything from choosing a lawyer as my negotiating agent to the handling of my investments. She has been everything I ever wanted in a woman until I met you, and now, much to my dismay, I realize I'd give everything except my children to be with you, Kari, the woman I love but can't have."

Again he paused, to let her absorb this, but she showed no real emotion, so he went on. "A young Latin ball player coming to this country today will never be far away from a bilingual person to assist him in his everyday life. Things are different now than they were five years ago. Today, many of the big league teams have permanent contingencies of their personnel set up in Latin America just to scout the kids and be a bridge between them and their parents when they leave to play ball in the U.S. Still, many of us choose to fight the prejudice we still encounter by taking a gringo lady as a wife. I may have married Vivienne for all the wrong reasons, but at least she's given me two beautiful children, and I believe she loves me very much, even though now I know, Kari, I wish I'd have waited for you. But then, they say, God always sees to it that things work out for the best." Manny stopped talking, and Kari turned off her recorder.

"Manny, who knows what the future holds? Certainly we don't! Here we are, professing undying love for each other in the face of what appears today to be insurmountable obstacles. Why don't we just accept our plight and enjoy the fact that we've joined in a lifetime friendship?"

"That sounds easy enough," he said, "but, in reality, if I'm ever around you, I know me well enough to know that I'll want to smother you with affection."

"And I, you," she said, "so we just won't ever end up like this, alone together in one or the other's hotel room." For a moment, they both were sharing the same unspoken thought. Who would ever know what happened here today but them? They came together, arms around each other, kissing passionately and long. The chemistry was not only still there, it was more and better. Each time they kissed, it was as if it was their last, and they lingered, not wanting the afternoon to end.

Kari knew that Manny was soon to leave her room and life, only to remain a friend and not her lover. Manny knew these were likely the last intimate moments with the woman he loved.

They did what they both felt like doing. Kari was no virgin, but on a scale of sexual inactivity, she was a nine-plus. Manny's gentleness was not only welcome, it was necessary. Penetration was difficult, but what pain Kari had was most enjoyable. Manny took his time with her, as he could tell she was a novice. Manny's manner was delicate in handling his innocent partner.

He made love to her continually for over an hour. The longer it lasted, the easier it became. Kari started climaxing after the first twenty minutes. At hour's end, sensing she was ready to get it all, Manny gave over and pumped harder until her vaginal cavity was filled with him. Then it happened, and, as Manny had timed it, it happened simultaneously. With his seminal vesicles at last completely evacuated, and Kari at the end of her sexual journey, Manny withdrew and rolled off her, holding her tightly in his arms for another twenty minutes.

Their crying and loving had taken them on an emotional roller coaster neither would ever forget.

Manny whispered sweet things in Kari's ear and then got up to go the bathroom. He returned, fully clothed and sat next to her on the side of the bed and said, "Kari, I did that so you could feel and always remember this day as the time you knew my true feelings.

"I'm leaving now, not because I want to, but because if I don't, I never will. What has happened this afternoon is ours and ours alone. Nothing either of us does with anyone else could change the time we had together.

"About your article," he continued, "if you need some kind of release or legal paper for me to sign to show my permission for you to use it, just send it to me and I'll sign it and return it promptly. If you should hit the jackpot with it and make a lot of money, set aside what you think you should for the underprivileged children in Dominica. Who knows, maybe someday you'll get to come down, and I'll take you on a tour."

"I'd love that, Manny. In fact, right now, I can't think of anything I'd enjoy more than following you around helping kids -- especially if they were our kids. I know you don't want to hear this, but I'd be tickled pink if some of that baby-batter we just mixed up would result in my having a little Manny!" She quickly added, "I meant that, but don't worry about it."

Manny smiled, looked at her and said, "Worry? Why, I was thinking the same thing myself." They both laughed.

"Manny, my love," she said as she wrapped a sheet around her naked body and followed him to the door, "I'll be there when you need me and probably when you least expect it."

He stopped at the door. Before opening it, he turned and again they embraced and kissed long and passionately. When they finished, he opened the door and left.

Kari went back and lay down on the bed to collect herself. 'Where to now?' she wondered. 'I'm not going to chase Manny, but I don't want to be far from him. What's the best way to do that?' she questioned herself. Then it came home to her. 'If Woody Justice wants to date me for awhile, I'll just do it. He is a nice young man, and he seems gentle enough, so I shouldn't have to worry about his getting out of hand on me. That's it,' she decided. 'To heck with feeling guilty about manipulating Woody. I'll be honest if it ever comes up and tell him I'm not ready to get serious with anyone yet, and that way I can at least keep up with Manny until I'm satisfied he's okay with what he said today about staying with his wife.

'I won't make any attempt to interfere in Manny's marriage,' she thought. Then it also occurred to her that no man could ever take her to the heights that Manny had that afternoon. She also wondered to herself if she had come anywhere near doing for him what he'd done for her. She didn't know. She ended her musing to herself while bathing and getting dressed to go out with Woody.

Chapter 13 -- THE DIVORCE

It was a gorgeous September day in Phoenix. Blossoms were present on top of the cactus, signifying fall was out all over.

Vivienne Hernandez arose particularly early this day. She toned down her makeup, put on her most conservative attire and whisked the children off to the sitter after feeding them breakfast.

She proceeded to an office building across from the courthouse known as the Luhrs Tower. She arrived at the tenth floor office of attorney Derrickson Henze and seated herself in his waiting room. Henze's office was tastefully but conservatively decorated.

Henze was a lawyer's lawyer, so to speak. As a young college student, he had worked several summers in Harrah's Casino in Lake Tahoe, Nevada, as a Keno runner. His summer job was his only opportunity to acquire 'street sense', as Henze was born of upper middle class parents and raised in a secure family atmosphere. He was a man of high ethical and personal standards, a complete opposite of Sammy Snider. He was the senior partner in an elite, five-man firm, and his huge corner office overlooked downtown Phoenix to the Northeast, which gave him a view of Camelback Mountain, where he made his home, in Scottsdale.

After only a few minutes, Henze appeared at his office door and invited Vivienne in. Then, after some prefatory small talk, Henze got down to the business at hand.

"Missis Hernandez, I have received nothing from anyone on behalf of your husband. Do you know if he has made any effort to retain counsel?" he asked her.

"No, Mister Henze, I don't," Vivienne replied, and continued, "however, I can tell you that my husband and I have talked, and he is fully aware of the consequences of my actions. He knows enough to contact counsel if he wants to, and I'm sure you realize, Mister Henze, that lawyers are commonplace in the lives of today's professional baseball players. Therefore, if my husband wanted one for any reason, including advice on this matter, he would have easy access."

Henze's facial expression gave away his more than idle curiosity with this unusual situation. "You realize, Missis Hernandez, that the judge we appear before this morning is likely to question you closely on this issue, don't you?" Henze asked.

Vivienne was armed and ready. She was treating this conversation as a dress rehearsal for the court appearance she was about to make. "Yes, Mister Henze, I do. I am prepared to answer any questions you or the judge may proffer."

Henze was going through a last-minute cursory inspection of the legal papers before him as he was preparing

Vivienne for her court appearance. He continued to talk to her as he turned the pages.

"I'm going to put you on the witness stand, Missis Hernandez, and basically go through your divorce petition out loud, asking you to verify, under oath in open court, what your sworn petition states. The judge may or may not choose to question you further. The essential thing for you to remember at all times during your court appearance is to tell the truth and do it in as few words as possible. An old saying that lawyers often tell their witnesses is, if you are asked what time it is, don't respond by telling them how to build a watch! Do you understand?" Vivienne nodded affirmatively.

Henze continued, "It is, to say the least, unusual for a man of your husband's prominence and financial standing not to be represented by counsel in a matter such as this, where the financial stakes are so high. One has to wonder why he stands mute and makes no effort to, at the very least, mitigate the judgment that is about to be assessed against him. Now, Missis Hernandez, have you an answer to such an inquiry, should the judge pose it to you this morning?"

"Yes," she quickly replied. "I can explain it to the court's satisfaction; of that I'm sure."

Henze concluded their pre-court conference, put on his jacket and led the way across First Avenue to the Maricopa County Courthouse. They passed through the metal detectors and caught an elevator to the ninth floor office and courtroom location of Judge Hughes, where Henze seated Vivienne and then proceeded to the judge's chambers, smiling at Judge Hughes' jovial secretary on the way by. He and the judge were old friends, and Henze wasn't required to observe the formality of going through the secretary to see the judge. The door to the judge's inner office was open, and the judge was alone, so Henze had the privilege of skirting the usual protocol and walked in and sat down in front of the judge's desk.

"Have you had a chance to review the Hernandez file that's on for default hearing this morning, John?" Henze asked.

"Not really, but then, that doesn't really matter, does it, Derrickson, since I can rely on you to accurately and objectively brief me on it," the judge laughingly replied.

"To be sure, Your Honor, to be sure," Henze chortled, and continued, "John, this is pretty cut and dried. The only thing that sets this case apart from the usual is the zeroes. This respondent is a foreign national, a Dominican, who was recently awarded a big-league baseball contract calling for over a million dollars. My client lived with him for several years and then married him and bore two children. What I'm going to tell you now is not in the record and won't be, but this fellow is Dominican and what we'd call a mulatto. In my opinion, that was the problem. This little lady is a good mother and a non-working homemaker who devotes all of her time to her kids. In my opinion, she just wasn't cut out for the fast lane a professional ball player travels in these days, and, although they have two beautiful children, I don't think she had any idea what she was getting into when she entered a racially mixed marriage. She tells me this fellow wants her and the children to go live in the Dominican Republic, and she's afraid if she does that he'd never let the children return. She doesn't bad-mouth him, and, like I said, this is largely my opinion, but if after hearing her testimony, you believe her, I'd appreciate your specifying that the children could not be removed from this country without the court's written permission."

"I have no problem with that," the judge said as he continued, "but pray tell, Derrickson, why a man of this financial stature has not obtained counsel?"

"I asked her the very same thing, Judge, in my office not over twenty minutes ago and told her you'd want to know just that. She said she was ready to tell you."

"Anything else, Derrickson?"

"No, Your Honor."

"Okay," Hughes said as he buzzed his secretary's intercom. When she answered, the judge instructed her that he was going to hear the Hernandez Default matter in his chambers and asked her to send in his court reporter and personal stenographer to record the proceedings.

Henze stepped into the courtroom and summoned Vivienne with a hand signal. When she arrived in the hallway between the courtroom and the judge's office, Henze spoke to her briefly. "Missis Hernandez, the judge is going to hear this matter in his chambers. This is nothing unusual or different in uncontested matters. It's done largely as a convenience to the court and counsel. But you must understand that, just because you are in a more relaxed atmosphere, you are under no less obligation to be totally truthful. It is an advantage to sit in the comfort of the judge's office and not have to testify in open court in front of total strangers, including meandering press and reporters, but the proceedings are nonetheless serious and not to be taken lightly. Do you understand that?"

"Yes, sir, I do," Vivienne firmly replied and then followed her lawyer into the judge's private office. The judge's secretary closed the door, and Vivienne was shown to a comfortable chair in front of his desk.

The judge commenced the proceedings. "This is Case Number DR 17572092 in the Domestic Relations Division of the Maricopa County Arizona Superior Court, entitled Vivienne Wilson Hernandez, Petitioner, versus Manny Hernandez, Respondent; let the record also show that Petitioner is present with her attorney, Derrickson Henze. The file duly reflects that the Respondent was personally served with a copy of the Petition over a month ago in Chicago, Illinois, and that he has failed to answer the Petition for Divorce in the allotted time. A Default Notice was duly filed by Missis Hernandez' counsel, and the matter comes on now for hearing in this court, presided over by John Hughes, Judge. Madam clerk, please swear the witness. Missis Hernandez, you may remain seated, but raise your right hand."

The clerk addressed Vivienne, who raised her right hand. "Do you solemnly swear to tell the truth, the whole truth and nothing but the truth, so help you God, in the matters now before this court?"

Vivienne demurely said, "I do."

"Mister Henze," the judge said, indicating that Vivienne's attorney could start the inquiry of his client.

Henze commenced. "You are Vivienne Wilson Hernandez, the wife of Manny Hernandez, the same being the Petitioner and Respondent, respectively, in your action for divorce?"

"Yes," Vivienne quietly answered.

"Missis Hernandez, you stated in your petition that you have been a continuous resident of Arizona for more than a year prior to your filing this action, is that true?"

"Yes," she replied, thereby satisfying the Arizona residential requirement for the court to have jurisdiction in the matter.

"You further state," Henze continued, "that you and your present husband, Manny Hernandez, were married in a civil ceremony performed by a duly qualified Justice of the Peace here in Phoenix, Arizona, on September 30, 1974, is that correct?"

Vivienne answered "Yes."

"Further that you and your husband continually lived together since that time, during which you, at all times, have faithfully demeaned and conducted yourself as his devoted and loving wife, is that correct?"

"Yes," Vivienne answered.

He then continued with the required questions: "Missis Hernandez, you state that the marriage relationship between you and your husband is irretrievably broken, is that true?"

"Yes," Vivienne said. Pulling a kleenex from her purse, she slowly dabbed the tears from her eyes.

"Missis Hernandez, you state that there are two children born of the union, Joseph, age four, and Marie, age two and a half, is this correct?"

"Yes," Vivienne answered.

"You further state that you have custody of these children now and that you are a fit and proper person to retain that custody, is that correct?"

"Yes," she replied softly and tearfully.

"You do want your husband to have reasonable visitation rights, do you not?"

"Yes," said Vivienne, now weeping openly, "if he just won't take them out of the country, and if he'll let me know a day ahead of time when he wants to see them. The children love their father very much, and it is not my desire to deprive him from visiting them at any reasonable time he can do it." Vivienne was personally pleased with her act so far. She realized, to her great satisfaction, that visitation could only be possible during the six months out of the year that Manny wasn't playing ball, and she had no fear of being unable to subvert his efforts during the other six months. As far as she was concerned, she didn't care if her children ever saw their father again. To her, the principal purpose for their existence was to guarantee and enhance her ability to extract all the money from Manny's income she could as long as he was actively employed as a baseball player in this country.

"Missis Hernandez," Henze continued, "I know this is very difficult for you, do you need a short break?"

"No," Vivienne tearfully replied, "let's get it over with."

Having covered the jurisdiction and venue issues, Henze now got to the reason Vivienne was really here, the money.

"Missis Hernandez," Henze continued, "you and your husband are the owners of certain real estate here in

Maricopa County, which is where you and your children now reside, is that correct?"

"Yes," she answered, "on East Thomas Road in Scottsdale."

"Is it your desire to remain there?" he asked.

"Yes," replied Vivienne.

"Missis Hernandez, at my request, have you brought copies of certain documents with you today that accurately reflect your husband's current income and financial status?"

"Yes," Vivienne answered as she handed Henze copies of the joint tax returns she and Manny had filed for the previous three years and several copies of Manny's recent payroll checks and the envelopes they'd come to her in, indicating that they had been directly mailed to her by the Cardinals' ball club.

"Missis Hernandez," Henze continued, after having the clerk mark each exhibit with a number, "would you please individually identify each exhibit which I've handed you in numerical order?"

"Yes," Vivienne said, and then went on: "Exhibits one, two and three are the copies of the joint tax returns filed by my husband Manny, and me, for each of the last three years. Exhibits four, five, six, seven, eight, nine and ten are copies of his payroll checks, which the St. Louis Cardinal Baseball Club mails directly to me on the first and fifteenth of every month. Let me explain... professional baseball players all get their payroll checks on the first and fifteenth of every month. The club withholds the payroll taxes and such, and gives the player his check. The player may elect to have his check sent to his permanent home, which my husband does, as reflected by these envelopes. Further, some players choose to be paid over a twelve-month period. Manny doesn't. He receives the full amount he is due for a season's play over the seasonal six-month period. During the off season or in the winter months, he doesn't receive a paycheck because he's been paid in full during the season. So, when the season is over at the end of this month, he'll get no more pay until spring training."

"With respect to this point, Missis Hernandez, have you given any thought to how your husband can satisfy any payments to you over the next few months that the court may see fit today to order him to pay?"

"Yes," Vivienne answered. "First of all, let me say that my primary concern is for my children. Also, it must be remembered that, although my husband's earning capacity may seem to be a large amount at this moment, his career could be over, due to injury, at any time, and under the best of circumstances will only last another few years. So the total amount of his current contract divided by the life of that contract is two-hundred-thousand dollars, but should he be unable to continue playing, due to injury, that million dollars divided by the number of years it takes to raise my children and then educate them, plus what little it takes for me to live on, is quickly reduced."

"That in mind, Missis Hernandez, do you want to tell the court what you would consider fair?"

Vivienne had set her hooks and was quite up to the task of reeling in, in the next few minutes, the biggest financial catch of her young life. She was reveling in these proceedings, but careful to continue to project the image of the loving and devoted mother who only wanted what was necessary for her to properly raise her children. Her dimorphic personality was at its best.

"Your Honor," she quietly said, while looking straight into the eyes of the judge, who at this point, unwittingly had become her ally in her efforts to financially strip her husband, "my husband loves the game of baseball, as do all of his countrymen. He would play for nothing just to get to play. I must do what I can now to insure the future security of our children. That sole purpose in mind, here is how it can be accomplished. I'm asking for his equity in our house. I don't want the money. I want the house. I want to raise our children there. Further, we have a two-hundred-fifty-thousand-dollar savings account. That was his signing bonus. I want that. I want seventy-five-thousand dollars a year in alimony and the same amount in child support. That would leave Manny fifty-thousand dollars a year, which you can see by our prior years' tax returns, is much more than what he needs. Also, I want the court to order that these payments continue to come directly to me from the Cardinals. There are two other things the court should be made aware of. Active players receive meal money while traveling. They can eat for nothing from a spread of food the club presents every day during the season in the clubhouse. I know for a fact that my husband eats in the clubhouse and pockets his meal money every day. I don't want any of that." At this point, Vivienne gave the judge a wry smile, as if she were offering something out of her own largesse. "Further," she went on, "players receive outside income nowadays in many ways, such as royalties from endorsements of products and pay for attending baseball card shows. Also, the major league retirement, which vests after five years of play, is the envy of every retirement plan in the country, and a player can elect to receive it at age forty-five. I'm asserting no interest in a share of any of these sources of income at this time. However, should the Cardinals get in the League Championship Playoffs, and today that appears to be assumed, and then should they play in the World Series, my husband's income could easily be increased this year by over one-hundred-thousand dollars, and I think the children and I deserve at least half of that." Vivienne paused to consider whether or not she'd left anything out, and then said, "That is all."

Henze and Judge Hughes had patiently listened during her discourse, and each now had some final questions. Henze asked, "Missis Hernandez, are the children in good health, and, along those lines, what kind of health insurance coverage do they have or need?"

Vivienne answered, "They are presently covered, along with me, by a group plan available to all players and their families, the cost of which is taken out of my husband's paycheck. I want to keep this coverage, and I think he should pay for it as he now does. The children and I are in excellent health, but I deem the coverage still very necessary."

The judge then interjected, "Missis Hernandez, I find it unusual that your husband would not retain counsel in a matter of this financial magnitude and importance to himself. Can you shed any light on that for the court?"

"I think I can, Your Honor, although I'd be the first to say that a large part of our basic problem has been his inattentiveness to our family life and everyday living problems. By way of background, let me say this first: my husband is a native and citizen of the Dominican Republic. His countrymen spend their whole lives just playing and watching baseball, whether they make it to the United States or not." Vivienne's demeaning portrayal of Dominican men was false, underhanded and suborning perjury, but she knew there was nobody there who could testify in opposition. She continued, "My husband's ignoring his responsibility to be here today is typical of the way he has failed to observe the responsibilities of our marriage. It grieves me deeply to say these things, but the truth is, he just doesn't care. All he ever desires to do is play ball, with absolutely no thought of where he and his family shall end up when he's too old to play.

"Your Honor, I still love my husband very much. Manny Hernandez is a wonderful man who's never mistreated me. But he's totally irresponsible and refuses to think in terms of what needs to be done today to provide for his children tomorrow." She started to cry again, as if what she was saying was almost too painful for her to relate. Then her lie continued in grand style. "It is only because he's ignored his kids and me that I'm here. He's gone entirely six months out of the year, and the other six months, he just doesn't care. No, Your Honor, let me say, the truth is, if you called him on the telephone right now, he wouldn't show up here even by your personal invitation."

The last statement Vivienne made created an idea in the judge's mind that could have derailed her little dog-and-pony show, but Vivienne didn't know it.

"In keeping with the seriousness of what's taking place here, counsel, do you or your client know of any attorney contacts the respondent has locally for any of his business matters?" With his eyes, Henze deferred to Vivienne to answer.

"Your Honor," she began, "attorney Sammy Snider handled my husband's contract negotiations during the off season last year and early this year."

The judge then asked, "Does anyone know if your husband contacted Mister Snider with respect to this matter?"

Vivienne quickly fielded the knotty question, which neither she nor Henze had anticipated. "I'm not sure, judge, but if you'll allow it, I'll go outside and see if he can be reached by phone and have him call you." The last thing Vivienne wanted now was to have Sammy receive a call from the judge before she had the chance to coach him on what had transpired.

The judge then said, "No, Missis Hernandez, that won't be necessary. First, let me say that there is a thin line between a judge, any judge, remaining an impartial arbiter of the parties' rights and his becoming an advocate. I don't want to cross that line and get into territory where the court doesn't belong. On the other hand, these are gravely serious matters here which, I don't mind you knowing, I'm inclined to declare in favor of you receiving everything you've asked for, especially since, from all apparent evidence before me at this time, your husband is not opposed to your having. However, to just assure ourselves that, should at some future time, your husband have a change of heart and hire counsel to seek to set my judgment aside, we can show that he was given every consideration under the law that he was entitled to."

Vivienne cringed inside. She had no idea what the judge was about to propose, but she trembled at the thought of her plan being upset just when it appeared that everything she'd planned for so long was on the brink of coming together.

Henze spoke up. "What do you have in mind, Your Honor? We certainly stand ready and willing to do whatever we can to put the court at ease in these matters. As the court realizes, I'm occasionally called as a substitute to sit when some of the judges are on vacations, so I'm aware of the problems and difficulties that sometimes arise. In that regard, I repeat, just direct us, and we'll gladly cooperate."

"Here's what I have in mind, Mister Henze and Missis Hernandez. You prepare the judgment and order, Mister Henze, according to what Missis Hernandez has testified to and asked for here today and send it over for the court's signature. In the meantime, contact Mister Snider and tell him what's going on. If he says anything contrary to what we're doing, tell him to see that a formal appearance is made before me to discuss it right away -- I mean, tomorrow. If I don't hear anything by the close of the court day tomorrow, as far as I'm concerned, the matter is closed. Now, Mister Henze, I shall have your word that you'll speak to Mister Snider today, unless he's simply out of reach, in which case you'll let the court know."

Vivienne breathed a deep, but undetected, sigh of relief. Her devious mind was already planning how to dispose of this problem.

Henze said, "Done, judge. I'll handle it as soon as I get back to the office."

The judge said, "I want these exhibits to remain in the court file, but my secretary will copy them for you, upon request."

Vivienne spoke up, "Judge, thank you, and may I ask one more question?"

"Sure," the judge responded, "what is it?"

Vivienne replied, "My husband, although not a violent man, is possessed of the quickly ignitable Latin temper. What could I do if, in a fit of anger, he just showed up unannounced and took the children and left?"

"I'm glad you mentioned that, Missis Hernandez, and I'll answer it this way: this court tries to avoid, if it can, setting visiting privileges at a time certain. It is my belief that two people who are old enough to bring children into this world are mature enough to agree on visitation that, from time to time, causes a modicum of inconvenience to both parties. Therefore, I tend to issue orders for reasonable visitation and leave it to the parties to arrive at what is reasonable after considering everyone's interests -- including the children's.

"Obviously, some parents are not mature enough to follow these instructions. If difficulties arise with this method, I'll step back in, upon the request of either party, and review the situation and make further orders, probably calling for time frames to be imposed and the issues to be settled accordingly. Do you understand?"

"Yes," Vivienne answered, "and I'll strive to abide by that, but, what if he simply takes the kids and runs away?"

"In that instance, I'm sure your attorney would advise you to consider bringing prosecution of him under the Federal Parental Kidnapping Act," the judge replied, trying once more not to appear as an advocate.

"Another matter comes to mind," the judge continued. "I have no authority to order the St. Louis Cardinal Baseball Club to do anything, with respect to your husband's payroll check. You will receive a valid judgment for an amount certain, but you'll have to seek ordinary legal avenues of enforcing that judgment, should your husband neglect or refuse to pay it. However, it would be my guess that if he loves his family as much as you've testified, he'll probably just let the matters continue as they are. In any event, Mister Henze can enlarge on this point with you; I'm sure he appreciates the inability of a state judge in Arizona to issue a valid order enforceable in another state. The Cardinal front office would just ignore such an order, and justifiably so."

After the judge's final comment, Derrickson Henze and his client, Vivienne Hernandez, exited the judge's office. While waiting for the elevator, Henze said, "I have to check on another matter, Missis Hernandez. Why don't you just go over to my office and wait for me; I won't be long."

Vivienne agreed. They stepped onto the elevator together, and when Henze stepped out, Vivienne said, "I'll be waiting in your office."

Vivienne then stepped from the elevator and headed straight to a pay phone and called Sammy's office. Shirley politely answered and put her right on through to him.

"Whew!" Vivienne said when Sammy answered. "Am I ever glad I caught you."

"What's up, Viv?" Sammy queried. "You're not calling for another 'quick Sammy fix' already, are you?" Sammy laughed.

"Be serious," she said, "and listen to me very carefully." She proceeded to repeat to Sammy what had happened in Judge Hughes' chambers, and then, out of breath, she asked him what they could do to ensure that she would get the judgment issued in her favor without delay.

There was a short silence as Sammy thought it through, then he spoke. "Have Henze call me right away, Viv, 'cause I've got an appointment soon, out of the office, so make sure he calls me right away; but, don't worry, I'll stay here until noon."

"But what will you tell him, dammit?" she insisted.

"I'll say Manny contacted me when he got the papers and I explained the seriousness of the matter to him and told him I couldn't represent him. Further, I told him if you two didn't reconcile that he should get a lawyer soon, because he only had twenty days from the day he received the papers in Chicago to make a court appearance. I'll tell him that Manny has not contacted me since. All of which is the truth. I'm sure not going to tell him that Manny was here in Phoenix, and don't you, either, 'cause that could open up a real can of worms for us. This Henze guy is a real boy scout, Viv, and if he even remotely suspects you're scamming him, Manny, and the court, he'll drop you like a hot potato. Unless, of course, he's under your spell like I am." Sammy laughed.

"<u>Stop</u> it, Sammy," Vivienne ordered. Her voice indicated her growing impatience with what she perceived as Sammy taking this whole matter far too lightly to suit her.

Sammy, sensing her impending anger, said, "Relax, Viv, and just have the man call me. Sammy has always taken care of your interests before, and he'll take care of them now. By the way, what did you tell the judge and Henze about the two-hundred-fifty-thousand dollars in my trust account?"

Vivienne carefully explained to Sammy that she'd referred to it as a 'savings account' and left his name out of it.

"Fine," Sammy answered, and again implored her to go to Henze's office and see to it that Henze called Sammy forthwith.

When Derrickson Henze walked into his office, Vivienne was waiting. He motioned her to follow him and be seated in front of his desk. As if on unspoken command, he picked up his phone and called Sammy. Vivienne couldn't hear what Sammy was saying, but it obviously had the desired effect, because Henze hung up the phone and told her he'd prepare the judgment and order, and would go over personally to have the judge sign it the next day and mail a certified copy to her. Vivienne, not wanting to delay getting the final papers in her hands, told him she would be down the next afternoon at four to pick them up.

As she was leaving, the astute lawyer told her that the judgment and order would not be final for thirty days after the date they were filed, as Manny had that period of time to appeal the court's ruling. Although Vivienne had completely overlooked that fact, her quick mental calculations put her at ease, because it appeared that the Cardinals were a mortal cinch to reach the championship playoffs, which would keep Manny busy until mid-October, and, should they get in the World Series, he wouldn't be home until almost November. In either event, she figured, the thirty-day appeal period would be over.

The deal was done. It had only taken her ten years, but Vivienne Hernandez felt like she had just accomplished a life's work. She most certainly had accomplished a life's ambition.

Chapter 14 -- THE TRAP

The Phoenix office of the Drug Enforcement Administration had just received a communiqué from the Office of the Comptroller of the Currency. The regional supervisor, after receiving it, called an afternoon meeting of several of his agents who had been involved in the Tino Borozi matters.

The meeting did not start until Supervisor Mike Patrick, a rabid baseball fan, turned off his radio. He had been listening to the opening game of the National League Championship Series between the St. Louis Cardinals and San Diego Padres.

"Gentlemen," Patrick began the discussion, "as you know, this office has been in gridlock with the U.S. Attorney over surrendering any of the funds we confiscated under the R.I.C.O. Act during the various indictments involving Tino Borozi and others. Two significant new events have occurred. First, we received a copy of an assignment from Borozi to a Missis Vivienne Hernandez. As far as our preliminary investigation reveals, she is a completely new player in Borozi's game. Write her name down and remember it for future reference.

"Today, this office received a separate piece of information, this time from the Comptroller of the Currency. We had asked them to 'flag' certain known bank accounts of people in Borozi's circle of influence. A routine report filed by Borozi's attorney's bank yesterday reflected a withdrawal of two-hundred and fifty-thousand dollars. The money was withdrawn by check from the trust account of attorney Sammy Snider and deposited in a bank account in Miami, Florida, in the name of a dummy corporation that has been under surveillance for some time. It is being used to launder drug money, and, as far as we know, the people who use the account for people like Borozi don't know we are watching it.

"First question," the supervisor continued, "who the hell is Vivienne Hernandez?"

The silence was broken by Agent Marion Henricks. "I think I know, Boss. If you listen to the rest of that game you had on the radio when we walked in, you'll probably hear something about her husband, Manny Hernandez, the Cardinal relief pitcher who is largely responsible for that club's winning their division this year."

"Pray tell me what a man like that would be doing getting an assignment of confiscated funds from Tino Borozi?" Patrick asked.

Henricks was quick to answer. "Boss, you said the assignment runs from Borozi to <u>Missis</u> Hernandez. Therefore, we don't, as of this moment, have more than a mere suspicion of her husband's involvement. However, there is a common denominator here that any local baseball fan would recognize, and that is in the person of their mutual attorney, Sammy Snider."

"Henricks," the supervisor ordered in an urgent tone of voice, "get on the horn and see if there has been a two-hundred and fifty-thousand dollar transfer out of the bank account in Miami, and get right back to me."

Patrick continued the discussion as Agent Henricks hurriedly left the room. "My next question involves the matter of refunding any money to Borozi; do you fellows have any comment?"

Agent Billy Long was the first to speak up. "Boss, we've been kicking this around among ourselves since Borozi was acquitted by a jury, and I think the consensus here is that it's just a matter of time before we nail Borozi again anyway. If we allow the refund now, he may lower his guard. We've had him under surveillance, and we know he's been to Panama, but it doesn't appear that he's brought any product back -- yet. This latest cash activity, I think you'll agree, is a pretty sure sign he's about to start."

"I see where you're going," Patrick interjected. "You're saying, give the money back now to lull him into a feeling of false security while intensifying the monitoring of his movements."

"Right," Long answered.

"Okay," Patrick continued, "let's set that aside for the moment and address the question of the involvement of one or more of the Hernandez people and whether there's a known connection between them and Borozi, besides having the same lawyer."

"I can't answer that, Boss, with any authority," Agent Long added, "but let's put it on the board and take a look at it."

Agent Long moved to the blackboard against the wall. He carefully drew an informational diagram on it.

Assignment of all confiscated funds
↓   ↓
Borozi   Hernandez
↓
Attorney Snider→ $250,000.00 check to Borozi

Miami Bank asks Phoenix Bank for expeditious handling of check

"There's still not enough to make a case against the Hernandez people -- either of them -- for conspiracy. We can assume that Borozi would not be assigning those funds to anyone except to further his own interests," Patrick said.

Agent Charlie Kelso spoke up. "Don't lose sight of the fact that, so far as the assignment is concerned, Borozi could be creating a decoy just to distract us." The others nodded cautious approval. Kelso continued. "The central question here is what, if any, is the connection between the assignment and the check which Borozi deposited in Miami? Once we've answered that, we could either dismiss it as coincidence or bring the Hernandez people into the loop."

"Boss," Kelso asked Patrick, "do we still have a solid informant in the Miami Bank that's involved here?"

"Yeah," Patrick answered, "that's who Henricks is calling right now." The words were barely out of his mouth when Henricks re-entered the room.

"What's going on in Miami, Marion?" Patrick asked.

"As you know, Boss, our informant has to speak cryptically when we call her at the bank, but she does that very well. The check for two-hundred and fifty-thousand dollars was put through for collection; however, ordinary collection has been circumvented by the mob's man at the bank. Borozi is to call tomorrow to pick up the cash, which our girl has the responsibility of counting and giving to him personally."

"Great!" Patrick said in a near shout. "That means we have some time." The supervisor started giving orders as rapidly as a lunch-time waitress in a ten-seat diner.

"Long," he barked, you get to Miami now! See that Borozi's pilot follows our instructions. You know the drill. It's a sure thing that our boy is on his way south sometime real soon to make a buy. Henricks, you go over to the U.S. Attorney's office and have them call Borozi's lawyer, Sammy Snider, and tell him the check's in the mail; that an order has been cut and a U.S. Treasury check will be issued to Vivienne Hernandez, according to the assignment from Borozi to her. Make sure you stay there until the U.S. Attorney calls Snider."

"Boss," Henricks interrupted, "a check for how much?"

Patrick answered, "Tell 'em three-hundred-thousand dollars. That represents only a fourth of what we actually got, albeit the whole amount was probably Borozi's." The supervisor's reasoning was simple. Borozi would rather have a fourth back than nothing, and the government will keep almost a million, plus several convictions. The 'big fish' got away, but the supervisor was acting fast to go right back after him.

Almost as an afterthought, Patrick reread the communiqué from the Comptroller of the Currency's office. This time he noticed a word he had overlooked in his hasty first perusal of it. The money was to be transferred from a SPECIAL trust account of attorney Sammy Snider. Patrick picked up his phone and called the Comptroller of the Currency's office in Washington, and left word for them to get back to him ASAP, with more definite information about the use of the term 'SPECIAL'.

Patrick then returned to the radio broadcast of the ball game, number one in the NLCS. It was the seventh inning, and the Cardinals were leading San Diego, one-zero, on a home run by rookie catcher Woody Justice. Manny Hernandez was entering the game to try to hold the Padres scoreless which the starter, Duffy McCoy, had done for the previous six innings. The last three innings took only an hour to play. Manny was brilliant in relief. The Cards won game one, and Manny and Woody were the heroes. Manny's exhilaration after the game was equaled by Supervisor Patrick's enthusiasm. The two were being drawn together by forces that Manny had no knowledge of, and that Patrick didn't yet understand. As Patrick listened to the post-game interview of the Dominican star, he wondered how a wealthy young baseball player with such a bright future could possibly allow himself to become involved with a hoodlum scumbag like Tino Borozi. 'God,' thought the DEA Supervisor, 'I hope I'm wrong on my supposition that Manny Hernandez is involved, but if I'm not, I'll treat him just like another dope-dealing defendant, star baseball player or not.'

Patrick's intercom signaled he had a telephone call on his 'URGENT' line, which he answered. It was from the Comptroller of the Currency's office in Washington, who had called Sammy Snider's bank in Phoenix to determine the significance of the word 'SPECIAL' relating to his trust account. It was explained that lawyers generally have a trust account as a means of holding clients' funds. In this instance, Snider had set up an interest-bearing account which had the designation 'SPECIAL' because it contained only the funds of one of Mister Snider's clients, and the voice on the phone concluded the conversation by saying that the clients whose funds were delineated as 'SPECIAL' were Manny and Vivienne Hernandez.

Patrick thanked his caller and stepped to the chalkboard to complete the diagram by drawing a line from the name 'Hernandez' to the name 'Borozi' and writing under it the figure, '$250,000.0 from SPECIAL TRUST ACCOUNT'.

The circle was complete, as far as Supervisor Patrick was concerned. Patrick shook his head in disgust. He had followed Manny's career with interest since Manny pitched for the Triple A Phoenix Giants in the Pacific Coast League. He had taken personal joy in the advancement of Manny's career. He is now having feelings of contempt for Manny, who, as far as Patrick's was concerned, had crossed the line. With Patrick, as with all drug agents, there was no shade of gray; you were either in the zone of black or white, and his premature and inaccurate opinion of Manny Hernandez had Manny firmly in Patrick's black zone.

The supervisor once more picked up the original communiqué and the assignment. He then realized the assignment was drawn in favor of Vivienne Hernandez. 'Maybe, just maybe,' he thought, 'Manny Hernandez isn't involved.'

Patrick's 'URGENT' line rang again. It was Henricks, who had gone to the U.S. Attorney's office. "Boss," he inquired, "they're all set to issue the request to Treasury to send the check, and they wanted me to double-check with you first to make sure the payee is only Vivienne Hernandez?"

"Hold on, Marion," Patrick ordered, "I have to go off the line a second."

"Sure," Henricks replied.

Supervisor Patrick put Agent Henricks on 'Hold' while he collected his thoughts. 'If the check is issued to both the Hernandez people, then it can't be cashed unless they both sign it,' he thought. 'If they both sign it, that will be the *prima facie* evidence that they both were in the deal together with Borozi. That's it!' Patrick reasoned. 'I'll have the check issued in both of their names. If Manny isn't in on it, then Missis Hernandez or Sammy Snider will just ask to have it issued in her name alone, according to the assignment, and I will have narrowed the field.'

Patrick went back on the line. "Tell you what, Marion, we've obtained further information since you left here. Tell the U.S. Attorney to have the check ordered out

204

payable to Manny Hernandez and Vivienne Hernandez, husband and wife. Those are the names on the special trust account that the two-hundred and fifty-thousand dollars is coming out of to go to Miami. The guy you're talking to should appreciate what I'm trying to do from an evidentiary point of view."

"I'm sure he will, Boss," Marion replied. "That would tie it together, eh?"

"Right," Patrick answered. "Now get on back here, Marion, as things are going to start happening fast, and you know where I want you at times like this." Agent Henricks was pleased with Patrick's compliment as they both rang off the line.

* * *

Agent Long arrived in Miami and went post-haste to a remote hangar at a small air service with a private air strip. "Hi, Paul," Long greeted the man who was servicing a handsome twin-engine aircraft.

"Greetings, Billy," the man replied, "what's up?"

Agent Long got right to the point. "Paul, when I helped your kid that time, I told you I may need your help someday," Long said, "well, that day is here."

"Sure, Billy, what do you need?" the pilot asked.

"We have reason to believe that a man named Tino Borozi will be having you fly him round-trip in a day or two to Panama. We know you've already taken him there at least once. This time, we're sure there will be a payload on the return trip. We need these little jewels put in that payload."

Long showed the pilot several small beeper tracking devices. Paul examined them and then placed them on a table. "You mean," Paul said, that if I do this for you, we're square?"

"We'll be square," Long replied.

Paul went on to say, "My kid never had no trouble after that, and you could have sent him to prison. I'll do it."

"Okay," said Long, "and once they've left you, give me a call at the number on this card."

"Okay," Paul said, and Agent Long departed.

Long's orders were to stake out the airstrip so he could personally observe the activities around it.

Chapter 15 -- THE PLAYOFFS AND THE WORLD SERIES

The next day, the day of game two of the NLCS, found Manny and Woody enjoying the notoriety that comes to big league stars who excel in post-season play. Kari was seeing Woody regularly, but still very much in love with Manny, whom she wasn't seeing much of, except as a reporter in the Cardinal dressing rooms.

The Padres were very formidable opposition for anyone. Their style of play was similar to the Cardinals, with the added punch of two well-established power hitters, Ralph Painter and Wilford 'Wil' Stark. Either of them could hit a ball out of any park in the league, and that they did in game two, tying the playoff series. Manny saw no action in that game, in which Woody got two hits, bringing his playoff total to four.

The first two games concluded, the Cardinal team was leaving for San Diego to resume play for the next three games. If a sixth and seventh game were required, they would be played in St. Louis.

Manny and Kari visited in the dressing room after the second game, and Kari let him know that she was going to San Diego to cover the games there. Manny responded by telling her that, although he wasn't sure she would come, he was going to try to have his wife, Vivienne, meet him in San Diego. Kari, wearing her feelings on her sleeve, was hurt by Manny's telling her this. Manny was only making innocent conversation, but it infuriated Kari and had the effect of driving her even closer to Woody. Kari hadn't realized it, but she was rebounding at full tilt. She was filling the vacuum that was left in her heart with the first man she could, and to Woody's great joy, it was himself.

The Cardinals were staying at the U.S. Grant Hotel in San Diego, and so was Kari. The third game was won by the Cardinals, and again, Woody got two hits. One of Woody's hits tied the game in the late innings, and Manny was called on to hold the Padres scoreless while the Cards scored once more and he got the win. There was much celebrating after the game. Woody and Kari ended up in Woody's room. Woody, of course, was cold sober. Kari, physically tired and emotionally wrung out, fell asleep on Woody's bed and didn't wake up before ten the next morning, still fully clothed.

Woody was in the shower when she woke up. She hurriedly fixed her face and rearranged her disheveled clothing, told Woody -- through the cracked bathroom door -- she was leaving and departed his room into the hall.

When the elevator door opened, to her embarrassment, there stood Manny. Their eyes locked, and both were speechless for what seemed a lifetime.

Manny was the first to speak. He said, "Good morning, Kari," and turned his body to hold the elevator door open for her.

As she stepped in, she meekly said, "Good morning, Manny." She wanted to shout, 'This isn't what it looks like!' but wisely thought better of it, because the noise of her actions would have drowned any words she could have offered.

Manny was polite, hiding the gut-wrenching pain he had not felt since that awful day in Chicago when the process server put the divorce papers in his hand. As he stepped away from the elevator door, Kari asked, "Is your wife here?"

"No," Manny weakly responded, "she's not, but it really doesn't matter; we'll be together soon."

Kari spoke as the elevator door was drawing closed between them. "Good, Manny, I'm glad everything is working out for you," she lied, still visibly embarrassed by what her rumpled appearance had implied to Manny.

As Manny walked to his room, his emotions were erupting inside him. 'It didn't take her long to find someone else,' he thought. 'It was God's will that things worked out with my loving wife. Where would I be now if I'd dumped Vivienne in favor of Kari just to have Kari dump me?' he thought. 'God surely does work everything out for the best.'

Kari went to her room, undressed, got into the shower and started sobbing. Her mind was posing questions much quicker than it could answer them. When she began to settle down and think things through, she decided there was nothing she could do about what had happened that morning between her and Manny at the hotel. She would just have to put that experience behind her. It didn't appear to make any difference anyway, as far as a relationship -- or possible relationship -- with Manny was concerned, because Manny was reconciled with his wife and had even gone so far as to tell Kari in St. Louis that he was hoping his wife would join him in San Diego.

That had to be the ultimate put-down, she thought. So what if he thinks I spent the night in bed with Woody? I couldn't damage a relationship that was already dead, she thought. Kari's mental gymnastics were identical to what she put herself through just a few weeks before when Woody had talked to her by phone from Los Angeles. She once again was excitedly jumping to emotional conclusions.

Woody's a nice guy, she thought, and with all the good publicity he's getting about his outstanding performance in the playoffs, any woman in America would give anything to trade places with me. She got out of the shower, her mind made up. Since things were definitely over between herself and Manny, she would take the relationship with Woody more seriously, something Woody had been doing since their first date.

* * *

Painter and Stark drove in a total of five runs in game four, tying the playoff series at two games each. Manny was not called on, and Woody continued his hot streak with two more hits. He now had eight hits for four

210

games. He was only three hits shy of the record of eleven held by several players for post-season play. Woody was looming prominently as the outstanding candidate for the Most Valuable Player honors. He was not eligible to be Rookie of the Year in the National League because he had been called up too late in the season to log enough qualifying play. He could be MVP of the playoffs, though, and was well on his way to doing so.

After game four, Kari and Woody met in the hotel dining room for supper together. Except for the occasional interruption of a well-wisher, they were having a quiet visit.

"I know you must have felt embarrassed the other night," Woody said. "After all, we've only been going together a short time -- hardly long enough for you to be sleeping over."

Kari, as she had originally been with Manny, was impressed by his seriously innocent mood. "Woody," she said, "I could not have been that relaxed if I hadn't felt totally comfortable and at ease with you."

These words were very pleasing to Woody, and he showed it. "Kari, I don't expect you to fall for me as I have for you." He paused, then continued in a noticeably more serious tone, "But, if I had my way, we'd spend the rest of our lives together."

Kari was at once pleased, nonplused and slightly confused. She felt sure that Woody knew nothing of her short-lived but serious affair with Manny. She therefore accurately reasoned that Woody had no reason to assume any conclusion other than that he, Woody, was the only man in her life. Armed with these thoughts, she countered his opening remarks by saying the obvious.

"We've only known each other a short time, Woody, and I'm deeply honored that you'd say such a nice thing to me."

"It's true," Woody said. "And as far as I'm concerned, I've thought it through very carefully. Do you mind if I elaborate on it?"

"Certainly not," she responded.

"In college," he began, "I worked very hard on two things: my grades and baseball. While others were out having a good time, I was laying the foundation blocks for my career. I've worked hard to get here, and I'm wise enough to realize that fame and fortune, especially as a professional baseball player, can be fleeting. I don't expect my career to end tomorrow, but if it does, I'll be ready for it.

"I have a lawyer who negotiates my contract. I have an investment analyst who takes care of my money. I concentrate on my physical well-being and mental toughness that has led me to what I've accomplished so far."

"And that's a lot," she interjected.

"The only thing that's been neglected, Kari, is my personal life, and now that you've come into my life picture, I know it's time to think about my future in that regard."

"But, Woody," Kari said, "your life's just beginning. Why, with all the press you've been getting, notwithstanding you're a great guy besides all that, you could have any girl you desired."

"I hope so," Woody said, as he took her hands in his and whispered, "because I want you."

Kari was at once flattered and all the more confused.

* * *

The fifth game ended in a Cardinal victory. They only needed one more to clinch the National League Championship. Woody's performance was continuing along a record-breaking path, and Manny recorded another save. The Cardinals would be going back to St. Louis with a one-game edge and the hometown advantage to help them win one more.

Kari had encouraged Woody to think through once more what he had proposed before they left San Diego. He told her he would, and that he would expect an answer from her by the end of the World Series, which everyone was confident the Cardinals would be in.

* * *

Manny returned to his apartment in St. Louis and promptly called Vivienne on the telephone, unaware that she was no longer his wife.

"Hi, Honey," he opened their conversation, "how're the kids?"

"Just fine, Manny," she answered. "You're having some fantastic post-season play, my love. We miss you horribly. Has anyone told you how much money to expect if you win the playoffs and get in the Series?"

"Not really," Manny answered; "why do you ask?"

Vivienne could not recall Manny ever asking a question that smacked of questioning her intentions, but she was ready for it. "Oh, I was thinking, the other day," she said, "that our kids will be grown before you know it, and it would probably be a good idea to start planning right now for their college education."

Her quick response put Manny at ease, and he mentally reminded himself of how fortunate he was to have such a loving and devoted helpmate who, to be sure, once again was just looking out for the future of their children. "Tell you what, Honey," Manny continued, "I'll sign the paper and tell the club to just send the playoff share to you -- and the one for the World Series also -- if there is one."

Vivienne was delighted. She had been reading the sports page of the Phoenix newspaper and knew such a figure would top one-hundred-thousand dollars, but she didn't let on.

"I have a little gift for you, Sweetheart," Manny said. He had found an import store in San Diego that stocked Vivienne's favorite perfume, 'Replique', and had purchased a three-ounce bottle and had it gift-wrapped.

"What is it, my love?" she purred.

"I'll just wait and surprise you with it," Manny said. "Now, let me speak to Joseph."

Vivienne put the phone to Manny's son's ear and told him to say 'hi' to his daddy. The little boy was thrilled and laughed out loud. Hearing his son's joviality reinforced Manny's decision not to leave his wife for Kari. He now felt stronger than ever that he'd opted the right way in preserving his family unit. Kari was gone, and it hurt, but with reinforcement like this, he could handle it.

"I was really sorry you couldn't make it to San Diego," he said, "but it won't be long before we're together again."

214

Vivienne was back on the phone with him. "I know," she said, "and I can hardly wait," she lied. "Okay, sweet Manny," she said, "we'd better ring off before we spend your post-season money on the telephone."

Manny knew she was right. He was so lonely for his family, he knew he could talk all day. Before she hung up, Vivienne said, "It's so good to talk to you. Honey, now don't worry about us, just concentrate on winning the playoffs and the World Series. In the meantime, your little wife and kids will be anxiously awaiting your coming home and our getting to be together all winter. And Manny, I have an itch that only you can scratch." She laughed.

Manny was so happy. Vivienne's last sentence had always been her ladylike way of telling Manny that he was the only man who could sexually satisfy her. Manny hung the phone up on an emotional high. At least, to his way of thinking, everything in his life was going in the right direction. Today being an off-day, he'd go to the Cardinal office and make sure they would send any post-season money straight to his loving wife.

* * *

The sixth game was a blow-out of the Cardinals. The Padres beat them by ten runs. The oddsmakers were aghast. Their disbelief was only exceeded by that of the Cardinal players and their fans. The Cardinal mainframe, in a word, had the come-aparts. Their whole National League season would now be decided by one game.

Manny didn't pitch in game six and didn't call home afterward. He knew he'd see action in game seven. Duffy McCoy was set to start the final game, and, at his best,

Manny knew Duffy could only go six innings, because the Padres' bats were hot, and Snake wouldn't hesitate to pull the string on Duffy at the first sign of weakness. Everybody knew that old Duffy had the nerve of a barker in a circus side show, and such had taken him beyond the bounds of an ordinary career. But now that the marbles were all in one basket, Snake would play it close to the vest, and therefore, Manny had correctly reasoned, that on the last day of the National League playoffs, he would be the one to throw the final pitches.

The atmosphere at Busch Stadium for the final game of the National League Championship Playoffs was electric. The odds were even on the morning line from Las Vegas. The California Angels had already captured the American League Championship behind the strong pitching of their right-handed fireballer, Tony Davis, himself a native of southern California. The Angels were anxiously awaiting their very first World Series appearance and were pleased to finally win a pennant for their owner, known affectionately as the 'Old Cowboy'.

The prognosticators deemed the Padres' momentum to be offset by the Cardinals' home-field advantage. It seemed to boil down to the basic question, how much did 'Old Duffy' have left? Of one thing all were sure: if Duffy's control was 'on' this day, the old man would be tough, and the quiet Duffy was prepared in his heart and mind not to let anyone of the Cardinal faithful down, especially himself.

Exactly fifteen minutes before game time, Duffy began his methodical warm-up tosses to Woody Justice under the watchful eyes of Bob Chastain. Snake was

216

engaged in taping a short pre-game TV interview to be
played during the game. In response to the interviewer's
opening question about his personal prediction of the game's
outcome, Snake said, "You know, this competition that's
been going on these last few days is what, on a larger scale,
life is all about. You have two teams of men from different
walks of life and ethnic backgrounds. They come together,
young and old, and cooperate to create a unified life force of
total teamwork. Some of them get along together personally,
and some don't, but these personal interests are set aside in
favor of the common goal; and that, of course, is winning. I
think our guys will win, but whether or not they do, I'll
promise you this: old or young, tired or fresh, they'll give it
all they've got, and with that, nobody will be disappointed.
This club's got guys like Duffy McCoy, who is easily old
enough to be his catcher's father. Woody Justice, Duffy's
catcher, replaced Augie Marido who, I can't overlook
reminding you, was as fine a catcher as this club's ever had.
I know Augie is listening, wherever he is, and I just want to
say our being here is a credit to the effort he gave us this
year, too."

Snake's speech was uncharacteristically long. He
was beginning to sound like one of those overly long-winded
recipients at the Oscar ceremonies. The interviewer
interrupted him with a comment he hoped would shut him
down, but Snake just seized the opportunity to continue. "I
want all of our loyal fans to know how much their support
has meant to us this season, and also, I want everybody to
know that a ball club, any ball club, couldn't have a finer

owner than Jack Hogan, who sees to it that we get plenty of good scouting and front-office help."

The announcer broke in and concluded the interview, which was starting to sound like the game had been canceled in deference to the Snake Fitch Show.

Halfway through his warm-up tosses, Chastain spoke to Duffy from his vantage point behind the old pitcher. "How do you feel, Duffy?" Bob asked.

"Pretty good for an old codger," Duffy answered, never breaking the rhythm of his warm-up as he continued the conversation. "The way I feel, I can go a strong six or so, and then let Manny wrap it up. I don't think we'll need any more help for me today than Manny. If the boys can just get me a few runs early, I'll relax and throw strikes and force them to put the ball in play and let our solid defense do the rest. That's my game plan. What do you say, Bob?"

"Stick with it, Duffy," the old coach went on, "if you can hold 'em, I think our boys can get you some runs."

"I know we can," shouted Woody enthusiastically, as he fired the ball back to Duffy at a higher velocity than Duffy was throwing it to him.

"Okay, Duffer," Bob said, as he walked away, "I'll go report to Snake."

Duffy finished his warm-up, and he and Woody made their way to the dugout to await the introduction of the starting lineups and the singing of the national anthem before the game began.

The preliminaries out of the way, Duffy went to the mound to begin his day's work. The early innings resulted in a run for each club, and they entered the fourth tied at one.

In the fifth, the Padres scored twice. Duffy walked a man and then threw a home run ball to Ralph Painter. Instead of being ahead, Duffy was now behind, and he was showing 'tired'. Snake called 'time', after ordering Manny to start warming up, and went out to the mound to talk to Duffy.

"Duffy," Snake asked, with Woody hanging on every word, "do you remember when you and I went goose hunting that time at Swan Lake?"

"Sure, Snake," Duffy replied, realizing his wily manager was just killing time to allow the resourceful Manny time to loosen up. "I remember you crippled a goose that flew back over, and I had to kill him," Duffy said.

By now, Woody Justice was fascinated with the conversation; he revered these two so much he simply overlooked the real reason for their palaver. Woody spoke up with wonder, momentarily forgetting the business at hand. "Do you mean to tell me that actually happened?" he asked, just as the home plate umpire approached all of them.

"Anybody bring a deck of cards, gentlemen?" the umpire asked jokingly, and then continued, "or should all cooperate and let this crowd of a mere fifty thousand start to get what they came to see?"

Snake and Duffy got big smiles on their faces, and Duffy said to the umpire, a long-time friend, "We were just waiting for you to get here, Jim... would you share that half pint you keep in your hip pocket?"

The umpire fought back laughter and said, "After this one's over, Duffy, we'll all probably <u>need</u> to share a half pint. Let's get on with it, Snake, does Duffy go or stay?"

With his left hand patting his right forearm, Snake responded with the signal that he wanted to change pitchers, and he wanted Manny. The umpire, Max Price, known as 'Jim' to the old guard (his middle name was James), took out his official score pad to pencil in the change. Woody accompanied him back to home plate. On the way, the umpire said to Woody, without looking at him, "Son, if you learn anything from those two old men out there, remember their philosophy of 'live and let live,' and you'll be here a long time. The game is changing so fast that it's becoming a game of too many self-centered individuals. Don't let that happen to you," Jim warned Woody as Manny commenced his warm-up tosses.

The last of the ninth arrived, and it came down to two out and two on as Woody had singled, along with Ike Wood. Big Glenn Ballenger came to bat, and the crowd was on their feet.

The Padres' pitcher was pitching very carefully to Glenn, a definite home run threat. He worked the count to three and two, and Glenn fouled off the next three pitches just trying to protect the plate. Bob Chastain said in the dugout that the Padres' pitcher, Bill Clinkenbeard, was tired and his curve ball was beginning to hang. Glenn hoped to see that hanging curve. On the next pitch, he did. From the moment it left his bat, there was no doubt about the ball's destination. Big Glenn hit a home run, and the Cardinals won the final game in the last of the ninth, four runs to two. The noise was deafening.

There was celebrating for several hours in the clubhouse. Kari congratulated Manny, but she could hardly be heard in the tumult. Manny just smiled. He was glad he couldn't hear her; it would just open old wounds for him.

The team took the next day off, but scheduled a light practice on Friday before the World Series opening game on Saturday. It would be against the California Angels in St. Louis.

On the day off, Kari and Woody packed a picnic lunch and went to Swope Park. They were getting along very well, but still had not slept together. It wasn't that they both weren't willing, but more because Kari wasn't going to force the issue, and the ever-shy Woody was too timid. His off-the-field demeanor was a real paradox compared to the tiger he'd become with his aggressive style of play. Once during the playoffs, he blocked the plate in front of a Padre runner who put what amounted to a cross-body block on him. When Woody stopped rolling, the umpire checked to confirm that he hadn't dropped the ball and promptly called the runner 'out' at the plate. It had been many years since the Cards had the services of a catcher with such bulldog tenacity. But around Kari, he was an altogether different personality. She noticed it, appreciated it and often complimented him on his manner and style of treating her.

The World Series went much the same as the playoffs. It went six games, with both teams winning three apiece. Woody went on another hitting binge, and Manny saved two of the Cardinals' three wins. In the seventh and deciding game, the Cards jumped off to an early three-to-one lead, and Manny was brought in to preserve it. He gave up one more run, and the Cards won the final game three to two.

The whole town celebrated all night. There was a parade the next day, and Manny and Woody were asked to say a few words, which they did.

Manny and Woody were chosen as Co-Most Valuable Players in the Series. The baseball writers could not give either the edge. Manny had three saves, and Woody had broken the record for most hits.

It was in this atmosphere that Woody and Kari had retired to a quiet Italian restaurant, Angelo's, on the 'Hill' in St. Louis, to discuss their future.

"Kari," Woody said, "I have something for you." He handed her a box, which she opened, exposing a two-carat diamond with another carat of smaller diamonds around it. She was overwhelmed at the sheer size of what he was offering her as an engagement ring. Woody, without waiting for her to respond, said, "Please put it on. I know you may feel that I'm trying to rush things, but I can't deny what's in my heart."

Kari just looked at him, tears starting to well up in her eyes. At long last, putting aside her ever-present feelings for Manny, she decided to accept his proposal and did so by saying, "Woody, I hope you know what you're doing; no man has ever been as sweet to me as you." 'Except one,' she thought, 'and I can't have him.' Aloud she said, "So I do accept; please put it on my finger."

* * *

The next day, Woody was aglow with the news as he was cleaning out his locker in the Cardinal clubhouse.

Manny was there, too. As soon as he heard Woody's good news, he walked up to him, stuck out his hand and said,

222

"Woody, I'm very happy for both of you. I know you'll have a long and happy life together. Please convey my heartfelt congratulations to Kari, and tell her how happy I am for both of you."

Woody thanked Manny and told him he'd remember him to his new fiancée.

They both left the ball park. Manny went to his apartment to clean it out and catch a plane to Phoenix, where he thought he was going to spend the winter enjoying his loving wife and children. He didn't let on to anyone that he was still suffering inside at the loss of Kari. He still loved her as deeply as she did him, but they had both decided, independently, that the passage of time would heal their wounds of the heart.

When Woody recounted Manny's words to Kari, she just smiled and said, "That's nice. I'm glad he got his family problems worked out and I hope he's as happy as we are." She was crying inside as she said it.

Chapter 16 -- THE HOSPITAL VISIT

Manny could not deny his feeling of despair over his loss of Kari. As long as she was unattached, she represented an alternative to Vivienne, should his marriage fail to work out.

Before leaving his apartment for the last time to take a taxi to the airport, Manny once again got down on his knees to pray.

He pleaded with his God to remove his heartache. He begged and bargained. Lastly, he gave thanks, as he did every day, for his many blessings.

He knew instinctively that things would work out for the best. After all, they always had.

A successful Major League baseball player, having grown up in Dominican poverty, knows inside himself that if he ever stops believing tomorrow will be a better day, he will have nothing more to live for. The tough times that Manny had successfully weathered in the past had prepared him for the eventualities of life's many disappointments.

When Manny finished loading his personal luggage into the cab, he directed the driver to take him to Lambert

Field by way of St. Louis Children's Hospital. He had one last stop to make. Quite by chance, he had met a lady doctor of German extraction who specialized in treating children with rare diseases, mostly untreatable by conventional methods. Her name was Doctor Hilda Workman, and she was forced to treat many of her youthful patients experimentally, there being no known cure for the maladies she encountered in her practice. When Manny had met the good lady doctor, he had urged her to feel free to ask him to visit any of the children who, in her opinion, would enjoy a personal visit from him.

The work done in this hospital was high on Jack Hogan's list of personal projects. When the club signed Manny, Jack envisioned that he could recruit him to also help in this endeavor, and he had personally taken Manny to visit the hospital after he signed his record-breaking million-dollar contract with the Cardinals. Jack's assessment of the effect such a visit would have on *Señor* Manny was correct. Jack knew nothing of Manny's childhood health problems, but he was an expert judge of men and their personal character. It was during Jack's and Manny's visit that Jack introduced Manny to the good doctor, thus leading to Manny's stopping there now on his way out of town.

The note Doctor Workman had delivered to Manny requested that he try to come before he left town, and Manny was more than pleased to oblige.

Manny handed the cab driver a ten-dollar bill and told him to go get a cup of coffee and wait for him. The cabbie was happy to do so, and Manny told him to take his time.

225

Manny made his way to Dr. Workman's office. She was on the telephone, but, upon seeing him, she waved him in and motioned for him to sit down while she continued talking on the phone.

Manny was fascinated with listening to her side of the telephone conversation.

"That's right, Congressman Ryan, we have a complete surgical team standing by in Des Moines, Iowa, who, together with their hospital, have all agreed to donate their time, skills and services. The only thing," she continued, "standing between this little girl and a kidney transplant is the air transportation of her mother and father, and the donor, her sister, from here to Des Moines." She paused while the Congressman was posing a question, then Manny heard her say, "We've tried commercial airlines, but they've refused on the grounds that they don't want to accept the risk of the little passenger dying en route. They told me it would be bad for business should it happen and their other passengers get upset. No, sir, the family doesn't have the money to buy one ticket, let alone charter a private plane," she answered impatiently and added, "I was calling merely to ask you if you could appeal to the local unit of the Air National Guard or Air Force Reserve and clear the way for them to help?" Her tone was fraught with frustration, but she wasn't about to show weakness in her determination to save her little patient's life with a much-needed kidney transplant. She signed off the conversation with the Congressman by thanking him for taking her call and reminding him that time was of the essence and that her little dying patient would not be reassured by hearing that the Congressman was 'going through channels'.

Hanging up the phone, Doctor Workman offered Manny a handshake and her usual big, optimistic smile and congratulations on his great season. She then sat back down and proceeded to tell him why she'd asked that he come. "Manny," she began, "many people visit our children only one time and leave by invariably saying to call them if we ever think they can help. Most of these people are very sincere, but what they really are saying to us is, 'I'll send you a check, but what I've seen here is too demoralizing for me to ever come back personally.' I knew when Jack Hogan brought you out here originally, you weren't one of those people. Please don't misunderstand. I'll be the first to say we need all the help we can get, and I applaud the financial help from any person, whether or not he or she can show up personally. However, many times, what one of these children needs is not possible just from money. It's just such a child that I've summoned you here to meet. I personally fear that he's not long for this world, a condition you certainly couldn't perceive by looking at him.

"This youngster is a baseball fan and a Cardinal fanatic. What's so cute," she continued, "is that, before you joined the Cardinals, he wasn't that crazy about you, but now you're one of his idols."

"What's wrong with him?" Manny asked, his question tinged with the sadness in his voice.

"When he was first brought here," she answered, "we thought it was what the public knows as Lou Gehrig's Disease, but it's much more complicated than that. His

227

ability to walk has deteriorated to the point we really don't want him to get out of his wheelchair unattended for fear he'll fall and suffer a fracture."

Doctor Workman could see that Manny was moved by what she was telling him.

"Doctor," he said, "I have brought some souvenirs of the Playoffs and World Series for you to pass out as you wish. However, if you'll excuse me a moment, I'm going down to the cab and get something special for..." Manny hesitated, because she hadn't yet told him the boy's name.

She interjected, "Donnie... Donnie Robinson."

"I'll be right back," he said, and left her office to get the gift for the dying child.

On his way to the cab, Manny's mind was dwelling on the telephone conversation he'd overheard when he entered Doctor Workman's office. 'Dear God,' he thought, 'all these doctors and the hospital have donated untold thousands of dollars to save this child's life, and they can't get her there because no airlines, not even the U.S. government will give her the transportation. I can't stand it,' Manny thought, 'so I'll see that she gets there if I have to hire this cab to take her.' The cabbie was waiting. Manny gave him another ten and told him to be patient. At those rates, the driver was more than happy to cooperate.

Manny hurriedly rummaged through his equipment bag, wondering to himself what item would most please the youngster he was going to meet. Suddenly, he dumped the bag on the ground, handed the driver another ten and told him to go buy him something to carry his equipment home in. The driver cheerfully assented, as he now realized who Manny was and could surmise what he was doing.

"Anything else I can do for you, Hernandez?" the driver offered, "while you're in the hospital?" Then he quickly added, "My God, man, it's not your kid you're going to see, is it?"

"No, sir," Manny responded; "he's not mine, but he is one of God's children, which we all are."

The driver was speechless to hear these words from the man who the morning papers were saying was the leading candidate for the Cy Young Award. That fact was the farthest thing from Manny's mind at this moment.

Manny re-entered the hospital and made his way back to Doctor Workman's office. Everybody turned and looked as the handsome athlete walked briskly by them in the hallways, carrying a black equipment bag with a red bird on it and the name 'St. Louis Cardinals' emblazoned in red, with his own name printed under the Cardinal name and logo. Sensing his urgency on this errand of mercy, nobody stopped Manny for an autograph.

He arrived back at her office just as she was concluding another unsuccessful bid to obtain air transportation for the child needing the transplant. When she hung up, Manny asked her, "Doctor, how much would it cost to send these people by air ambulance?"

"Way too much, Manny," she answered. "These people couldn't afford air mail postage, let alone air ambulance."

Manny still hadn't gotten an answer to his question, so he persisted. "Just how much, Doctor?"

At last, Doctor Workman got the drift of his question. This man wasn't making an idle inquiry; he wanted to help, and she just now realized it.

"Manny," she said, "I honestly don't know. I haven't asked, because I knew the family couldn't afford it."

Manny modestly told her, in a tone of voice so quiet she thought he was whispering, "Well, Doctor, it's time to find out."

She just stared at him for a moment, then broke the silence, saying, "Tell you what, Manny, while you're visiting with Donnie, I'll just do that. His room is only two doors down."

Neither the patients nor their parents, and certainly nobody outside of hospital personnel knew it, but, as a child moved closer to the end of his terminal illness, Doctor Workman moved him closer to her office. This dynamo of a treating physician wanted no time lost when getting from her office to the side of a very sick child.

"Does he know I'm coming?" Manny asked.

"Yes and no," she replied. "The staff has sort of been bragging on your performance during the Series and telling him that it wouldn't be unusual for you to just pop in on him, but we've been careful not to promise him you'd come. Actually, now that you're here, I'll confess we have a little plan. You take all these souvenirs with you, 'cause after you've visited with Donnie for awhile, we're going to start bringing a few more kids to his room, sort of a 'Manny Party', you see."

Manny smiled his approval, packed all the presents for the kids in his equipment bag and headed for Donnie's room. He carried Donnie's special present, Manny's personal ball glove, in his hand hidden by the bag.

Little Donnie Robinson, age ten, was sitting up in his bed watching TV when Manny walked in. A nurse tripped the TV 'Off' button as soon as Manny was in the door. The big, strong athlete walked straight to the child's bedside, put the equipment bag on the side of the hospital bed, stuck out his right hand and said, "Hi, "I'm Manny Hernandez, and I've been wanting to meet you."

The youngster's mouth flew open in awe as Manny continued, "I'd have been here before now, but those darn Pittsburgh Pirates and California Angels were kind of keeping me busy."

The boy still just stared, and momentarily, Manny was afraid he'd come on so strong he'd scared him. Actually, the strong come-on was Manny's way of masking his grief. When he saw an American child like this, it reminded him of the many sick and underprivileged children in his homeland and how much he wanted to take care of all of them. 'Kids are all so beautiful,' he thought, 'before they get old enough to learn the awful things that separate them, like racial prejudice.'

Donnie found his voice when he saw the Cardinal logo on the equipment bag. Still awestruck, the child asked, "Is that a real Cardinal equipment bag?"

Manny responded, "Yes, Donnie, "I've personally carried that bag all year to every ball park in the National League and to the World Series against the Angels in Anaheim. The reason I'm giving it to you now is because the season is over, and I don't need it, but I know you'll be needing it to pack your things when you leave the hospital." The encouraging words had the desired effect on young Donnie. This was the therapy the doctor was referring to which money couldn't buy.

Manny continued, "Also, Donnie, I want you to have my personal glove. I know you saw the Series on TV. Well, this is the glove I was wearing when you saw me pitch. My own son, Joseph, isn't old enough to use it, so I thought you might like it."

"But Manny," the child innocently asked, "won't you need it for next year?"

Manny just smiled and said, "Sure, Donnie, but in the meantime, you can have it, and when I need it, I'll come back and borrow it from you." When Manny told Donnie he wanted to sign the glove for him, a nurse handed Manny a soft-tipped pen. On the glove, Manny inscribed, 'To my good friend Donnie Robinson, here's my personal glove that I used in the 1979 World Series -- your pal, Manny Hernandez.'

By now, other children started to come into Donnie's room. Seeing them, Donnie shouted proudly, "Hi, everybody, come and meet my pal, Manny Hernandez, of the Cardinals. He just gave me his glove!"

Manny handed out autographed baseballs and met and talked to all the children individually. He could do this ad infinitum. The only children he enjoyed more were his own. He was eternally grateful for the good health his own children enjoyed as he visited with the lesser fortunate. Why God allows these young innocents to be stricken with dreaded diseases was a question Manny often thought about.

Manny said his good-byes to the children, especially the beaming Donnie, and promised he'd see them all next spring. He was always careful when concluding a hospital visit like this to not say he would 'be back' to see them, for fear it might imply to the youngsters that he expected them to always be there. By saying he'd 'see them' at a future time, he could mean at the ball park, or anywhere besides the hospital. Before he left Donnie's room, at the dying boy's request, Manny wrote down his Phoenix address because the stricken youngster told him he wanted to write to him.

Manny re-entered Doctor Workman's office, where she opened the conversation. "I'm ready to give you some answers to your questions now, Manny, about the cost of sending the family to Des Moines by air ambulance. The fact is, the family could travel separately by commercial airlines while the kidney recipient and donor and attending staff could go in the air ambulance. This would create a substantial savings in the total amount."

Manny interrupted her, saying, "I don't know much about these things, Doctor, but if it were my little girl, I think I'd like to travel with her."

Doctor Workman replied, "I was hoping you'd feel that way. In that case, the total one way would be seventy-five-hundred dollars. There is no discount for round trip, and no reason to book the passage that way, for the obvious reason -- the donee may not live to come back, and there would thus be no need for the ambulance and attending personnel."

Manny contemplated how to accomplish this without telling Vivienne, who always objected to his spending money on anything that she didn't control. He found it much easier to conceal such things from her than to argue with her about it.

He asked, and received, permission from the doctor to use her phone and called the Cardinal front office. "Mister Hogan, please," he asked when his call was answered. "This is Manny Hernandez speaking." It was obvious to the doctor that Manny's call had been placed on hold. "Hello Mister Hogan, this is Manny," he said after the short wait for Jack Hogan to come on the line. Manny continued, "Boss, I'm with Doctor Workman right now, and I need a favor. Could you withhold seventy-five-hundred dollars from my World Series money -- no, I mean fifteen-thousand -- and disburse it as Doctor Workman wishes? I don't want to go into it now, just help me get the money to her and I'll tell you all about it later."

Jack agreed, and asked to say hello to the doctor. She briefed Jack on what was taking place, much to the joy of both of them, and then handed Manny the phone. Manny thanked Mister Hogan and signed off.

Manny then looked at the doctor and in his most serious voice, he said, "Doctor, for reasons I won't go into, don't send me anything in the mail about this matter. If there is something further I must do to help this little girl and her family, just call me personally at my home in Arizona. If you call and my wife answers, please don't mention any of this to her."

The doctor assured Manny that she would keep it between herself, Manny and Jack Hogan. The doctor discreetly didn't pursue that part of the conversation any further.

Manny said good-bye to Doctor Workman and returned to his cab. The cabbie was very proud to be carrying a celebrity and told Manny he'd already tipped him enough, but would appreciate an autograph, and Manny happily obliged him.

At last, he boarded the aircraft bound for Phoenix. Because of the extended side trip to the hospital, Manny had to change his original reservation, which now called for a layover in Dallas and would not allow him to reach Phoenix until that night.

In the meantime, Vivienne had picked up certified copies of the divorce judgment and decree and lodged a copy with the Scottsdale Police Department. She did so, telling them that her husband was likely to show up after the World Series and threaten her and the children. The desk sergeant who interviewed her told her the police couldn't intervene until she was actually threatened, but that the department would keep the papers on file to expedite the handling of the complaint, should one arise.

Vivienne proceeded to change the door locks on the house and was ready to deal with the situation with rapid dispatch.

Manny slept most of the way to Phoenix, grabbing a sandwich in the Dallas Airport, and reading the sports pages in the Dallas newspaper about his being the favorite to receive the Cy Young Award.

What was about to happen to him could only be likened to a person with a hangover waking up at Pearl Harbor on the morning of December 7, 1941.

Chapter 17 -- THE HOMECOMING

Vivienne had purchased a telephone answering machine, which allowed her to receive Manny's call telling her of his arrival time, without having to talk to him. Manny called her from the airport in Dallas to let her know of his change of plans and late arrival. After playing the message from Manny, Vivienne alerted the Scottsdale Police Department of his expected arrival that night. There was feigned fear in her voice as she pleaded with the desk sergeant who took her call, imploring him to please see to it that she was protected and not physically abused by what she described as a violent ex-husband who was coming to town for the sole purpose of doing her bodily harm. The desk sergeant passed the word on to the patrolmen assigned that evening in the Scottsdale area of the Hernandez home.

Vivienne already had gone over with Sammy what she anticipated happening between her and Manny upon his return.

Sammy knew that, at some point in the brouhaha, Manny would be calling him, so Vivienne and Sammy already had decided what Sammy would do when that happened.

It was in this setting that the unsuspecting Manny stepped off the plane in Phoenix on a beautiful October evening in Arizona.

He obliged several fans with autographs and small talk as he made his way to the cab stand outside. He had harbored a happy thought that maybe Vivienne would surprise him by showing up with the children to meet him. When she didn't, he quickly dismissed it from his mind. Such thoughts had never been more than wishful thinking for Manny, but he was never resentful.

The cab driver recognized Manny from his picture, which had appeared frequently in the Phoenix newspaper over the past season. He engaged Manny in non-stop conversation all the way to his home and even up to his front door, where he'd placed Manny's belongings and finally departed. The house was dark. Manny fumbled in the darkness for his house key. Finally he located it and stuck it in the front door lock. It wouldn't turn. It went in smoothly, but it wouldn't turn.

Finally, in his frustration, he rang the door bell. No answer. He then walked to the garage door, for which he had no key, and it, too, was firmly locked shut. He went to the fence door in the rear of his home, a door he had never known to have a lock on it, but it, too, was tightly secured and would not open. Then he heard what he thought was Joseph's voice from inside the house. He couldn't make out what his young child had said, but he was sure he had heard him.

Joseph had been asleep when his father arrived. It was the noise of Vivienne moving about in the dark inside the house that awakened the young boy. Vivienne made her way to the telephone and called the Scottsdale Police Department. Her frantic tone of voice frightened Joseph, who now was calling for his mother in a loud voice.

Manny returned to the front of the house, where the porch light was on. He tried to open the glass outer door, but now it was locked, a situation that puzzled him, because it was not locked a short five minutes before when he had opened it to try to unlock the front door. However, the porch light having obviously been turned on from within, Manny wasn't alarmed that the outer door was now locked. He passed that off as the natural act of a protective mother alone, who had answered her door in the darkness to find nobody there.

He rang the doorbell again, and began shouting, "Vivienne, Joseph, it's me, Manny; I'm home. Come unlock the door and let me in, I'm home."

There was excitement in his voice, as he had missed his family very much during the baseball season. Also, the anxiety brought on by the several recent emotion-packed events in his life had led to his mood at this moment climbing to a happy crescendo. The excitement continued coming through his voice as he kept on hollering for Vivienne to hurry up and let him in.

The arrival of the police car went completely unnoticed by Manny until one of the officers said, "Calm down, sir, and show me some identification." Manny noticed the two officers, one on either side of him, and realized their seriousness. Once again, he misinterpreted what was going on. After all, he thought, he should be grateful that his family was given such protection when he wasn't around. He thought they had just been driving by and stopped to investigate what appeared to them to be a potential burglar. Manny quieted himself, reached into his pocket for his billfold and produced his Arizona picture driver's license to identify himself. He handed it to one of the officers, who looked at it under his flashlight.

The other officer broke the silence. "Is it him?" he asked his fellow officer.

"Sure is," came the reply. The second officer produced some papers and handed them to Manny, while holding his flashlight so Manny could see them. "Can you read English?" he mordantly asked.

Manny was bewildered, but he replied, "Just wait 'til my wife opens the door, and everything will be cleared up."

The second officer then repeated his question so sternly that Manny knew he had to answer. "I read English, sir, yes, I read English." Manny still had not looked at the papers the officer had handed him.

The officer explained, very impatiently, "What I have handed you are certified copies of the Divorce Decree and Judgment that have been duly issued by the Superior Court in this county. Now, don't stand there and tell me that you don't know what I'm talking about!" By now, the officer's voice was degenerating to anger, because both of the officers had pre-discussed the matter and decided they weren't going to buy any act of innocence or plea of ignorance should the same come up, and, sure enough, that's exactly what was happening, and they wanted none of it.

"Look, Mister Hernandez," the first officer said in a pleasant, but firm, tone of voice, "we don't want any trouble out of you. Here's the deal. Your wife and you are divorced. She owns this home. She has total custody of your children." The officer's tone was more condescending than courteous, as he continued, "You have reasonable visitation privileges with your children, which you must pre-arrange with your wife. We're here because you have not made such a visiting arrangement; therefore, your wife called and asked us to remove you from her property which, under the law, we are required to do unless you want to cooperate and peacefully remove yourself, an act which we and your wife would very much appreciate."

When the officer paused, Manny asked, "You mean this is no longer my home?"

"You're beginning to catch on," the officer sarcastically answered, still totally skeptical of Manny's bewilderment.

"You're telling me that you two are here to see to it that I leave, and I can't even see my wife and kids?" Manny asked, in a tone projecting grief, minus anger.

"Mister Hernandez," the second officer said, "the woman who owns this home is not your wife; she is your ex-wife, and you may see your children by appointment."

It still hadn't sunk in. Manny's emotions were going in every direction at once. Skyrockets were going off inside him. His gut was wrenching, his heart had sunk, and, as usual, when he was getting very angry, he was about to cry.

The bigger officer placed his hand behind Manny's arm, and Manny jerked away upon being touched. The smaller officer, sensing a fight was about to begin, spoke up. "Look, man, we don't enjoy standing here having a conversation like this."

Manny interrupted, now pleading, "Just let me see my children and talk to my wife for one minute -- in front of you -- right here. Ask her to open the door."

Suddenly, the door did open, and Vivienne said, as she reached through the opened outer door with some papers, "Here, officers, he's probably lost his set. Here, give him these copies of what you've been trying to get him to look at; give them to him and get him out of here."

Vivienne had momentarily released her hold on Joseph. The youngster, upon seeing his father, darted out the door, screaming with glee, to his father's side. Manny knelt down and picked up his happy son, then started crying openly while hugging and kissing Joseph. Then he said to the officers, "See, this is my son, see how glad he is to see me?" Joseph was giggling his approval when his mother ran out the door, grabbed him away, re-entered the door and locked it.

Manny just stood there for a moment and stared at her. Then he said, "I thought you said everything was all right."

Vivienne snapped, "Everything is all right. We're divorced, Manny, so get that through your thick Dominican head. This is my house, and every time you come around here, for any reason, this is what you'll get." She once more opened the door and started shoving his remaining belongings out into the yard.

At this, the bigger officer said, "That's it, man, you're coming with us," and led Manny away, depositing him in the rear of the patrol car without applying handcuffs. Actually, because Manny cooperated in walking to the patrol car, the officer didn't want to stop to cuff him, for fear the well-proportioned athlete might resist, an alternative neither of the officers wanted to occur.

The other officer started carrying Manny's gear to the patrol car and depositing it in the trunk. When everything was loaded, they drove away, amid Joseph's frantic screams calling for his daddy.

The patrol car sped down Thomas Road for several blocks before the smaller officer, riding on the passenger side, said, as they neared Scottsdale Road, "Why don't we drop him off somewhere instead of booking him?"

The other officer, welcoming the question, replied, "I really don't want to book thus guy, but what if we don't and he goes right back out there?"

Manny, hearing this, remained silent. He wasn't going to lie. He was sure he was going back out there. However, he was equally sure that the next time he went would be on his terms and not Vivienne's. He just kept quiet until the smaller officer turned his head around, looked squarely at him and said, "Mister Hernandez, you are not the first man we've ever talked to in a situation like this. If you would have just read the Court's Judgment and Decree, you would have known better than to have gone out there tonight in violation of the Court's Order."

Manny wanted to speak up and tell the officers that he would have read the papers had he seen them before tonight, but he hadn't. When he had first faced the language, culture and racial barriers in the deep south as a young immigrant ball player, one thing he learned quickly was not to fight back until he understood the problem completely. This night he knew he had absolutely no understanding of the problem, so he kept silent. No protest, no complaint, he just stood mute.

The officers, neither of them, could entice Manny into conversation, so they ended up in the parking lot next to the officers' entrance to the Scottsdale Police Department. They had informed the night watch commander that they were bringing him in and asked for a Spanish-speaking interpreter, who, in this instance, was a young Arizona State University student from Venezuela who was helping pay for her education by working part time at the Police Department. She was attractive and wisely met the patrol car when they parked it. She started talking to Manny in Spanish as the officers opened their doors to get out.

"*Señor* Hernandez," she said in their native tongue, "I'm Juanita Armas. I have a cousin, Tony Armas, who is a pro ball player; maybe you know him."

Manny responded in Spanish, "Sure, I know him; he's a very good power hitter. I pitched against him in the National League before he was traded by Pittsburgh to Oakland."

Sensing that the young lady had calmed Manny down, the two patrolmen stood to either side and let the linguist open the rear door. She asked Manny very politely to come with her and took him by the hand and led him into the headquarters building. They did not break their conversation, which definitely had the desired calming effect on Manny.

The young lady asked that she be permitted to talk to Manny alone. The officers assented and left them in a small room with a table and two chairs. The two officers then went to an adjoining room, where they could observe Manny and the lady linguist through a one-way viewing device, which from Manny's side, appeared as a mirror.

Manny, animated, pleading, crying, but not showing any sign of violence, talked to the pretty young woman, non-stop, for an hour. She carefully reviewed the court papers which Vivienne had handed out the door, and when Manny would question her, she would read the Judgment and Decree and then answer him in Spanish.

When the young lady felt she had taken him about as far as she could, she excused herself, ostensibly to go get Manny a drink.

She walked straight to the adjoining room to speak to the two officers and the watch commander. She opened the conversation by saying, "Fellas, he says she sued him for divorce, but then told him she dropped it. He therefore had no lawyer handle it for him. He says he talked to her during the World Series, and she didn't mention a thing to him about the divorce. He has agreed to go to a hotel and not go back out there tonight. But he is adamant about seeing his kids. He says he has a lawyer, Sammy Snider. He doesn't want to call him now. He says he'll call him tomorrow. I got him to agree to follow the Court Order in the future, as far as going around his wife and kids."

"Do you believe him?" the W.C. inquired.

"I do," the young lady said. "This actually is a familiar scenario, in these circumstances... at least, to me."

"Okay," said the W.C., "don't book him, but be sure he's checked into a hotel so we can have them call us if he grabs a cab out of there after we leave. I'd say take him to that one up on Scottsdale Road, near Curry."

"Right, boss," one of the patrolmen answered.

"Juanita," the W.C. said, "give him your name and the department number and tell him to call you before he does anything foolish."

"Good idea," she replied. She got Manny a cup of water and returned to explain things to him. Manny agreed, again, then followed her back to the patrol car and got inside.

The officers took him to the motel, watched him check in and then took him to his room and helped him unload his gear. From all outward appearances, Manny had calmed down. The courteous and helpful demeanor of the pretty interpreter was a sharp contrast to that of the two officers whom Manny first encountered. Vivienne's efforts to predispose the policemen's minds had not found their way to Juanita Armas, and, fortunately for Manny, it was she who finally enlightened him on what was at the bottom of his problem.

The officers departed after a final warning, not to go back to Vivienne's house. Manny wished them 'good night' and sat down, head in hands, and sobbed. Pleading aloud, he said, "God, where are you?" He was letting it all out. He had experienced several sessions like this as a young, confused, distressed ball player in a foreign land, and every time, he sought the solace of solitude to cry it all out before trying to figure out the solution. So this night, he did, indeed, sob himself to sleep.

Manny awoke, still fully clothed, on top of the bedspread, having cried himself to sleep without bothering to undress or pull back the covers. He proceeded to shower, change clothes and attempt assessment of damage to aid himself in figuring out a solution. What he wanted the very most was to see his children, especially Joseph. He knew he must do this in a way which would not incur the wrath, or attention, of the police. He wanted outside advice, but couldn't decide who to turn to. On the one hand, he didn't want anyone to know of the very embarrassing position he was ignorant enough to get himself into. On the other, he wanted his movements concealed and wasn't sure at this point whom he could trust and whom he couldn't.

He wasn't resorting to prayer. He was angry that his God had let him down. His anger had him motivated to accomplish his decision, whatever it should turn out to be, by any means necessary, legal or not. He didn't consider what had happened to him to be fair and above-board, therefore, did not concern himself with what was legal, proper or fair, but rather what was expedient to do what he desired. The overriding thought that kept recurring was about his children. Manny cringed inside at the memory of Joseph calling for him last night as the police took him away in their patrol car.

Manny suddenly recalled Rennie Parker, the old black lady who ran the boarding house in Mobile, whom he had come to know and trust as a young, confused and distraught ball player. He knew he had her phone number somewhere in his billfold. He had used it to call her every year at Christmas just to thank her for the unselfish and loving care she'd treated him with at a very crucial time in his young life. Times were crucial again, he thought. 'Who needs God? I'll call Rennie.'

Finding the number, he obtained the desk clerk's permission to charge the call to his room. Vivienne had kept both their telephone credit cards. She told Manny he could always call her collect, and she didn't want him running up their phone bill by calling his parents in Dominica. This didn't stop him from calling his parents but did prevent his use of a telephone credit card, another situation where he capitulated rather than argue.

Soon he had the elderly Rennie Parker on the phone, and she greeted him in her characteristically happy voice, as she recognized his voice before he had a chance to tell her who was calling.

"Manny!" she exclaimed, "I'm so proud of you! I've been following you in the paper every day. God has been very good to you," she added.

Ignoring her last remark, Manny proceeded to explain to her, as best he could, what had happened to him. She heard him out, then said, "You're in a tough spot, child, but, with the help of your God, I know you'll find the right answer."

Manny was becoming personally agitated with Rennie's 'God-talk'. After all, he reasoned, it was his so-called 'loving God' who allowed all this to happen, but he

247

was careful not to verbalize that thought to Rennie. "Rennie," Manny blurted, "I don't know what I'm going to do, but I'll call you when I decide."

When they finished their conversation, Manny still had both feet firmly planted in mid-air. He went for a walk. He returned after walking almost five miles. His head was throbbing, but his brain was still disengaged, as far as any answers were concerned. He bought a morning paper and read it in the coffee shop while having a soup and sandwich lunch.

He was relieved at finding no mention of his police involvement in the morning news. It had been his observation over the years that the prominence of being a star ball player, when mixed with police involvement, led inexorably to unwanted press coverage that often was very deleterious to a man's career in baseball, regardless of his ability. Manny had learned, early on, that there were many promising ball players just waiting their chance, and a club nowadays wouldn't allow itself to be identified with a scandal when they could avoid it. He felt much better this day when he didn't see his name in the paper except, again, on the sports page, where the writers were singing his praises as the front runner for the Cy Young Award, to be announced shortly.

It was when his eyes fell across the display ads in the travel section that a solution began to formulate itself in his mind.

Manny thought it through and then placed a call for Sammy Snider, who wasn't in his office. Shirley Simmons responded to Manny's urgency by assuring him that she would have Sammy call him as soon as he returned.

Chapter 18 -- REASONABLE VISITATION

Manny, driven by his plan, was formulating it as he went along.

His phone rang. It was Sammy Snider.

"Hi, Manny," Sammy said, "congratulations on a great year!"

Manny's tone was subdued. "Hi, Sammy," he came back; "thank you."

"What can I do for my star client?" Sammy asked.

Manny was unimpressed by Sammy's cavalier attitude. "Do you remember those papers I gave you at Aunt Polly's?" Manny asked.

"Sure," Sammy answered, "what about 'em?"

Manny carefully chose his words. "Sammy, Vivienne has divorced me." He waited to assess Sammy's reaction to his words.

He didn't have to wait long. Sammy responded with a loud "No!" in his most surprised tone of voice.

"Yes," Manny went on, "I just found out last night." Manny went on to tell Sammy everything that had happened to him and then said, "Sammy, all I want is to see my kids, and I have to do that by appointment. Would you call Vivienne and ask her to have them in your office in the morning, and I'll have them back there at three o'clock. That's reasonable, isn't it?"

Sammy quickly responded, "Sure, Manny, I'll be glad to. Gee, I had no idea this was going to happen. I hope you believe me."

"I do believe you, Sammy," Manny lied, "so I'm just trying to make the best of a bad situation."

"I understand, Manny," Sammy said, "and you know I'll help you in any way humanly possible," Sammy lied back. "Tell you what, Manny," Sammy went on, "you just be here at ten in the morning, and I promise you I'll have them here."

Manny thanked Sammy and rang off. His plan was in motion.

Sammy called Vivienne, who opened the conversation by asking him if he'd heard from Tino.

"No," Sammy reported, but, after all, he didn't expect to for a few more days. Sammy then told her of Manny's call. They agreed to placate him by letting him have the children at the agreed time the next day.

Manny went to the Phoenix airport. There he rented a car, using a credit card for the first time since it had gratuitously arrived for him at the ball park in St. Louis, provided by an aggressive bank seeking new business. For reasons he couldn't explain, he hadn't bothered to share it with Vivienne, probably because he really never intended to use it. Now, it was most helpful to Manny in carrying out his plan.

After obtaining the rental car, he drove it to the motel. He then went to the desk clerk and paid two more night's rent. He loaded his gear in the rental car and carried it to a self-storage, retaining only one small bag for his toiletries and a change of underwear and socks. He then drove the car to a large vacant lot near the Phoenix Zoo and parked it.

Everything was now in place for what he was going to do when he had his children safely in tow.

Manny waited. He watched TV. He agonized. He didn't pray. His God had deserted him, so he decided on self help. Where he was going with his children, he knew all the Arizona Court Orders in existence wouldn't reach him. He obviously had to get on friendly turf if he was going to thwart the recent turn of events and convert the odds to his favor. He placed a call to Juanita Armas at the Scottsdale Police Department. He thanked her for helping him during the ordeal with the police and told her of his plans to see his children -- by permission. She told him she was glad everything was working out.

On the surface, Manny appeared to have accepted his plight. Vivienne, not Manny, was the one on the receiving end of the false security treatment this time, as she was on the verge of getting the surprise of her life, a condition she definitely was unaccustomed to.

Manny was in Sammy's office at the appointed time. He patiently waited while Sammy engaged in courteous small talk, most of which Manny merely responded to with a polite 'yes' or 'no'. Manny had detected a side to Sammy during his last two visits that was unlike what he'd seen before. Sammy's nervous politeness now reminded Manny of the Dominican peasant being nice to his chicken before he beheaded it. Manny decided he'd been wrong about Sammy, but now would be an inappropriate time to announce it. He refused to take Sammy's cue to tell an 'inside' story about the Playoffs or Series. Manny did put Sammy at ease by telling him that his World Series share would be in Sammy's office soon. That was what Sammy really wanted to know, anyway. Sammy asked Manny where he might be spending the winter. Manny was proud of the lie he dreamed up on the spot to answer that one. He told Sammy that the Cardinals had already hired him to scout some A.S.U. and rookie league players, ergo, he would be spending the winter in Phoenix. The lie served Manny's momentary purpose, conveying several impressions he wanted in order to put everyone at ease with his presence.

Vivienne then arrived with the children and asked to speak to Sammy personally, then left Manny and their children in the waiting room, admonishing Shirley to let her know, should Manny attempt to leave with the children before she finished talking to Sammy. This was the first Shirley knew of any problem between Manny and Vivienne, but she agreed, as Vivienne went into Sammy's office and closed the door.

Sammy told her everything Manny had said before she arrived. They finished talking, and Vivienne opened the door and re-entered the waiting room. She looked Manny sternly in the face and said, "Manny, the Court Order clearly says the children cannot be removed from Arizona without the Court's written permission. Do you <u>understand</u>?"

Manny nodded 'yes' and then audibly answered the same way. Vivienne then asked, "Where are you going to take them?"

"To the zoo," he answered as his young son squealed his approval and repeated the announcement to his sister.

Manny's ready answer took Vivienne aback, but she approved of the answer to her question. She was confident Manny wouldn't lie to her. "That's fine," she said, "just be sure you have them back here by three o'clock." Manny reassured her, once more thanked Sammy and Shirley, and departed. Vivienne discreetly followed them to the street and watched as they got into a cab going east on Washington, which was the direction of the zoo.

She went back up to Sammy's office and asked him to call Tino just to say hello. Sammy got Tino's answering service, which dutifully took the message and told Sammy that Tino would be returning the call soon. This was the answer they always used when Tino was out of town. Sammy shared this information with Vivienne who, for the time being, was pacified.

Arriving at the zoo, Manny spent the next two hours enjoying his children. As they started to get tired, he fed them and made his way to the rental car. The children fell fast asleep as Manny sped out of the city bound for old Mexico. By his calculations, he would be out of the country about the time he was supposed to return them to Sammy's office.

He returned the rental car to the company at its installation on the Arizona side of Mexico. He then walked across the border into Nogales, Mexico. He took a hotel room for the night and enjoyed frolicking with his children after taking them out for green-turtle soup, a dish this little tourist town was famous for the world over. Manny had side-tripped there many times when the Phoenix Giants traveled to Tucson to play the Toros.

The first leg of his trip had gone smoothly, much to Manny's satisfaction. He hoped it would continue this way all the way to his intended destination, his home town of San Pedro de Macoris.

He began telling the children of their grandparents, whom they'd never met. Joseph was excited and enjoying every minute of it. His joy was contagious, although the younger Marie would occasionally call for her mother. Manny knew she would be fine, once he got her to her grandmother's house.

Manny now had a healthy and abiding fear of the Court Orders that Vivienne had reminded him of, as he departed Sammy's office. He began posing the various questions to himself concerning how he could accomplish his intended goal of getting to his parents' home with his children, without attracting the attention of any law enforcement authorities.

He had plenty of cash. Rising above the poverty he was raised in left him indelibly reminded that such an existence was one he never intended to return to. Thus, in spite of Vivienne, Manny always kept enough cash on hand to assuage his former feeling of insecurity, brought about by the poverty in his background. If Manny had a million in the bank, he would still have ten grand in his pocket.

Manny was smart enough to know that the first place the Scottsdale Police would look for him was at the hotel where they had deposited him. He also accurately assumed that, by leaving a few personal things in his room and paying the rent a day ahead, they would be looking for him to return there. By the time the paper trail on the rental car had been ferreted out, he figured he should be safely in his parents' home in Dominica.

The question confronting him now remained: how should he implement the last leg of his journey? He had heard of celebrities landing their private planes at the beautiful Casa de Campo Resort near La Romana, Dominican Republic, where he had played winter ball. 'That's it,' he decided, 'I'll get a private plane to Casa de Campo.'

For two days he and the kids enjoyed the environs of Nogales, then he chartered a private aircraft. They stopped once to re-fuel on the Yucatan Peninsula before striking out for the private airstrip at Casa de Campo Resort, a thousand miles away. They crossed the Gulf and soon found themselves over the Atlantic. Careful to avoid Cuban or U.S. air space, the competent pilot found his way to their destination. Manny and his children exited the airplane and thanked the pilot. Manny had already given him the required four-thousand dollars as compensation for the flight.

Manny checked into the resort for one night, because the children were exhausted from the trip. The next day he bought himself and the children, to their delight, some new clothing and luggage to carry it in. After lunch at the resort, they boarded a bus for San Pedro.

Alighting from the bus, Manny hailed the first car he saw. It wasn't a taxi, but in his home town, <u>every</u> car was a potential taxi for a celebrity such as Manny. The driver recognized Manny and was glad to take him and his children to his parents' home. Manny offered compensation, but the young man refused, wished Manny well and drove away.

Manny went into his parents' home. It was not the home he had been raised in, as his parents had built a new home with the money Manny had generously sent them from America.

His mother was in the kitchen when she heard Manny calling as he entered the front door.

Angelica Hernandez greeted her grandchildren for the first time with tears of joy and words, Spanish words, of her love. Angelica Hernandez couldn't speak a word of English. His father, Alejandro, was at work, as were his brothers and sisters.

Soon Grandmother Hernandez had the children comfortably moved into a vacant upstairs bedroom she had reserved for them, should she ever get to receive them in her home. She was resigned to the fact the day probably was never going to come, which greatly enhanced her feelings at this moment.

Grandmother Hernandez' happiness exceeded her bounds of verbal expression. She would hug the children and love them, and then she would pour them more lemonade. She would then pepper Manny with questions about them. It appeared she just wouldn't run down. Then it dawned on her, and she asked Manny in Spanish, "Where's your wife, where's Vivienne?"

Manny told her it was a long story and for now he simply asked her not to worry. He said he would explain everything when his father got home.

Angelica Hernandez spent the rest of the afternoon busying herself with the joy that comes with a doting grandmother seeing her son's children for the very first time. The two pictures on her dressing table had come alive today for the first time in her home and her delight was beyond measure.

Angelica tucked the children under the covers for a nap and sent Manny to the market for groceries. The presence of her grandchildren from America caused her to pleasantly depart from the usual meals and eating schedule in the Hernandez home. After talking it over with Manny to determine what the children were used to, she made a grocery list and gave it to Manny.

Manny gone, and the children asleep, the gloriously happy Angelica Hernandez began to wonder more at the absence of Vivienne. She hadn't met Vivienne, but telephone conversations between the two, short as they had been, had left Angelica Hernandez with bad vibrations. She prayed that something bad had not happened to her son's wife.

Manny's father, Alejandro, and two of Manny's brothers, came home shortly before Manny arrived back from the market. They were all very happy to see Manny and his children, and after they settled down, Angelica pressed Manny for an explanation about Vivienne.

Manny obliged and told them the whole story, from his receiving the summons in Chicago to his being led away from the front door of his home by the two policemen.

His family was shocked. His mother then asked him if he would get into any trouble by bringing the kids to Dominca. This was one question that Manny had put out of his mind when it came up, but he couldn't ignore answering his mother. "I'm not sure," he said, "Except I know I am in violation of the Court Order. What the punishment for that is, I just don't know."

Angelica Hernandez spoke. "Manny, you and your children are loved and welcomed here in this home at all times. That understood, you still have to live with yourself. If you think there is any chance of having your actions come back to haunt you later, I think you should do whatever is necessary to meet the problem head on, right now. You know your mother well enough to know," she continued, "that right is right and there simply is no other way."

Manny knew all along what his mother would say, once she knew all the facts.

"Mother," he said, "I know you are right, but I also know that, once I am back within her reach, Vivienne won't rest until I'm in jail. Please try to see my side of it," he pleaded.

His mother just kept saying, "Right's right and there's no other way." His mother's opinion on how one should conduct one's life left no shade of gray.

* * *

Supervisor Patrick back in Phoenix had been successfully monitoring the movements of Tino Borozi, Gus

Kirby, Sammy Snider and Vivienne Hernandez. As yet, to Patrick's pleasant surprise, Manny Hernandez' presence was not to be detected in the Borozi scheme of things, but Manny's movements were being furiously investigated by the F.B.I. because of Vivienne's kidnapping complaint.

Manny's paper trail with the rental car led to the supposition that he'd left the country. Vivienne Hernandez was in the F.B.I. Office daily, demanding the return of her kids.

The Bureau had information confirming the children's whereabouts and their apparent safety, but Vivienne demanded that Manny be indicted under the Federal Parental Kidnapping Act. The District Attorney's office delayed prosecution of Manny, thinking it would impede the D.E.A.'s ongoing investigation, which they couldn't reveal to Vivienne, especially since she was a target. Also, the government had not discounted the fact that Vivienne and Manny could be in a ruse trumped up by both of them to decoy attention away from the dope deal.

The less the U.S. Attorney's Office seemed inclined to act against Manny, the more vocal Vivienne got. Finally, they placated Vivienne during one of her daily 'bitch trips' to the F.B.I. by telling her that they had unofficially confirmed that Manny was bringing the children back to Phoenix. They refused to give her any more information. They assured her that when he returned, he would be arrested and the children returned to her.

They refused to tell Vivienne that the information they were relying on was Manny's having made an airline reservation from Santo Domingo to Phoenix for himself and his children. He was currently slated to return at the same time Tino Borozi was expected back with twenty kilos of pure cocaine. The government was still curious to find out the relationship, if any, between Manny and Tino. Their grip was closing on Tino, Gus, Sammy and Vivienne, but they still didn't have enough evidence on Manny's involvement to include him in their planned bust, a fact which wouldn't matter, because, once they had him in custody on the Parental Kidnapping charges, they could always file additional charges against him. Everything was going smoothly in the government's direction right down to the beeper tracking devices in the payload, which indicated Tino's already having returned to Miami from Panama. He was then bound for Phoenix after refueling, a fact confirmed by agent Billy Long from Miami.

Chapter 19 -- THE RETURN

The few days spent with his children in the Hernandez home in Dominica were like a dream come true for Manny, his Dominican family and his children. The family warmth and attention had a tranquil effect on the children, who failed to mention or miss their mother from the time they entered the Hernandez home.

The children were taken to the homes of various relatives for short visits, with Manny growing more proud of his progeny everywhere they went. It was a vary happy time despite Manny's nagging thought of what he had to do to straighten things out.

Manny feared jail. The only jails he knew anything about were Dominican jails. In Dominica, as Manny knew, unless a prisoner has family support or money, he can starve there. Manny had never had a personal jail experience, therefore, his imagination ran riot and was based on what his friends who had been there had told him. At any rate, he didn't like even the thought of it. On the other hand, he knew his mother was right, as she always had been. He had even thought of taking one of his brothers back to America with him for moral support and to bring him food if he were put in jail. He ruled this out because none of them spoke English. He didn't realize that prisoners in American jails were clothed, fed and provided reasonably comfortable accommodations. Manny probably wouldn't have believed it if somebody had tried to tell him that, because of the practice and procedures in jails where he was raised and learned of such things.

His mother and he continued to have long talks about his plight, until at last, he was ready to return to Arizona and start getting out of his problem and into its solution.

Manny was unaware that his movements were being carefully monitored by the F.B.I. His advance plane reservations for himself and the children were reported within minutes to Supervisor Patrick in Phoenix.

When the day for their departure from Dominica came, Manny and his two children were given a grand send-off by his parents. After all, under the circumstances, Angelica Hernandez could not be sure that she wasn't saying good-bye to her grandchildren for the last time.

During their visit, Manny's mother had tried to rekindle his faith in God, to no avail. Manny was still in rejection of the God he was positive had abandoned him. Manny's recalcitrance surprised and disappointed his mother, who kept reminding him that God didn't take vacations and he shouldn't give up on his God. Respectfully, the much frustrated Manny chose to change the subject, rather than argue with his mother over a matter where their two opinions, at this juncture, were polarized.

As the aircraft carrying her beloved son and grandchildren lifted off Dominican soil, Angelica Hernandez watched with trepidation while clenching her hands together in silent and concentrated prayer. Her mood was given away by tears rolling down her cheeks. She was not unlike a mother watching her son go off to war, never knowing whether she would see him again.

The government agencies, F.B.I. and D.E.A., had set up a central control to monitor their coordinated efforts in the investigation. Now dubbed by the code name, 'Cleanup', the operations included the kidnap charges now lodged against Manny and the dope trafficking charges about to be brought against Vivienne, Tino, Sammy and Gus. There were still some loose ends to be pulled together before other charges could be added against Manny, but, for the moment, all government personnel involved in 'Operation Cleanup' were pleased with their progress.

Tino's cash withdrawal had been reported shortly after it occurred by the informant in the Miami Bank. Tino's movements to the private airstrip and his departure had been eyeballed by Agent Long, as had his return and subsequent departure for Phoenix.

The tap on Vivienne's phone revealed her illicit affair with Sammy, but, more importantly, her constant impatience to hear something from Tino. Her voracious greed had driven her to daily telephone calls to Sammy seeking progress reports on Tino. Tino was too smart to tell Sammy his itinerary, but he didn't have to. The government had managed to track Tino without help from the phone tap.

Vivienne was happily anticipating her first installment payment from Tino, Manny's Playoff and World Series shares and the return of her children.

Sammy was on the golf course, basking in the Phoenix sun and the thoughts of his next encounter with Vivienne, which he was planning on happening that afternoon.

The plane carrying Manny and his children touched down in Miami and they made their way through customs. The Inspector took a cursory look inside Manny's lone suitcase to delay him while an unseen camera recorded the ongoing chain of events.

They had a short layover in Miami. Manny's mind was awhirl, as he was trying to decide whether or not to call Vivienne. The fact he had not contacted her was eroding the government's suspicion that he was engaging in a decoy tactic. Even the best decoys, experience had taught the G-men, call home once in a while. The closest he came to calling was during a short layover in Houston, when he got some change and walked up to a pay telephone. At that time, Joseph, seeing his father's picture on a tabloid cover, pulled on Manny to get his attention. The story was the announcement that he had won the Cy Young Award. Manny didn't buy the paper, but his concealed elation distracted him from making the phone call to Vivienne. The significance of this oversight was never known to Manny. His young son had just made a great contribution toward lessening the harrowing experiences which his unsuspecting father was on the edge of being hurled into. Manny's monitored movements could be likened to a great meteorite that was about to crash and burn.

Knowing he had won the coveted Cy Young Award made Manny very happy, the only distraction being that he had absolutely no one to share his good news with. His young son could not have understood it, even if Manny had tried to explain it to him.

The last leg of the trip back to Phoenix found Manny experiencing a myriad of emotions, and they ran the gambit from extreme joy to deep sadness. The mental confusion he had been going through before he hustled his children off to Dominica paled now in the face of what he was anticipating to be very troublesome times for himself. Once his thoughts even turned to Donnie Robinson, the dying youngster in St. Louis Children's Hospital and to the little girl needing the kidney transplant. When these thoughts occurred to him, he would look at the sleeping Joseph and Marie and feel very fortunate at their good health. Manny still refused to include God in the retinue of his thoughts.

Supervisor Patrick was in Project Central conferring with his F.B.I. counterpart, Jim Wade, and the question under discussion was how to handle the Manny Hernandez return to Phoenix. "We can arrest him any time we choose," Wade said, "but we wanted your thoughts on that, Mike... so, what are they?"

Agent Patrick, realizing Manny's flight would be on the ground in a matter of minutes, replied, "Jim, our people still don't have enough evidence of his involvement to bring him into the loop. The check from Treasury will probably get to his Scottsdale home in a day or two. He hasn't contacted his wife at all, and frankly, I'd like to wait and see what he does. He hasn't done anything that gives focus that he's in the dope deal, or even knows about it. The money Borozi got from the special trust account was taken out under lawyer Snider's signature. We can prove through the assignment and the phone tap that Missis Hernandez was in on it from the get-go, but such incriminations just don't appear for her husband. Given a trial by jury tomorrow, Manny Hernandez would show up innocent, and there's a real good chance that he is, at least, so far as the dope deal is concerned."

Wade then said, "Just the opposite is true of our parental kidnapping charge. We've got him hung, drawn and quartered right now. Okay," Wade continued, "let's see what he does after he gets here. We'll both sit right here next to our radio contact with the field agents and order them to follow and observe only until we order his arrest from here. What about Tino Borozi?" Wade inquired, "when do you plan to take him?"

Patrick responded, "We've got him tracked like a cat in the snow. That brazen bastard has stored the coke in the trunk of a Mercedes Benz in the parking garage adjacent to his office building. Ever since we advised his lawyer of the three-hundred-thousand-dollar refund from his last bust, Tino's been acting like a burglar with a license to steal. Trouble is, he's a 'one-trick' pony. He's not even half clever. He's been on the horn lining up several of his distributors to come to his office tomorrow to pick up product. It looks like he and his people-pet, Gus Kirby, are going to stay up all night and cut it. Our plans right now are to take their distributors as they exit his office, and then take Tino and Gus, or, in the alternative, we'll just take them all in his office. In either case, we won't be making our move until tomorrow. So you can float with Manny Hernandez for at least twenty-four hours if you want to."

"Sounds good," Wade answered. "I guess we should plan on just staying here and letting it happen."

"Right," Patrick agreed.

It wasn't long before the radio reports started coming into Project Central concerning the movements of Manny Hernandez.

"He's disembarked with the two children, obtained his baggage and is in line to catch a taxi," the observing field agent reported. A little later he continued, "Subject is going over the Hohokam Freeway into town... subject is north on Forty-Fourth Street... subject is turning east on Thomas Road."

Patrick and Wade looked at each other. Patrick spoke first, "He's going home! The son-of-a-buck is going home! I don't believe it... well, we've got him now. He and 'mama' are probably going to soon be laughing about having pulled the wool over our eyes. Boy, do we have some surprises for him!"

The two supervising agents were gleefully anticipating that Manny Hernandez was about to reunite with his wife, thereby confirming their original theory, never abandoned, that Manny was in the conspiracy all the time. However, their balloon of mutual admiration and personal smugness was about to be deflated by a puncture of truth.

The cab stopped in front of the Hernandez home. Manny and the children walked to the front door. The cabbie carried their luggage to the door and departed after Manny paid him. Vivienne observed all of this from inside. As Manny rang the doorbell in front of the excited children, Vivienne retreated to the bedroom to call the Scottsdale Police Department. The latter had not been informed by the Federal Agents of either the kidnapping or narcotics investigations. The G-men had strongly desired that the massive publicity to be garnered from the bust of such a prominent athlete be shared only by them. They had omitted the local boys, on purpose. When the call came from Vivienne to the Scottsdale Police, they acted quickly to dispatch the patrol car in that area to the Hernandez home, expecting to simply arrest Manny for violating the court's order in the divorce proceeding. The charge would be in the nature of contempt for removing the children from the state without the court's written permission.

The presence of the two F.B.I. agents in their unmarked car had gone unnoticed by Manny. They just sat there reporting to Project Central and awaiting orders.

What happened then wasn't in anyone's forecast of what to expect.

Secure in the thought the Scottsdale Police were on the way, Vivienne wanted to get her licks in before the police got there. She was furious, so she ran from the bedroom to the front door. She flung it open and began a caustic, loud, verbal tirade, while simultaneously jerking the children violently into the house. She returned to the outside and started kicking and swinging at Manny, screaming vile expletives at him at the same time.

The video-cam in the F.B.I. agents' hands was capturing the commotion. The other agent keyed the mike and said, "Boss, you're not going to believe this, so we're getting it on tape. This Hernandez woman is beating the crap out of her husband and screaming dirty words at him at the top of her lungs. He's retreating from her, shielding his face with his arms, and she's staying right after him. Wait a minute, the Scottsdale Police are pulling up. Two uniformed officers are getting out of their car. One of them is trying to calm Missis Hernandez down; the other one is just standing there next to Mister Hernandez. Mister Hernandez has dropped his guard now and is just standing there. The one officer is having a hard time getting Missis Hernandez to calm down. My God, he's picked her up, bodily, and is carrying her into her house. Any orders for us?" the agent asked.

Patrick and Wade just looked at each other quizzically. Patrick spoke, "It's your call, Jim, but the Hernandez guy still hasn't stepped into our loop. In fact, the goings-on we just heard about seem to militate entirely in his favor, as far as our side of the matter is concerned."

F.B.I. Agent Wade nodded approval of Patrick's assessment and then said into the radio mike, "Presumably the Scottsdale Police are going to take him away. Follow them. Before they book him, talk to them and see if they'll release him to our Parental Kidnapping Warrant. If they agree, you may promise them that we'll return him any time they desire to make him. Try to get Hernandez out of there before they book him. Once they book him, we'll have the added problem of dealing with some Magistrate. Do the best you can," Wade concluded as he signed off.

The F.B.I. agents shut down their video-cam as the cooperative Manny was placed in the police car and taken to the Scottsdale Police Department.

After a certain amount of wrangling, Manny was turned over to the Federal Agents. The Scottsdale Watch Commander was nettled at the matter being handled in such a way that the Federals didn't enlist their support until they were forced to. He was assured that due credit would be given his men for the 'collar', an eventuality which the G-men knew would only occur at <u>their</u> discretion, because, after their intervention, the S.P.D. didn't go on and book him. Fortunately for Manny, although he had no way of knowing it, the latter point ultimately would be moot anyway.

Manny was taken to Project Central for questioning. Upon his arrival there, he was read his rights and ushered into an interrogation room, soon to be joined by Agents Patrick and Wade. Wade brought in Agent Sam Hammock, who would spell either of the two senior agents who might be called back to the radio at any moment. All of them were about to be confronted with a candor the level of which they had never experienced.

"Do you know why you're here, Mister Hernandez?" Agent Patrick asked.

Manny answered, "Because I took my children to Dominica and made their mother very mad."

"Any other reason you can think of?" he was asked.

"No, sir," Manny politely but emphatically replied.

271

Patrick then asked, "Does attorney Sammy Snider handle your money?"

Manny answered, "No, I always left that up to my wife... ah, I guess I should say my ex-wife."

"You mean to tell me," Patrick continued, "that a millionaire ball player like yourself doesn't have <u>any</u> say-so over his own money?"

Manny answered, "Vivienne does all that, I don't even carry a check book."

The agents were aghast at what was unfolding out of Manny's innocent mouth. "Suppose I told you, Mister Hernandez," Patrick continued, "that we know about a special trust account held by attorney Sammy Snider, but consisting wholly of funds belonging to you and your wife?"

This line of questioning puzzled Manny, but, having nothing to hide, he saw no harm in cooperating. Manny answered, "Yes sir, there is such an account and it draws interest and is there for us to draw on, if need be, but we never draw it out. We figure we're less likely to squander it if we have to go through Sammy to get it."

"You mean," Patrick continued, "that you, Manny Hernandez, have never authorized Sammy Snider to use it?"

"That's right," Manny replied, "and hopefully <u>we</u> won't have to use it, unless the children need something."

The agents continued to be flabbergasted. Either this guy was the penultimate con man, or the victim of a con game pulled off by his ex-wife and lawyer.

"Manny," Agent Wade asked, "do you know you've won the Cy Young Award?"

Manny acted ignorant. "No, sir," he answered, then followed by asking, "Have I?"

"You sure have," Agent Wade said with a big smile, "and this is a helluva way for you to find out about it."

The agents were impressed with him. Manny's answers were crisp, quick and quite obviously honest. Nevertheless, he had, by his own admission, violated the Federal Parental Kidnapping Act, and the agents' responsibilities in this regard were to arrest him for that and place him in custody, for which purpose they utilized the Maricopa County Jail where they took him, to await his arraignment before a Federal Magistrate the next day. The Magistrate would set his bond. All of this was totally new to Manny. The only good thing that happened to him, to his welcome surprise, he didn't go hungry.

He was booked, issued a jail uniform, green in color to signify he was a federal prisoner, and placed in a holding tank with about twenty other men. He kept to himself, only speaking when spoken to, until he picked out a man he'd decided he'd speak to, to find out what to expect. Manny carefully chose the one who looked like he'd had the most experience. The man carefully explained to Manny what was going to happen the next day. Manny was pleased to hear about his ability to be admitted to bond, and he relaxed in the knowledge that there was a way out of there, even if he didn't clearly understand it. In Dominica, he remembered, if a well-known celebrity was arrested and paid enough *mordida*, he could get out of almost anything, but by now his 'pocket money' was almost exhausted.

* * *

Kari Robins had finished her piece on Dominican baseball players and submitted it to her publisher, who liked it. The publisher wanted Kari to expand it from article to book status and feature Manny's life in it. Toward this end, she was given a ten-thousand-dollar advance. The only drawback was the fact the legal department demanded a complete release from Manny before publication. Kari remembered Manny's telling her of his willingness to sign such a document and so informed her publisher. Kari was then dispatched to Phoenix to obtain Manny's signature on the release. She arrived there with no idea of where to find him, but she soon found out from a headline in the morning paper, which announced:

'Hernandez Wins Cy Young
Then Jailed for Parental Kidnap'

She read the article over several times and then retrieved one of the tapes which bore the conversation between them in St. Louis the day they made love. The inadvertently-recorded words between two lovers she found herself playing several times lately, hanging on every word and wishing she were engaged to Manny and not Woody Justice. She fell asleep the night before Manny's arraignment listening to their loving words spoken to each other in the recent past, but which seemed like eons ago because of their parting.

The next morning, Kari looked up a local bondsman. She impressed two things on him --she wanted Manny out of jail at any cost, and the fact <u>she</u> was paying for it must remain anonymous. Under no circumstances was her presence in Phoenix to be revealed to Manny. The bondsman, Harry Keets, agreed, and went to the Federal Courthouse to await Manny's arraignment and arrange for his release.

Chapter 20 -- THE BUST

After a short visit, Vivienne deposited Joseph and Marie at the sitters and returned to the Hernandez home to await the arrival of Sammy. Sammy finished his golf outing, called Shirley and his wife and announced that he'd been called out of town, a practice he had employed successfully in the past to enable him to stay overnight with one of his female conquests. In this instance, he planned to sleep over with Vivienne in the Hernandez' home. Sammy was not aware he was under the watchful observation of the D.E.A. Agents who were tailing him. Neither he nor Vivienne noticed the unmarked van parked near the Hernandez home, which was one of the field command posts for 'Operation Cleanup'.

It was almost dark, ergo the parking garage was all but vacated when Tino ordered Gus Kirby to commence bringing the pure coke, in grocery sacks, from the trunk of the Mercedes to his office.

Tino had errantly assumed that the District Attorney's call to Sammy, announcing the decision to return the three-hundred-thousand dollars, was an indication that the heat was off for awhile.

"You know, Boss," Gus said as he paused to rest, "you've really done some amazing things these past couple of months. First you beat the rap with the jury. Then you make a deal in Panama with Raphael, talking to him like King Kong, when we don't have enough cash to pay the rent. Then you really slicked the slicker; you bearded the lion in his own den, when you got the two-hundred and fifty g's from Sammy."

Tino and Gus had no remote suspicion that D.E.A. Agents, posing as janitorial personnel, had infiltrated their office while the two of them were out of town, and, under court authorization, installed listening devices known as 'bugs'. A person couldn't pass gas anywhere in Tino's office without being recorded.

Tino thanked Gus for his praise and said, "The reason the broad we got the money from didn't want us to know who she was, was that her husband, the big-time ball player guy, didn't know she and Sammy were dipping into his money for us."

The words were barely out of Tino's mouth when the agent monitoring them placed a call to Supervisor Patrick to advise him of what he had just heard and recorded.

"Looks like Manny Hernandez has really been taken for a ride, doesn't it?" Patrick said upon hearing the latest information, and he continued, "That's it; cross Manny Hernandez off the target list. He's got all he can say his prayers over anyway. There's newspaper speculation that he could be suspended from baseball, pending the outcome of the kidnap charges. Boy, his fortunes really went from the sublime to the ridiculous in one day," Patrick concluded. He complimented his field agent and hung up.

Sammy arrived at the Hernandez home. As usual he parked in the garage and entered the house through the adjoining door. Vivienne greeted him buoyantly. "It's all happening, Sammy," she said. "Today I got the kids back, Manny's in jail for kidnapping and the world's best lover just walked in my door."

Sammy had one piece of serious business he was anxious to dispose of. "Viv, is there any indication that Manny knew I was dipping into your trust funds?" he inquired.

"Why, no, why do you ask?" she questioned.

Sammy continued, "Because he could make a complaint to the Bar and I'd have big problems."

"Don't sweat the little things, Sammy," she said reassuringly, then continued, "the only things you have to worry about are scratching my itch and making sure Tino makes his payments on time."

The words were flowing into the tape recorder in the government sound truck outside, which was painted up to resemble a telephone company truck.

"Tino finally figured out who you were," Sammy told her. "He probably wouldn't have if Manny hadn't made the surprise trip home to find out about the divorce papers you had served on him in Chicago. Manny ran me down at Polly's with Tino, as you know, and Tino just put two and two together. That won't inure to your detriment, though, because you have me as a buffer."

Sammy's words were simultaneously loosening the noose from Manny's neck and tightening the ones around Vivienne and himself.

Supervisor Patrick had now assumed full control over 'Operation Cleanup' at Project Central. The F.B.I.'s official involvement ended with the arrest of Manny Hernandez. They would be called upon to reiterate his verbal confession when necessary, but, other than that, his arrest had the effect of closing their file on him.

The information from the various field agents prompted Patrick to order Agent Henricks to call in the group of men he had pre-selected to make the arrests of Sammy, Tino, Gus and Vivienne. It was midnight when the last of these men and women arrived at Project Central to be briefed before making the various arrests.

Patrick opened the meeting. "Ladies and gentlemen, you have been hand-picked to make the arrests in this operation because of the unique qualifications of each of you. What I'm about to say, many of you will find repetitious, but it bears your serious attention. Tonight we are taking the first step toward eradicating from the public venue a slime-ball lawyer whose nefarious methods have landed him in concert with his clients in the financing of a cocaine importing scheme. His one client loaned to his other client the funds to make the buy in Panama. We have stood by patiently from the embryonic stage of this criminal association, just waiting for this evening to get here. When I leave this room, Agent Henricks will instruct you on your specific responsibilities, but, before I do, I want to leave you with some very important overall procedural instructions.

Because of the investigation of the people involved, you do not -- I repeat do not, have to read them their Miranda rights during the initial arrest period. We know none of them will make any incriminating statements anyway, so don't bother to waste our time by 'Mirandizing' them.

"Next, and most important," Patrick went on, "safety first. I can't overemphasize this point. It is our belief that the only gun in Attorney Snider's possession is the one between his legs, and I have it on reliable information that, by now, he's out of ammunition." With that announcement the room erupted with laughter. "Seriously," Patrick continued, "as you all are painfully aware, most of us get wounded or killed by the people we're not expecting it from, so be careful. As for Tino Borozi and Gus Kirby, those of you going in there should expect them to be armed and dangerous. They are both unconvicted killers. Don't hesitate to use your weapons if threatened. We prefer to take them alive; in fact, I'm instructing you to take them alive." Patrick made the latter comment, upon recalling some of his men having to recently submit to skillful cross-examination by a very competent defense lawyer who made them repeat, in open court, all of their pre-bust instructions, much to their embarrassment, and his.

Patrick closed his brief part of this meeting by saying, "In my humble opinion, the arrest and conviction of a dirty lawyer is worth the arrest and conviction of twenty-five importers. The arrest and conviction of one importer is worth the arrest and conviction of twenty-five distributors, and so on down to the street or consumer level. Tonight we have the rare opportunity to have in our net a dirty lawyer, an importer, street distributor and the added bonus of collecting one of the worst types of offenders. The one who, in our opinion, is the prime mover of all the others, and that is the one who provides the money. In this case it is Vivienne Hernandez, wife, or ex-wife, of star baseball player Manny Hernandez, who, I am pleased to announce, was not involved in any of this." His last comment brought whoops of joy from the ones who were fans of baseball, and of Manny.

"Missis Hernandez should be handled carefully and isolated," Patrick continued. "She's the one link in the chain of bad guys who we feel is the most likely to turn state's evidence against the others. After her arrest, bring her here first for me to interrogate personally. Take the others to the Maricopa County Jail. They'll all be arraigned in the morning."

Patrick left the room and Henricks gave the search and arrest team their final instructions.

"Ladies and gentlemen," Henricks commenced his part of the briefing, "tonight your mission is to serve federal arrest warrants on the following people: Tino Borozi, Gus Kirby, Missis Manny 'Vivienne' Hernandez and Attorney Sammy Snider. Borozi and Kirby are in their office in the Briggs Building in the Central Corridor and have been under constant surveillance. There may or may not be street distributors present when you go in. Take note. We always find some new faces in a situation like this, which adds to the total unpredictability of what we may expect from them. Such unpredictability spells D-A-N-G-E-R.

"Naturally, after serving the warrants and securing the area, we expect you to conduct a thorough search of the immediate premises, including all desk drawers and all imaginable places where money or contraband could be hidden. In a word, tear the place apart! You heard me correctly and I didn't stutter. <u>Tear the damn place apart.</u> Rip open seat cushions, take pictures off the walls and remove them from their frames. Do it all. Also, any contraband in unopened containers will have with it certain of our own beeper tracking devices. These should be retrieved and carefully marked and preserved as evidence. Our 'bugs' tell us none of these devices have been discovered by the bad guys. Any questions?" Henricks concluded.

Agent Pat McFadden raised his hand. The grin on his face telegraphed that he was about to crack wise. "Boss, if our raid at the Hernandez home should amount to 'coitus-interruptus', my colleague, Agent Kinnaird, wants to know if he may be substituted for Lawyer Snider to perform 'coitus-continueatus'?"

All the men joined in the laughter as Henricks replied, "Please, Agent McFadden, don't you and Agent Kinnaird be so thoughtless and rude as to deprive the very caring and tender Mister Snider of his last piece of pussy as a free man." The laughter was renewed.

The meeting adjourned after Henricks turned it over to the team leaders to iron out any last-minute questions on the operation. The meeting then ended. Each team got into separate vans bound for their several destinations.

By prior agreement, the warrants were to be served on Tino and Gus and anyone else in their office first. After all, until the cocaine was confiscated and field tested, the illegal purpose of the conspiracy could not be proven beyond a reasonable doubt. So that arrest team went in first.

The first team of agents arrived in the parking garage adjacent to the Briggs Building. They moved with the uninterrupted and silent precision of a twenty-one-jewel railroad-approved pocket watch. Their communication consisted of hand signals only, as they sealed the elevators and staircase. Arriving on the floor containing Tino's office, they surprised two arriving distributors who had just knocked on the locked outer office door. They quickly subdued the distributors after shoving them into a bathroom and replaced them, awaiting admittance. The unsuspecting Gus opened the door to the greeting, "Federal officers, you're under arrest! Lie down and spread your arms on the floor, palms up!" When Gus hesitated, he was thrown down.

The arrest team filled the office, arrested Tino and hurriedly escorted Tino and Gus to their waiting van.

The agents followed their instructions to the letter. They spent the next two hours ransacking Tino's office. Each piece of evidence, from the kilos of cocaine to the beeper tracking devices, was collected, sorted, tagged and preserved as evidence. Agent Negial Brisco sat to one side, making a voice recording of everything that was happening and specifically who was doing what, a practice initiated in the Phoenix District Office by Supervisor Patrick. It was abundantly helpful, especially months later during trial preparation. Additionally, each agent wrote down notes about his own actions. Patrick had been repeatedly commended by the Justice Department for the innovations he had created which assisted them in developing their case at a later date.

Also following instructions, Tino, Gus and the various distributors were not Mirandized. Finally, Tino broke silence after an hour and a half in the van. "Dammit, when are you pigs going to read me my rights and let me call my lawyer?"

"Patience, little man," Agent Ronnie Ollis quietly informed him. "We won't be wasting our time reading you your rights for the simple reason that we aren't interested in anything you have to say and certainly don't need any of your words to seal your fate. Simply put, little man, and that includes both of you, we've got you guys on more film footage than was ever made of Charlie Chaplin. And, as for calling your lawyer, if you act nice, we'll even recommend that you get to share a cell with him tonight."

Tino's indignation was exceeded only by his surprise when he learned that Sammy was included in the bust. Without thinking, he blurted out, "What about the broad?" before he was able to restrain himself.

The agent obligingly answered, "Oh, she'll be there, too, except that I don't think jail regulations will allow her to bunk in with the rest of you tonight."

Tino growled his disapproval. 'How could this happen to him at the very moment he was about to get back on his financial feet?' he queried silently. Then he thought to himself, as Manny had many times lately, 'Is there no God!'

The first phase of the D.E.A. mission completed, so attention was focused on the Scottsdale home where Sammy

Snider and Vivienne Hernandez were fast asleep after an evening of wine and sex.

Team Two of the D.E.A. surrounded the house, covered all available exits, windows and doors, and then the team leader commenced repeatedly ringing the front doorbell, which awakened Vivienne, who shook Sammy until he, too, woke up. Her first words to Sammy were, "That God-damned Manny! He's gotten out of jail and come back, so I guess I'd better call the police."

This time, the federal agents had advised the Scottsdale police of their intended actions. When Vivienne's call reached the duty officer at the Scottsdale Police Department, he advised her to put the phone down and go confirm who it was at the front door. Vivienne followed his suggestion. She turned on her porch light and was greeted by a female agent who identified herself and asked Vivienne to open the front door. Vivienne thought they had come there looking for Manny, so she quickly unlocked the two doors. The agents streamed through the open door, lit up the house lights and discovered Sammy, sitting up erectly in the bed, clothed only in a satin sheet.

A female agent got Vivienne dressed, Mirandized her and quickly transported her to Project Central to join Supervisor Patrick and Agent Henricks in an interrogation room.

Sammy was allowed to dress himself and then was handcuffed and removed to the Maricopa County Jail.

Sammy and Vivienne protested vehemently, but their prostetations fell on deaf ears. The agents saw to it that the two were given copies of the arrest warrants and took them with them.

The home was searched, revealing no incriminating evidence. The bugs were removed after their locations were photographed. The listening devices were packaged and marked. Each agent handling such things would attach to each package a piece of tape with an impression of his own right index finger imprinted on it, the final touch to coordinate each piece of evidence with the identification of the agent who gathered it.

Sammy was silent but puzzled at first by the quick separation of Vivienne and himself. He caught on, though, as he began to wake up, and shouted at her as she was being led out of the house. "Keep your mouth shut, Viv, and just let me handle it."

The female agent escorting her couldn't resist saying, "Yeah, Missis Hernandez, you do that, especially since he's given you such god-damned good advice already." Vivienne subconsciously at that moment suffered the final large chink in her armor.

At Vivienne's request, the crying children were taken by the arresting agents to their sitter's house and left there only with the explanation that Missis Hernandez would be in contact with them.

Chapter 21 -- THE PLEA BARGAIN

Vivienne, now wide awake, was seated when Supervisor Patrick and Agent Henricks entered the small interrogation room at Project Central. There was no one-way viewing mirror. Mike Patrick introduced himself and Marion Henricks and began the conversation.

"Missis Hernandez, I remind you of the Miranda Warning that you've been given and also inform you that this room is equipped with very efficient recording devices to preserve everything that is said here." Vivienne started to speak, but Patrick cut her off short and asked her to "Please hear me out."

She sat back and elected to listen.

"I know how clever you think you've been," Patrick continued. "I also know that when one operates in league with their lawyer they feel, shall I say, very secure. That in mind, let me favor you with some knowledge that we have. Then I'll tell you what we want from you and more importantly, what we're willing to do for you if you choose to cooperate with us. While I'm talking, if you need to go to the toilet or want a refill for your coffee, please tell us."

287

Vivienne slowly shook her head 'yes' and the supervisor continued.

"A few weeks ago, a check was drawn on Attorney Snider's special trust account that contained funds provided to him solely by you and your husband, Manny Hernandez. This check was made to 'cash', but the real payee was Tino Borozi. Borozi took it to a bank in Miami, Florida, to cash it. After cashing it, he flew to Panama where he purchased raw cocaine powder, twenty kilograms of it. Borozi returned to Phoenix to sell and distribute the cocaine, but we arrested him and several of his distributors before it hit the street. Borozi and his first lieutenant and several of the distributors were arrested tonight, as you and Attorney Snider were. Borozi gave you personally, in your name alone, an irrevocable assignment for valuable consideration, that being the two-hundred and fifty-thousand-dollar loan, of all funds belonging to him, Borozi, in U.S. custody, having been confiscated by us in a previous case involving Mister Borozi. We have enough evidence to convict all of you. We don't have to have your cooperation. However, based on our experience, we know it is always prudent and desirable if we can achieve the cooperation of someone on the inside of any illicit activity. And, in this instance, we've chosen to give you the first opportunity to cooperate."

Vivienne couldn't resist interrupting, and said, "You're telling me that Borozi was arrested with twenty kilos tonight here in Phoenix."

"Yes," was the quick answer.

Vivienne then blurted out, "But the bastard told me that stuff would not be brought to Phoenix, that it was going

288

to doctors and lawyers on the east coast. I'm not sure now which one said it, but it was Sammy or Tino, one! Why, those dirty liars!" After her announcement, she sat back quietly.

"Missis Hernandez," Patrick continued, "people in our business never cease to be amazed at how the likes of a Tino Borozi or a Sammy Snider can persuade people who otherwise appear to be law-abiding citizens to join in their illegal schemes. We believe this to be the first time you've ever done so, and it's because of that fact that we've chosen to give you a break. Don't get over-confident. These charges are not going to just go away; but if you will fully and unreservedly cooperate with us, starting right now, we will see to it that you don't get any jail or prison time. We will also see to it that when you appear before the U.S. Magistrate later this morning, you are released on your own recognizance."

Vivienne was smart enough to realize that she was caught in a web, from which her only possible means of extrication would be to cooperate. First, she had a question. "Mister Patrick, if I am willing to do as you suggest, what happens to my children? Also, would I be in any potential danger of being the target of Mister Borozi's revenge?"

Patrick nodded his understanding of her concerns and said, "Your children are at the sitters, where you told us to take them. You can pick them up there when you're released. There was no contraband found in your home. Therefore, we will see to it that your home is not confiscated by the U.S. Attorney under the R.I.C.O. Statutes. Thus, you can collect your children today after your court appearance and go home.

"The next part of your question is not as easy to answer. Borozi is only part of the problem. His Colombian contacts can go anywhere and hurt somebody and be back in Colombia almost before their deeds over here are discovered. That understood, here are the alternatives: you can enter the Federal Witness Protection Program, in which case, you will be given a whole new identity and taken to live in what our very competent intelligence system deems a safe place. I'm sure you've heard about this through the news media and so on. As for the matter of your retaining custody of your children, that is a matter that the Arizona Courts have the reputation of jealously guarding. We would be glad to appear before such a judge and give witness to your cooperation with us. However, we have absolutely no control over whether or not your husband shall seek to change the custody order now in force, or if the court, being advised of your recent conduct, would want to change the custody. I would say -- and this is only my own speculation -- that if your husband chose to change the custody, and all things being equal, you would have a fight on your hands, regardless of how much we testified for you.

"My best advice, Missis Hernandez," he went on, "is to take first things first and solve each problem as it demands solving. If Manny Hernandez wanted to contest the custody of your children, I don't think he would've brought them back to you from Dominica."

"You know about that, too?" she asked.

"We know just about everything you, Snider, Kirby and Borozi have done for the last month," he answered.

Agent Henricks then spoke for the first time. "Missis Hernandez, your ex-husband is in jail right now on the Parental Kidnapping charges. It just might be a good time for you to contact him and make your own trade-out with him on the custody issue. Unless the Domestic Relations Judge has something brought before him by your husband, it is very unlikely that the custody decree in effect will be reconsidered."

Vivienne sat there trying to leave no stone unturned. She was inclined to cooperate. She liked the idea of being released from custody, picking up her children and going home. She broke silence by asking, "Will Borozi and Kirby be let out of jail before trial?"

"Yes," was Henricks' quick answer. "We don't like it, but these days, a judge can't set a bond that a narcotics operative on their level can't make. They take pride in their ability to foil the system. However, when they are released -- and we doubt it will be today; that is, at the same time you are -- we will see to it that they are sternly warned of what to expect if you become threatened."

Vivienne quickly said, "It really doesn't make me feel any better that they'll be warned, and I'll tell you right now that if they should kill me, I won't be concerned about what penalty is assessed against them. Do you people understand me?"

Then came the government agent's stock and often-repeated answer. "Missis Hernandez," Patrick said quietly, looking her straight in the eyes, "we didn't create this problem -- <u>you did</u>. However, we shall endeavor through any and all means at our command to help you through it. If you want to be kept in protective custody today, we'll do it. If you want to enter the Witness Protection Program, we'll do it. If you want to go pick up your kids and go home, we'll take you. But if going back to your home is what you choose, we can't protect you twenty-four hours a day."

Agent Henricks then spoke up. "Why don't you do this, Missis Hernandez... why don't you go pick up your kids later and go home. We'll alert the Scottsdale police <u>and</u> set it up for you to periodically call us to let us know you're okay. As long as nothing happens -- meaning you're not threatened -- we'll continue in this mode. If you become uncomfortable, we'll do something more drastic. Certainly we'll change our approach if we find out that you're in any danger -- which we often do before the intended victims even suspect it. Let's take the one-day-at-a-time approach."

Vivienne seemed to be satisfied, then she asked, "Now will I be taken to jail?"

"No," Patrick answered her. "Here's your schedule. One of our agents will escort you home, where you can prepare for your court appearance. After your court appearance, you will be taken to the jail to be photographed and fingerprinted. The jail lingo is 'booked'; you'll be booked. Then you'll be taken home. Later on, as we need to, we'll call on you to provide any information for us that may assist us in the prosecution of any of your co-defendants. We are only aware of your acquaintance with three of them -- Borozi, Kirby and Attorney Snider."

Vivienne's interview concluded, she got up to leave. As an after-thought, Patrick asked her, "Oh, yes, Missis Hernandez, there is one more thing you can clear up for us right now. Did Manny Hernandez ever have any knowledge or role in any of the transactions involving you, Snider, Kirby and Borozi, that led up to these arrests tonight?"

"Manny," she smirked, "<u>never</u>, not Manny. Why he's so squeaky clean, he wouldn't say shit if he had a mouthful. I even have to laugh when I think about him being in jail. Knowing him, if he's in there very long, he'll have the joint converted to Christianity and a gospel choir organized."

She left them in the company of an agent who was assigned to take her home before returning her to court.

Patrick and Henricks just looked at each other and grinned. Patrick spoke first. "You know, Marion, sometimes I'm happier to find out who the 'bad guys' aren't than who they are."

Henricks agreed.

Chapter 22 -- THE COURT APPEARANCE

The majuscular sign on the door read:
'Thomas P. Strong
United States Magistrate
District of Arizona'
The courtroom of the U.S. Magistrate was filling gradually with curiosity seekers and press.

Manny Hernandez was shackled by a chain around his waist, to which his handcuffs were attached, as were all of his fellow inmates taken to court en masse.

The jail was two blocks from the courthouse. Those making court appearances had been transported in the early hours and placed in a holding tank in the federal courthouse. Manny, Tino, Gus and the latter's co-defendants were now all together. Gus and Tino were so busy singling out their fall partners, admonishing them, one by one to keep faith with them and not turn informant, they didn't recognize Manny. The absence of Vivienne didn't loom as unusual to them, because they knew she wouldn't have been transported and held in the same quarters as the male defendants. When they were all finally escorted into the courtroom and seated, her conspicuous absence detonated the fear alarms in Tino.

The bailiff appeared and whispered something to the U.S. Marshal. In response, the marshal and his assistants ordered all of the men who'd just been brought to the courtroom, except Manny, to get up and follow the escorting assistant U.S. Marshals right back to their cells.

In the confusion, Tino and Gus still didn't recognize Manny, no doubt because he was in surroundings they would never have associated with him. In this setting, he was to them, just another Hispanic face.

Manny was the only defendant in the courtroom when Vivienne walked in through the public entrance. They saw each other immediately. Vivienne was not in a jail uniform nor in any restraints. Manny had no idea why she was there, but his mind was sure it wasn't for his benefit.

Vivienne whispered to her female escort, who in turn, whispered to the assistant U.S. Marshal standing guard in the courtroom over what appeared to be the only federal prisoner present, Manny Hernandez. The assistant U.S. Marshal nodded his approval, and Vivienne was permitted to walk over and talk to Manny.

It was during this time that Manny was so narcotized by his ex-wife's presence that he failed to see Kari quietly enter the courtroom and take a seat among the gathering crowd. Kari watched with more than idle curiosity as the woman she'd never met walked over and started talking to Manny, who just sat expressionless and without emotion.

"Manny," Vivienne began, "when you get out of jail, we have to talk. There isn't much time now, but just remember, I won't call the cops on you any more, and we need to talk to each other as soon as possible."

The urgency in her voice was unmistakable, and somehow he knew without asking that what was on her mind was more than something about the children. Vivienne withdrew as Manny meekly said, "Okay, sure, I'll call you." He was not familiar with courtroom protocol, so the fact she was seated in front of the bar held no particular significance for him, as it did to the watchful but undetected eyes of Kari.

The bailiff opened court as the judge made his appearance. The assistant U.S. Marshal had to motion Manny to stand and then to sit back down.

The judge read aloud. "United States versus Hernandez; Vivienne Wilson Hernandez, please come forward." Manny was thunderstruck as the judge continued. "Missis Hernandez, the U.S. Attorney's office has contacted me prior to our being together this morning and indicated their desire to have you admitted to bond on your own recognizance. Are you represented by counsel?"

"No, Your Honor, not at this time," was Vivienne's reply, as the judge continued.

"It is unusual for me to consider releasing a defendant on his or her own recognizance in cases of this nature. Are you aware of the charges against you?"

Vivienne quietly answered, "Yes, I am, Your Honor."

The judge then asked her, "Do you waive formal reading of the charges?"

"Yes," she answered.

The judge then announced, "It is my decision, then, even in the face of these serious charges relating to conspiracy to traffic in narcotics, that you be released on your own recognizance."

The judge had made his little speech to let the assembled press know he wasn't getting soft. Everybody in the courtroom immediately assumed, correctly, that Vivienne Hernandez was now an ordained government witness, to be treated with appropriate protection. Thus was Kari Robins indirectly introduced to Missis Manny Hernandez, and the effect could not have been more electric.

Before the judge excused Vivienne, he posed a question to her. "Missis Hernandez, is that your ex-husband?" he inquired, as he pointed to Manny.

"Yes, Your Honor," she answered.

The judge then said, "In the interest of saving the court's time, I would ask you if you have any fear of this man repeating his recent conduct involving taking your children out of the country?"

"None, Your Honor," was her sincere and immediate reply.

"Thank you, Missis Hernandez; you may be excused, and I think the Marshal wants to run you through the booking procedure before you are released, is that not correct?" the judge asked as he looked at Vivienne's escort, who spoke up.

"Yes, Your Honor."

"Very well," the judge said, as he called the next case on his docket, "United States versus Manny Hernandez."

Manny was escorted before the judge, and the courtroom was quiet. So many things had just happened in front of him so quickly that his brain was gridlocked trying to digest it. The judge started going through the formalities of arraignment, none of which Manny understood, but he managed to nod his head the proper way at the appropriate time. The judge had been much more detailed in Manny's matter than he had in Vivienne's. He knew the gathered press were there to witness what was happening to the latest winner of the Cy Young Award.

As the last thing he said to Manny, the judge announced that his bond was to be set at ten-thousand dollars. He explained to Manny that under the Federal Bail Reform Act, he could be released by posting one-thousand dollars cash, or ten percent, with the clerk. At that moment, Manny didn't have one-thousand dollars, but something much more important was on his mind, so when the judge asked him if he had any questions, he meekly asked, "Judge... Your Honor... " He hesitated, "Please be kind enough to tell me why my ex-wife was just here."

The courtroom broke out in laughter. Manny stood there expressionless, waiting for an answer. His question bore no levity for him. He was dead serious. So was Kari, still unnoticed by Manny; she was anxiously awaiting the judge's answer to Manny's question.

The judge was not given to answering defendants' questions that were grounded in curiosity, and especially when they weren't pertinent to the case of the defendant who was posing the question. This judge routinely answered such questions by redirecting them to counsel, but Manny was not appearing with counsel.

With a pitiful look, and realizing that his words would soon be heard literally around the world, and with the fore-knowledge that Vivienne Hernandez had opted to cooperate in the prosecution of her co-conspirators, the judge looked at Manny and began by saying, "Mister Hernandez, you've been in jail, so you really don't know why your wife was here, do you?"

The courtroom was as quiet as a morgue at lunchtime as the judge said, "Your wife -- or, I should say -- your ex-wife, Mister Hernandez, appeared before this court this morning charged with a serious crime against the United States. Don't be confused. The matter that she appeared to answer to has nothing at all to do with the matter you have been called to answer to. She was released, and, as soon as you post bond, you, too, shall be released. It can be assumed that she is the principal complaining witness against you; that is the role she'll play in your case. In the case against her, she will have to defend herself, and to these ends, you will both need counsel. The main point I think you need to understand at this moment, Mister Hernandez, is that you stand charged with one thing, and your wife with another. Now, I really must get on with the rest of my docket, so please be seated and address any further inquiry you may have to your lawyer."

Kari's mind was really on fire with more questions, but she would have to wait for the answers.

Manny sat down, still unaware of Kari's hidden presence. The judge called for the rest of the criminal defendants to be returned to the courtroom and relaxed the decorum while the U.S. Marshal followed the court's directive. The gathered press were excitedly discussing their morning findings. They were all surprised and eagerly awaiting the balance of the court's docket.

Bondsman Harry Keets was in the federal clerk's office, busily arranging Manny's bond. Kari quietly joined him and reminded him again of her insistence on anonymity. She returned to the courtroom after requesting Keets to insist of Manny that he know where to find him at all times. Kari told him that she would soon be needing to talk to him, Manny, so for Keets to be sure she could find him. Keets readily agreed. Kari gave him an extra two-hundred and fifty dollars over the bond cost to ensure his cooperation. Latinos are not the only ones who understand *mordida*.

When the prisoners were returned to the courtroom, Manny was again thrown into shock. This time, in their midst, was his attorney-agent, Sammy Snider.

Sammy, like Vivienne, had been interrogated separately. So far, he had agreed to cooperate, but had not agreed to testify. Sammy's priorities were firmly established in his mind. His would be a posture of avoidance. He wanted to avoid losing his law license and avoid losing his life. The cooperation that Vivienne had pledged, with an ease born of ignorance, had been partially withheld by Sammy, due to his awareness of what Tino could and would do to anyone who dared to agree to testify against him. Sammy knew that such intimidation against possible witnesses had been the real reason for his recent successful defense of Tino, rather than Sammy's legal prowess, as he, Sammy, had so often bragged.

The bailiff recalled the courtroom to order, and the co-defendants were all brought before the court together. Their names were separately read, and then the charges were read to all of them. Manny listened attentively. He noticed that Sammy was clean-shaven, dressed neatly in coat and tie and unshackled. This didn't mean nearly as much to Manny as it did to Tino.

Ultimately, Tino's bond was set at one million, cash; the other defendants, at five-hundred thousand, cash; and Sammy's at ten-thousand cash. Sammy's wife was there with the necessary funds, and, as Sammy walked around Tino to go to the clerk's office, Tino whispered so only Sammy could hear him, "You'd better know what you're doing, you son-of-a-fucking-bitch!"

The words had their intended effect of striking fear to the depth of Sammy's being, a fear he hid by smiling and saying, "See you later," words he thought would suggest to Tino that he intended to talk to Tino and not to the government. Tino wasn't impressed and held Sammy in his steely gaze until he was out of the courtroom.

Somebody in the assembled press offered to go Manny's bond, but Keets, returning to the courtroom and enjoying the attention, told them it was already taken care of 'through his office', but would offer no further explanation. It was assumed that Jack Hogan had taken care of it.

Kari had listened to the other arraignments and deduced that Vivienne and Sammy had been acting in concert, sans Manny, in the illicit drug deal. The morning's

301

court session had raised more questions than answers for her. She had heard the court's reference to Vivienne as Manny's ex-wife, which now permitted her to put the name with the face, and had looked closely at the attractively dressed Vivienne as the latter left the courtroom.

Kari Robins was silently ticking off in her mind a replay of the morning's events. She had seen Manny's ex-wife make a court appearance on a dope charge and be admitted to a meager bond by a reluctant judge, who was busy trying to keep his backside covered. She had seen Vivienne have a short, but apparently friendly, exchange with Manny. She had watched while a bewildered Manny was able to gain enough compassion from the judge to elicit information which Manny was obviously ignorant of before entering the courtroom. And she had seen Tino, who stood out as the ringleader of the dope deal, whisper something to Manny's player agent with what could only be described as a mean-mouthed expression. She had correctly identified Tino as a very dangerous man, and especially so when he was backed into a corner.

Kari returned to her hotel to reflect alone, in the quiet of her suite, upon how her entire life might be affected by what she'd just seen and heard. She was slowly awakening to the fact she'd entered the engagement with Woody more because of the vacuum created in her heart left by Manny's absence than her love of Woody. 'How could all this be straightened out?' she wondered to herself. She was in a dilemma, and the more she tried to figure it out, the more perplexed she became. She fell asleep, fully clothed, on her bed, her mind having tired from overwork.

She was now convinced that Vivienne had been providing Manny an apocryphal account of her home life with their children, while plotting and scheming to divorce him and strip him of all his money and property. She knew this in her heart, just as she knew that Manny was the only man she had ever been in love with, but she wasn't ready to contact him yet. Least of all did she want Manny to be attracted to her now for all the wrong reasons. She was unaware that he had tried to call her before she departed for Phoenix, but would not leave his name with her answering service.

Manny was pleasantly surprised to learn of his pending release upon being returned from court to the jail. He was taken through the routine of returning his personal property and walked out of the jail to be met by Keets, who introduced himself. Keets walked him down the street to his office, and, following Kari's orders, engaged him in conversation. Manny was reluctant to say much to Keets, so Keets carried the conversation to him.

"First of all, congratulations, Mister Hernandez, on your winning the Cy Young."

Manny meekly acknowledged the compliment, and then said, "I wish somebody would explain to me what's going on."

The effervescent Keets was glad to oblige. He slowly and efficiently explained to Manny, until he was sure Manny understood, the answers to many of Manny's questions. Finally, Manny asked him, "How come you got me out of jail?"

Keets explained, "That's my job, Manny. Just like your job is to pitch for the Cardinals, my job is to get people out of jail."

"I know who pays me," Manny said, and then asked, "who pays you?"

"Usually," Keets answered, "the people I get out of jail pay me, but in your case, a friend of yours paid me, and they won't let me tell you who they are."

"Was it Mister Hogan?" Manny asked.

"No," was Keets' reply. "I will tell you that it was not your wife or your lawyer or anybody in baseball. I guess you'd just have to say it was a friend. A friend who very much wanted to do it for you without being given any credit for it."

Manny's curiosity was piqued, and, oddly enough, his thoughts had not brought Kari to mind in this context. In point of fact, Manny would be very embarrassed if he thought Kari knew what had been happening to him. His most remote imagination would never suggest to him that she was, at this moment, resting in a hotel suite less than five blocks from where he was sitting.

Kari awakened from her nap and called Harry Keets. He told her where Manny had indicated he would be staying. It was a hotel in Scottsdale. She got the name and number from him and then lay back down to continue meditating on what would be the best way to approach Manny, a fact she wanted to accomplish in a manner that would be pleasantly meaningful to him and effectively revive what she errantly thought were feelings for her that he had set aside. In truth, although she hadn't been in his thought pattern since being

304

unable to reach her by telephone, he had never stopped missing Kari. He was still very much in love with her.

Manny checked into the Scottsdale Hotel and immediately called his ex-wife at the Hernandez home.

Chapter 23 -- THE REPRISAL

Vivienne and the lady agent assigned to help her retrieve the children from the sitter's home, arrived at her home, and she was once again carefully briefed about the steps to follow for her self-protection and then left alone with her children. She hadn't stopped long enough to allow the gravity of the situation to fully impact her.

Vivienne was a survivor. These instincts within her being had taken hold from the moment she became fully aware that her 'house of cards' was tumbling down. She felt comfortable with the fact she had wisely acted fast to cooperate with the government and, as yet, felt no apprehension about her personal safety. She didn't like losing the two-hundred and fifty-thousand dollars she'd given Tino, but she still had her house, automobiles and children, plus a six-figure bank account that she had kept secret. She was still well-heeled, and these thoughts distracted her from considering any more of a worst-case scenario than she and the children having to move. If that had to happen, at least she knew it would all be at the expense of the government. Actually, her consideration of the damages she'd undergone during the preceding twenty-four hours were added up in her mind under the headings of 'financial' and 'inconvenience'. Her thoughts had just turned to how she was going to strike a deal with Manny over custody of the children when his call was ringing in on her phone. She answered, and their conversation began.

"Viv," Manny began, "how are you?"

"Oh," she said, "none the worse for wear, I guess you'd say. How are you, Manny, dear?"

Her attempt to sound affectionate was ignored, as Manny continued, "I'm really not sure how I am," he said. "Things have happened so fast the last couple of days that my mind hasn't caught up to them yet."

She was fumbling for words but knew there was always one subject he couldn't resist. "The children really miss you," she offered.

Manny appreciated her words, as he missed them, too, but, still being shell-shocked by the turn of events, he didn't take the bait, as she was accustomed to his doing.

"Would you like to come over and see them?" she asked.

Manny answered, "You know I would, Viv, but I don't want to get into any knock-down and drag-out argument with you in front of them."

"What makes you think that might happen?" she purred, in a tone reeking of subdued, false indignation. But Manny, for the first time in their relationship, was genuinely stand-offish. "Okay, Manny," she said, "spit it out... whatever you don't understand, I'll tell you now, so just ask."

Manny was confused even more. She had changed her whole approach. He could see her, in his mind, flaring her nostrils and showing her teeth like a menacing dog about to bite. He didn't like the direction the conversation was going. Vivienne had gone from affectionately willing to invite him over, to defensively speaking in tones that he could only interpret as abusive. He wanted some answers, though, so for the only time since he'd met her, he was determined not to excuse what she had done to him and to press her until she was honest. He would never understand, because he was personally incapable of being any other way, that she was equally incapable of cleaning up her act this late in her life.

Manny changed his approach. "Just tell me what I did to you, Viv, to cause you to do all these things to me." These words underscored his true feelings. Somehow, Manny still could not perceive himself as blameless.

Vivienne, sensing she could convert this suggestion to her own benefit, picked up on it immediately. "I'll tell you what you did, Mister Manny Hernandez," she started, raising her voice and adding venomous sarcasm; "what you did was abandon me and these children for six months every year, and then sit and talk about your home and family in Dominica the other six months."

Her words cut Manny deeply. Her vitriolic diatribe left him depressed and hurt. When she stopped to breathe, he sadly asked, "Is that all you wanted to tell me?"

Vivienne suddenly realized she shouldn't be engaged in the alienation of the last friend she might have in the entire world and one from whom she needed a huge favor. In her true chameleon form, she at once went from piranha to pussyfoot.

"Manny," she said, returning her tone to friendly and sensual, "I know you must hate me, and I deserve it, but we do have two children, and they need us both. I want you to come over, and let's grill some steaks and talk this out. I'll make an effort not to lose my temper, and you try your best not to get too angry with me. Let's just agree I've been wrong, and you're not perfect."

These words, although he was not sure he agreed with them, made more sense than anything she'd said yet, and he responded by laughingly saying, "I hope you have some money, Viv, because I don't."

She laughed back and said, "Manny, I've been holding out on you. I've got ten grand stashed in a shoe box under our bed."

Her admission momentarily rendered him very vulnerable. After all, if she was starting to come clean with him in such matters, maybe she wasn't so bad after all, was his fleeting thought, until his guard went back up. "Tell you what, Viv," he offered, "you get the steaks and things, and I'll be over about six. I need to clean up and get rid of this jail smell."

She agreed, and almost automatically signed off their conversation, saying, "I do love you," which pleased him, although he knew in his heart he couldn't trust or live with her again. He did realize, now more than ever, that you don't have children with someone and later achieve the ability to completely write them out of your life.

Vivienne knew that if she were going to persuade Manny not to try and take the children away from her she would have to drop her complaint against him. She also knew that, once she refused to testify against Manny, leading to the *nolle prosequae* of the charges, Manny could then change his mind and attack her for custody of the children, she could have a very had time opposing him.

It all boiled down, she reasoned, to the bedrock point of convincing Manny that her keeping custody was truly in the best interests of their children. She was smart enough to realize that if Manny finally got a good lawyer, as opposed to one she had chosen for him, and if such a lawyer paraded before the court the evidence of her many misdeeds, that Manny would beat her, hands down. Her tack, she was thinking, would be to simply make friends with him. That would include her permitting him to take them whenever and wherever he pleased, even back to Dominica for a visit.

It was close to four-thirty now, so Vivienne took the children and drove to the grocery store to shop for supper. She was pleased, now that her mind was at ease with the latest plan she'd concocted to manipulate the always-unwitting Manny in her chosen direction.

* * *

While Vivienne was on her sojourn to the grocery store, a lone male figure entered her home through the unlocked door leading from the garage to the kitchen, the same door Sammy always used. The man made a thorough inspection of the Hernandez premises. He went from room to room, first to make sure that he was the only one in the house, and next, to choose a vantage point from which to perform the sordid task he'd come to do, plus allow himself a clean getaway. After his inspection of the interior, he went into the backyard and walked around the pool. His presence was concealed from outside vision by the same privacy fence Vivienne had erected to allow her to carry on her naked poolside trysts with Sammy and others before him.

He smelled the burning charcoal, telling him that his intended target, after her return to the home, would at some point be outside to tend the charbroiler. He found the door in the fence secured shut with a chain, originally placed there to prevent Manny's entering through it. He carefully unwound the makeshift lock chain and left it sitting in such a way as to avoid suspicion by less than a very close look. He then concealed himself in a small opening between the privacy fence and a storage building used to house lawn-care equipment. When he chose to act, he could step from behind the storage building and have about twenty feet between himself and his intended victim standing at the grill between him and the pool. He could afterward continue in the same direction he'd stepped from behind the building. In another forty feet, he would be out the door. There was a large, vacant lot behind the Hernandez home. He felt that, once he made it out of the Hernandez backyard and into the vacant lot, he could safely leave the premises and get away. He carefully removed a nine-millimeter semi-automatic weapon from his shoulder holster and screwed a silencer on the barrel.

Now all he had to do was wait. He had been assured that he would not be confronted with more than the usual logistical problems, which he was accustomed to dealing with. So far, everything was precisely as he'd been led to expect.

Then Manny showed up, before Vivienne got home with the children. Manny also entered the house through the garage connecting door.

The unwanted intruder, hearing the male voice, was not daunted. It simply meant that the unexpected company might have to also be killed. He had been told in his instructions that the children were not to be targets, unless killing them was somehow necessary to accomplish the murder of their mother. In any event, it wasn't in this hit-man's bag of tricks to shoot kids. His reserve did not extend to adults who happened to be at the wrong place at the wrong time. The unsuspecting Manny was facing potential death at the hands of a man he not only knew nothing about, but who was there to silence forever the mother of his children. All of Manny's and Vivienne's life problems were about to be extinguished with their pending execution.

Manny heard Vivienne pull into the garage and park, so he went to help her carry in the groceries. Joseph lit up with approval upon seeing Manny, and Marie squealed her delight.

Vivienne drew near to Manny as they were emptying the car and rubbed her breast against him, acting as if it was inadvertent. Manny just went right on unloading the grocery sacks and ignored her overture. He wasn't there to get re-involved with Vivienne. He had resolved to strike a plan with her that they could both live with, as far as their children were concerned. He might be willing to engage in a little roll in the hay later, if it wouldn't get in the way of the business at hand.

She still hadn't mentioned the two-hundred and fifty-thousand dollars in Sammy's special trust account. He probably wouldn't have even thought about it amidst all the turmoil, except that they had reminded him of it when he was being interrogated. He didn't want to mention it now, though, because he was enjoying playing with the children.

The gunman stood poised to perform his gruesome duty on a second's notice, but he remained patient and unanxious. He was satisfied now that his job could be accomplished, so his thoughts were more in terms of <u>when</u> to do it and to assure himself of a safe getaway. He was used to waiting; it was a fact of life in his business. He was confident now that the quarry he had come for was his, anytime he chose to take it, and he had no reservations about including Manny, although he felt a small tinge of remorse about leaving the children with <u>no</u> parents. This feeling didn't last long, and he was ready to follow his chosen line of work at all costs, even his own life. One thing he was also sure of, he'd leave no live witnesses to identify him later if he was seen and subsequently caught.

Manny put the steaks on the grill and went back inside to help Vivienne with the salad. She began talking to him. "Manny, for what it's worth, I'm sorry," she said. "I know it's over for us, and that's as it should be, after all I've done to you."

Manny just listened. He was wary and untrusting. He wanted to ask her again what he had done to bring all this on, but did not want to ignite her temper as he'd done over the phone. He finally just simply asked her, "What do you want for yourself, Viv?"

Given the opening, she told him. "As it stands now, the house and cars are mine, and I get what amounts to two-hundred-thousand dollars a year child support and alimony. I want to keep that in place and custody of the children. For your part, I'll let you keep fifty-thousand dollars out of your annual salary, and I'll drop the charges pending against you for parental kidnapping. You can keep your per diem and endorsement money, or, for that matter, any other money you make."

"Is that it?" he asked.

"Generally, yes," she answered, always afraid she'd think of something later she'd overlooked.

Manny then asked, "What about my seeing the children? If I agree to all this other stuff, can I have the kids when I want them, maybe even take them to see my parents again?"

"Yes," she answered.

Manny stopped slicing a tomato, dried his hands and embraced her, whispering in her ear, "I know I haven't been the perfect husband, but we must think of the children. I also know a smart lawyer would say you're screwing me, but I don't care about that. If you'll drop the charges and not call the cops when I come to see the kids, you can have everything you've asked for, and I won't complain."

Vivienne was relieved. She kissed him, not sensually, but in gratitude. Then her old greed horned in, and she said, thinking maybe she had let him off the hook too

314

easily, "Manny, will you split your World Series money with me too?"

Manny just smiled, sighed, pulled her close to him and said, "Sure, I don't mind, whatever you want; but remember, don't get between me and Joseph and Marie."

"I wouldn't think of it," she answered. Vivienne then said, "No man will ever satisfy my appetite in the bedroom like you, Manny, do I feel something coming up between your legs?"

"You sure do," he whispered, and he was ready.

"I'll meet you in the bedroom," she said, "right after I turn the steaks."

"Okay, honey," Manny answered, and turned the other way to walk to the bedroom. Manny didn't undress. He relieved himself in the adjoining bathroom and then sat on the bed to await Vivienne. The children were watching TV in the living room. There were no unusual sounds.

After about five minutes, Manny returned to the kitchen to see what was keeping Vivienne. Through the window over the sink he saw her lifeless body in the swimming pool, face down. He rushed outside and jumped into the swimming pool and dragged her body to pool's edge and pushed it out of the water. He noticed the fence door was swung open and the chlorinated blue water was turning red from her blood. He then saw the bloody bullet holes in her blouse and could see that she was not breathing.

He ran into the house and called 911. The response was rapid. In five minutes, the emergency medical team and the Scottsdale Police were there.

Two patrolmen in a police car saw the gunman walking down the street behind the location where their radio had told them there had been a shooting. They attempted to catch up to the man to check him out. He turned and started shooting at them. They killed him, but not before one of the officers was wounded.

In thirty minutes, D.E.A. Supervisor Patrick was there. Manny recognized him as he entered the Hernandez home. Manny was sobbing, grief-stricken. He could hardly answer questions through his tears. At first, the Scottsdale Police thought Manny might have shot her, and they told him he would have to undergo a paraffin test. Then, when the gunman's pistol was taken from his lifeless hand, the Scottsdale Detectives relented, as it was apparent that the much disturbed and aggrieved Manny was not the assailant.

Her body was removed to the County Medical Examiner's office for a post-mortem examination, which is required in all homicides.

Manny's identification of her, along with Agent Patrick, made a trip to the Medical Examiner's office unnecessary. Manny finally regained control of himself and took the children to his hotel room. He was completely at a loss for what to do next, but he knew he must soon be about the task of preparing for her funeral.

He called her parents to tell them what had happened. They insisted on having her remains returned to them, which Manny agreed to do. He called his mother, who was deeply saddened and encouraged Manny to pray. He told her he would call her again when his head had cleared.

One of Vivienne's last acts had been to go out to her car and bring in the mail, which she'd taken from the box as she returned from the grocery store. She was in a hurry to turn the steaks and join Manny in the bedroom, so she had failed to examine it. On an end table in the living room, among the usual bills, form letters and junk mail, was a blue envelope from the U.S. Treasury addressed to 'Manny and Vivienne Hernandez' and a box addressed only to Manny, with a return address in St. Louis, Missouri. These items had been completely overlooked by Manny and remained undisturbed where Vivienne had placed them.

There was a knock on Manny's hotel door. It was D.E.A. Supervisor Patrick and Agent Henricks. The children were asleep. The two visitors extended their sincere condolences to Manny. It was then that Manny obtained a complete and thorough explanation of his deceased ex-wife's involvement in the dope deal with Tino, Gus and Sammy.

The older men had encountered every kind of situation imaginable, but neither could remember one like this that had touched even their hardened hearts. They explained to Manny how the law worked in Vivienne's favor when he didn't answer her petition for divorce.

The government men stayed with him until the early hours of the morning. This session with Manny was unofficial. They had truly come to see if they could help him in his hour of grief. However, it did serve the dual purpose of convincing them thoroughly of his innocence. Men who have been investigating dope-related crimes as long as these two, develop an ingrained suspicion of everyone they encounter. They are not quick to give up on these suspicions.

In this instance, the first either of them could remember, they had at last met the most innocent man they had ever known. And, besides that, they began to like him.

It was these two men who helped Manny make the funeral arrangements for Vivienne. He had decided on a simple and private memorial service for any of their friends who might wish to come. Then he arranged for her body to be shipped up to Medford, Oregon, to her parents.

Patrick and Henricks had not mentioned the refund check which, unknown to Manny, was still on the end table in the living room of the Hernandez home. Neither had the two agents interrupted Manny's train of thought to ask him the identity of the woman who paid the bondsman securing his release from jail. They were provided with the information as soon as it happened, and a check on the name 'Kari Robins' through the NCIC and other channels came back 'subject unknown'.

The only people at Vivienne's funeral service were reporters, government agents, Manny and their two children. Vivienne's penchant for privacy had left her friendless. Even next-door neighbors didn't know her. Any locals who may have thought about going, such as her hairdresser, chose to avoid it because of the now well-publicized circumstances under which she had died. Flowers were everywhere, mostly sent by people like Jack Hogan and others in baseball. There were two hymns sung, a preacher provided by the funeral home, who read the Twenty-Third Psalm, and a closing prayer.

The most significant thing that happened occurred after the service was over. Manny was standing in front of

Vivienne's casket with their two children, looking at
Vivienne for the last time, when a familiar voice from behind
him whispered, "Hello, my dear Manny." It was Kari
Robins, who then whispered, "I'm sorry."

Chapter 24 -- THE MARRIAGE

Manny at once noticed there was no engagement ring on Kari's left hand. Its absence left a white circle around her otherwise tan finger.

He introduced her at once to the children and to Patrick and Henricks. The latter were pleased to find out who she was. Failing to have her identified had nettled these two thorough investigators.

When the hearse left for the airport, Manny took Kari and his children back to his hotel room so they could change clothes. It had been his original plan to spend the rest of the day getting the house cleaned up and ready to put on the market. Kari volunteered to help. A quick stop at her hotel room enabled Kari to put on her jeans. She accepted Manny's invitation to stay with him and the children.

Manny had an uncomfortable feeling, upon returning for the first time to the scene of Vivienne's murder. Kari sensed his uneasiness and suggested they start by just sitting in the living room and visiting. It was then that Manny first noticed the unopened mail. He handed some of it to Kari to assist him. She instantly recognized the familiar blue-colored envelope from the U.S. Treasury and handed it to Manny, saying it was likely some kind of tax refund, although it did seem odd to her that such would be arriving this time of year.

Manny stopped midway in opening the box from St. Louis and opened the blue envelope Kari had just handed him. Upon seeing the contents, he was awestruck. He handed it to Kari, who said, "Honey, this is a check to you and Vivienne from 'Uncle Sam' for three-hundred thousand dollars; did you expect some kind of tax adjustment or something?"

"Not that I know about," Manny replied. He immediately called the man he'd found so helpful during the last several days, Supervisor Patrick. Patrick explained it to Manny and assured him the money was his under the law of survivorship. Manny then asked him to explain it to Kari, in case he missed something in the interpretation of Patrick's explanation, so Patrick went through it again with her. Kari followed the agent's explanation easily.

By the time she had gotten off the phone, Manny had unwrapped the box from St. Louis. He was sitting there with a baseball glove on his hand, crying like a baby. Kari went to him, but Manny jumped up and ran into the bedroom, handing her the letter that he had removed from the box. Kari sat down to read, opting to leave Manny alone for the moment. The letter read:

'Dear Mr. Hernandez:

We shall forever be in your debt for the unselfish way you gave of yourself when you came to visit our child, Donnie Robinson, at the Children's Hospital here in St. Louis.

Donnie is gone now. Before his death, he enjoyed
many hours showing this glove to his last visitors
and telling them all about his receiving it from his
friend, Manny Hernandez. In his last conversation
with his father and me, Donnie made us promise to
return the glove to you after he was gone.

Donnie was sure in his mind that you would need it
next season. He also wanted us to ask that you think
about him during next year's World Series.

My husband and I join to wish you the very best of
everything. It is our opinion that a loving God shall
always hold a special place in His Sacred Heart for
men like you.

Sincerely,

Mr. and Mrs. Jerry Robinson

P.S. Dr. Workman said for us to tell you that the
kidney transplant was successful. She said you'd
understand.

All our love and good wishes,

The Robinson's

     Kari carried the letter to where Manny was in the
bedroom, and they both openly wept. While sitting on the
bed, Manny remembered Vivienne mentioning the shoebox
full of money she had hidden under where they were sitting.
He pulled it out and opened it. Vivienne had unwittingly
provided the funds to pay for her own funeral and shipment
of her body back to Oregon.

     Manny stopped crying and sat there with his eyes
transfixed on Kari. Finally, he broke the silence. "There
really is a God," he said. "Not only is there a God, but He's

talking to us right now. I'm sure that He's talking to us through the signs we've just been shown."

"What's that?" she asked.

"As far as I'm concerned," Manny said, "God has sent you to stay with me and the children forever. He's given us more than enough money to start our life over, and He's reminded us where our real happiness shall come from, besides each other. He handed us the box from little Donnie Robinson's parents so we wouldn't forget that true happiness only comes from helping others."

Now Kari started to cry again as she said, "Manny, do I hear you proposing to me, or is it just my wishful thinking?"

Manny quickly responded, "I've been proposing to you in my dreams since our first evening together in my hotel room in Chicago."

"If that's the case," she joyfully announced, "I accept."

They fell back on the bed and embraced. Both of them had longed for this moment for what seemed many lifetimes, and they were savoring it.

The next day, while the house was being cleaned by a commercial service, Manny and Kari took the children and went off to be married in Las Vegas, Nevada.

They returned and put the finishing touches on the house-cleaning before offering it for sale. The attractive home sold quickly. Manny had agreed with the Realtor, Mike Cavanaugh, to offer it at a reduced price because of the recent tragedy which had occurred there. A young couple snapped up the bargain. The funds from the house sale were

placed in a conservatorship for the benefit of Joseph and
Marie, the heirs of Vivienne. She had died as the home's
sole owner, due to the divorce decree.

Sammy Snider could not keep up the payments on
the strip center in Scottsdale, so he deeded it to Manny and
Kari, in lieu of foreclosure. They promptly sold it to the
anchor tenant, Randee Spencer, who enlarged her already
successful lunch and antique business, known as the "Line
Dancers' Paradise".

Manny signed the authorization which had brought
Kari to Phoenix, and they stopped in New York on their way
to Dominica to deliver it to her anxiously waiting publisher.

Kari was granted unlimited leave of absence from
the newspaper. Her boss, Brendan Ryan, encouraged her to
use her time in Dominica, when she wasn't honeymooning,
to dig up another best-selling baseball book.

As she, Manny and the children were flying over the
Atlantic to be united with the Hernandez family in San Pedro
de Macoris, Kari was ogling what she thought was her
sleeping new husband when a smile worked its way slowly
across his face.

"What is it?" she asked. "Darling, what's so funny?"

He opened his huge, beautiful green eyes and,
looking into hers, said, while retaining his happy smile, "You
know, dear, I just can't get over it; there really is a God."

She smiled and agreed as the latest addition to the
Hernandez family joined in the return of her husband to his
homeland to begin their quest to help needy children, while

enjoying a mutual love that had remained unsullied through the worst imaginable circumstances.

You may purchase copies of "CAUGHT STEALING"
by mail-order. Call toll free, 1-888-600-9922. All
major credit cards accepted. Or visit our website
www.caughtstealing.com
$7.99 per book plus $3.00 postage and handling.